HOLD ON!

Season 1

PETER DARLEY

HOLD ON!—Season 1

Copyright©2015

PETER DARLEY

www.peterdarley.com

Cover Design by Peter Darley and Christy Caughie.

Lyrics from 'Highway of Love' by Shining Line used with permission.

Other Titles in the Series:

Go! – Hold On! Season 2

Run! – Hold On! Season 3

Hold On! - Tomorrow

"To the victims of all forms

of tyranny and oppression,

past, present, and future,

and to all of the world's lovers,

this work is respectfully dedicated."

Prologue

Four minutes left. Brandon gazed at a digital clock on the mantelpiece: 14:26. His heart rate quickened as though he was a condemned man four minutes away from his own execution. The fluttering in the pit of his stomach wouldn't stop.

He sat on the edge of his leather sofa with a blazing log fire before him. It was so comfortable he was sorely tempted to stay there where it was safe. His left hand trembled as it rested on a smooth, black helmet beside him.

14:27.

A series of papers lay strewn across the carpet—layout plans for a skyscraper he'd spent two weeks committing to memory. Despite knowing them, his urgency persisted in driving him toward an obsessive last-minute revision, not that there was any chance of him being able to concentrate.

He gathered the papers in his clammy hands to fold them—anything to delay the terrifying moment when he would have to leave.

Bundling the plans became a desperate procrastination, a traumatic dance through his own Gethsemane. If he were caught, there was no saying how long he would be sent down for. But he had no choice.

He'd already attempted the easy option by alerting the victims to a forthcoming attack one month earlier. No one had believed him, and hundreds of innocent lives had been lost. This time, there was no alternative. He couldn't live with any more deaths on his conscience, no matter the cost to himself.

He placed the papers on the living room table and picked up the helmet from the sofa.

Draped across the armrest were a black Kevlar jacket, leg-wear, and a tool belt. With fearful reluctance, he picked them up and hooked them across his left forearm. With his free hand, he picked up a pair of black, rubber-soled boots from beside the sofa.

Through a window, gray-hued sky shrouded a snow-covered landscape. The bleak overcast perfectly mirrored his anxiety-ridden frame of mind.

Bracing himself, he accepted his fears and made his way toward the door, shivering.

One

Inferno

February 7th, 2014

Belinda gazed out a window across the Denver skyline. She glanced at her watch. *Only two hours to go.* It had been yet another five days of tedium, relentless painted smiles, and painstaking tolerance. But tonight was Friday night. Party night.

"Ms. Reese, where's the report from Manning Enterprises?"

The sound of Barton Carringby's humorless tone startled her. "I'll get it for you, sir."

She moved away from the window in a hurry and back to her desk. As much as she disliked her employer, he wasn't someone to disappoint. Carringby had authority wherever he went. A man of tremendous wealth and influence, he didn't have to speak but merely to appear in a room and the world would seem to freeze.

Carringby Industries was involved in almost every media, from telecommunications and crop rotation, to oil refining. As Carringby's secretary, Belinda performed her tasks with the utmost efficiency, but in her heart she wanted to be somewhere else. Anywhere else. Life as Carringby's assistant was boring, and her only true interest in the company was her weekly salary. She couldn't deny her resentment that this was all four years of college and a degree in marketing had managed to earn her. Her time

3

studying had been even more harrowing because she didn't have a passion for the subject. She'd worked with self-discipline and desperation in the hope it would lead her out of her financial rut.

Her relationships with men had led to one break-up after another. The problem arose from her longstanding trust issues, and only coming into contact with men who were corporate types when she wasn't a corporate type. She did, however, make a convincing impersonation of one when necessary.

At twenty-seven, she was a woman upon whom life had inflicted great frustration. It wasn't the first time Carringby had caught her daydreaming, always wishing to be taken away to a place of fulfillment.

As she handed him the file, she noticed the serial number, XD-47, on the first page. Of late, she'd processed hundreds of papers containing that particular number. She was slightly curious as to its meaning, but the instant Carringby took the file from her, she'd forgotten all about it.

He stood before her for a moment, flicking through the pages. At six feet tall, with strong gray eyes and sharp, chiseled features, Belinda had often considered he would have been handsome in his youth. Nevertheless, he was pushing sixty, and even if he hadn't been, he was still a suit.

"Please make some coffee, Ms. Reese, and get the best china out." He glanced at his watch. "I have a meeting in the conference room in ten."

"Yes, sir."

Belinda worked with haste to prepare the coffee for Carringby's guests. He habitually dropped tasks on her at the last minute, frequently forcing her to contain her anger.

4

She entered his vast, luxurious conference room pushing a refreshments trolley before her. Fifteen men in suits sitting at a circular table all turned to look at her in silence. It was a painfully unnerving moment, but she said nothing. She simply had to provide them with coffee as quickly as possible, and then get out of the room.

As she performed her menial task, she noticed, through the sprawling, semi-circular window, the sky was turning a dark shade of blue. Her heart fluttered with excitement. It had been almost a year since she'd last ventured into town with her college friends, and this night might be her chance to meet the right man. Or, at the very least, some guy who wasn't a suit.

As she served the coffee, her gaze anxiously latched onto the clock on the wall: 17:36. *Less than an hour.* The idea thrilled her enough to enable a genuine smile as she poured the last suit's coffee.

"That's fine, Ms. Reese, thank you," Carringby said.

He clearly wanted her out of the room so they could discuss their business in private. Dutifully, she departed.

"Good night, Ms. Reese. Have a good weekend."

Belinda looked up from her desk to see Molly Rigsby, one of the cleaning personnel, smiling at her. Belinda had always found her to be warm and charming. "Thank you, Molly. You too."

With only ten minutes remaining until she could leave for the weekend, Belinda paid a quick visit to the ladies' restroom. She immediately heard Carringby and his entourage exiting the conference room, filling the reception area with voices. Sighing with frustration, she hoped he wasn't going to reprimand her for leaving her post at that moment. She couldn't be sure if it mattered to him at all. The man was impossible to read or predict.

She hurriedly applied her lipstick then checked herself in the restroom mirror. She'd always been insecure about her appearance and was committed to making the best of herself. Despite her reservations, she knew men thought she was beautiful, at five-eight, with a lithe shape sculpted from two years of hard work in the gym.

As she made her way toward the restroom door, the bottom fell out of her world.

An explosion threw her off her feet, taking her breath from her. *An earthquake?*

The sound of muffled machine-gun fire came from the lower floor. Her heart pounded. The gunfire grew louder, echoing through a stairwell, until she heard a door burst open. They were on Carringby's floor.

Belinda froze, trembling with the horror of what she could only hear.

Summoning every iota of courage she possessed, she stood and inched her way toward the door. Every step was a marathon. She didn't know if it was even safe to peek through the slightest crack in the door.

With trembling fingers, she pulled it open a mere fraction of an inch and pressed her right eye into the gap. She could barely make out six men in ski masks opening fire upon members of Carringby's entourage. Her hand came across her mouth to stifle a whimper of terror.

Carringby came out of the conference room with his arms raised in surrender, but his look of stoicism remained.

"Where are the blueprints?" one of the assailants demanded.

Another gunman kicked every door open along the corridor and aimed his machine gun into the rooms. Satisfied a room was empty, he would move on to the next, and he was coming closer.

Panic stricken, Belinda moved away from the door and looked around trying to locate another way out. If she set one foot through the door, she knew she would be met with a hail of bullets. But there was nothing. No escape.

Unless.

She looked at the ceiling and found an air vent grill.

After climbing onto the counter, she found her palms could touch the grill with ease. She prepared to push against it only to discover it was merely a cover and wasn't bolted down. It flew from her fingers into the vent, giving her the opportunity to grasp the opening. The sound of doors being kicked in outside was growing closer.

Strength the likes of which she'd never known infused her muscles as she pulled herself up and crawled into the steel shaft.

Even as adrenaline pumped through her veins and terror clouded her mind, one last thought for survival occurred to her—the vent cover. She grasped it, slid it from under herself, and managed to turn around in order to cover up the hole again.

At that moment, the door burst open.

She pulled her head back and held her breath, watching the gunman through the grill. He kicked in each stall door, and then stood in the middle of the room looking around. To Belinda, he seemed to be moving in slow motion.

Unaware he was being observed, he removed his ski-mask and rubbed his face with his free hand. Ordinarily, she would've considered him handsome, with thick, blond

7

hair falling in his eyes. But in that moment, she couldn't see him in any positive light whatsoever.

Watching him with unbearable fear, she almost lost control of her bladder. If he knew she could see him, he would kill her.

Finally, he put the mask back on and exited the restroom.

Exhaling with overwhelming relief, she gathered her thoughts before moving along. She crawled through the vent aimlessly, not knowing where it would take her.

She closed her eyes and froze as another barrage of gunfire rang out from below. *Mr. Carringby.*

Another explosion rocked the building, knocking her from side to side into the walls of the vent. The belief that she was going to die grew stronger with each passing moment.

As she went farther through the ventilation shaft, turning corners endlessly, she was overcome by a need for her mother. It was an obscure feeling given she and her mother had been at each other's throats ever since she was a child.

She'd never been a religious person. A strict and abusive Catholic upbringing had long since put her off the idea. But in that moment, she reached out in a state of jabbering hysteria for even a semblance of comfort. "Ourfatherwhoartinheavenhallowedbethyname . . ."

She came to another grill and tried to push it, but it was bolted into place.

With barely enough space to maneuver her body, she desperately twisted onto her back and kicked at the grating, but to no avail.

Repeatedly, she pummeled the grating with the soles of her feet, but it wouldn't give way. Her heart raced with panic at the thought of being entombed inside the ventilation shaft. The possibility of her life ending like this was an unbearable thought. Her panic shifted to resentment, and then to rage.

Another explosion shook her as her feet collided with the grill one last time. The force of the detonation loosened the bolts, and the grill finally broke away.

Sobbing with relief, she pulled herself forward until she could make out a storage cupboard below her. The door appeared to be ajar from what she could see through the rising smoke.

She dropped to the floor and pushed the door open to be met with a wall of flame, causing her to instinctively recoil. She gave herself a moment to compose herself before seizing a break in the fire.

Darting to the left, she found herself in the maintenance stairwell. Below her was an inferno. It wasn't possible for her to go back down.

In a desperate effort to escape the fire, she ran up the steps with the smoke engulfing her.

By the time she'd reached the next flight of stairs, only a few steps from where she'd started, she fell to her knees in a coughing fit. Her eyes stung, watering from the smoke, but she persisted.

Despite her initial determination, she became convinced she wasn't going to make it. She couldn't see anything ahead of her, and her consciousness was slipping away.

She thought she could see a dark shape coming down the stairwell toward her, through the smoke. As it came closer, she could make out a man decked out in black. *It has to be one of them.*

Through her squinted eyes, she could see he wore a shiny black helmet, similar to the type worn on a motorcycle, although far less bulky. It seemed to cover his head with a slender, streamlined fit. A reflective, black visor covered his face.

In her weakened condition, she resigned herself to the belief she was going to die. The fight was leaving her, and smoke inhalation was stealing her consciousness. She couldn't be certain whether or not she was dreaming the man in the black helmet.

And then, she felt strong, gentle hands cradling her face for just a moment. "P-please don't kill me," she mumbled.

"I'm not going to kill—"

Belinda passed out.

She woke without a sense for how long she'd been out. Had she been unconscious for seconds? Or days? Why was everything upside down?

She felt a tight grip on her legs below the knees, and sensed herself moving quickly with a jerking motion. The smoke seemed to be clearing, and blood rushed into her head, bringing her back to consciousness. She saw the white surface of the steps from her inverted position and suddenly understood. He was running up the stairwell while carrying her over his shoulder.

Moments later, the ground turned black and she felt herself being turned upright in the freezing cold. Dazed, it took her a few moments to realize she was outside.

The stranger knelt down beside her and she trembled. "Who . . . are you?" she said.

"Your only way out of here."

"Where are we?"

"We're on the roof. We can't go back down. The place is a torch."

Belinda couldn't place his tone, but there was a masculine depth to it that was genuine and sincere.

"Please, trust me," he said. "Can you stand up?"

"Yes, I think so," she replied, but her coughing resumed.

He waited for the attack to abate before speaking again. "I'm going to get you out of here. There's only one way."

As he helped her to her feet, she realized how high up they were with the skyscrapers all around them.

"I need you to listen to me," he said. "What's your name?"

"B-Belinda. Belinda Reese." She quivered, and hugged herself tightly against the chilling effects of shock and the brutal February wind.

"All right Belinda, I need you to come over here with me." He motioned toward the edge of the roof. "There's nothing to worry about, trust me."

He walked toward the edge before her. Once he was standing on the ledge, he reached out and beckoned her to join him.

She placed one foot in front of the other, but froze when she saw him taking a gun-like device from his tool belt.

"It's OK," he said in a reassuring tone. "This isn't what you think it is. I swear to you on my life, I'm not going to hurt you."

With trepidation, she resumed her steps toward him.

"That's it," he said. "Just a little closer."

Belinda stopped inches away from him at the ledge. He aimed the device toward a skyscraper opposite and brought a small targeting sight to eye-level. Although it bore a resemblance to a gun, it didn't have a barrel, but rather a tennis ball-sized bulb held fast by his palm.

He depressed a button on the top of the metallic casing and a thin, high-tensile, steel cable jettisoned from the nozzle toward the building opposite. The cable reached the other side and a small steel claw at the end of line clasped a maintenance rail in the center of the roof. Pulling on the cable, he ensured it was secure, and stepped away from the edge.

He hurried across to a maintenance stairwell next to the entrance and climbed three steps. Once he was in position, he wrapped the wire around an iron step above him. From the height of the roof's ledge, Belinda estimated the step was approximately twelve inches above his own height. Reaching height.

With a flick of a switch, the cable was locked inside the bulb casing.

Belinda watched him, bewildered. "What are you doing?"

He didn't reply, clearly focused on his task.

Returning to her, he took a black metal tube from his belt, approximately fourteen inches in length, and pulled out two hand-grips from either side.

Belinda noticed a small pulley wheel on the underside of the tube, which he clipped onto the wire. He'd created a zip-line between the two buildings.

She panicked, believing he intended for her to hang from the hand grips and glide across to the adjacent building. "I can't do this. Please, I'm begging you. I can't do it."

He stepped back up onto the ledge. "You don't have to. I do. Now, take it steady and join me here."

She raised her right leg so slowly she thought she'd never put it down. Eventually, the tip of her shoe settled onto the ledge.

He gently placed his hand upon her shoulder. "All right. I've got it from here."

He grasped her under her armpits and lifted her onto the ledge. She trembled with vulnerability and vertigo. "Oh, God, please don't let me fall."

"You're not going to fall."

As he carefully placed her arms around him, she detected the solid base underneath his black, bullet-resistant attire. It was clear that, beyond the Kevlar, he was muscular, which heightened her sense of safety with him. With shaking hands, she held onto him for dear life.

He gripped the pulley with his left hand and lifted the visor with his right. Belinda looked into his deep green eyes. He looked exactly the same as his voice sounded—strong, but kind.

The moment ended and he pulled the visor back down into place.

Holding the right hand grip, he looked at her again and gave her the most unnecessary piece of advice she'd ever heard: "Hold on!"

Two

Night Flight

Belinda closed her eyes tightly as she held onto the stranger. The secure footing of the ledge disappeared. Her feet instinctively scurried in mid-air, hungry for the security of solid ground. She dared not open her eyes as she soared five hundred feet above ground with him. He hung from the grips of the pulley as a motor system within it rapidly launched them across to the adjacent skyscraper.

Sheer terror gripped her heart again as they reached the halfway mark. "Don't let me fall!" she screamed.

In a rugged whisper, he repeated, "You're not going to fall."

Within seconds they reached the rooftop. He raised his legs, gliding them over the ledge to land gracefully on the surface. Belinda squealed as her heels lightly clipped the edge.

"Are you all right?" he said.

Slowly, she settled her feet onto the roof, looked up at him and tried to speak, but no words formed. She simply nodded.

Satisfied she was unharmed, he let go of her and made his way across to a maintenance entrance door. He quickly discovered it was locked with a security code. There was no conventional method of entry without the code.

Getting into the Carringby building had been so much easier. The time he'd spent committing the architecture to

14

memory had been invaluable. Breaking in through the rear entrance and taking the service elevator had been a sound plan. However, halfway to Barton Carringby's office, he'd heard the gunfire and the explosions and realized his information on the timing of the attack was wrong. He'd had no choice but to continue to the roof. From there, he'd made his way back down the maintenance stairwell in search of survivors.

This time, he got lucky.

He took a small, chrome projector a little larger than a pen from his belt. With the push of a button, a slender orange beam was emitted onto the door. As he twisted a dial back and forth around the projector, the beam increased in intensity.

Despite shivering with the freezing cold, Belinda watched, awestruck, as the laser rapidly burn through the steel door lock. The stranger casually drew the projector around in a circle until the two ends of the incision met.

He switched off the device, stepped forward, and kicked the circle in with his right heel. The lock mechanism shattered and the door came open to the shrill wailing of alarm sirens.

Belinda clasped her hands over her ears, barely muffling the ear-shattering sound.

Urgently, he said, "Come on. There's not much time."

She followed him through the open door and along a dark corridor.

They came to a fire exit stairwell. Fueled by adrenaline and nervous energy, she managed to keep up with him, although everything seemed to be happening in slow motion.

They faced forty stories before they would reach the ground. On each floor, they hid as security guards ran past the windows of the fire exit doors.

After an exhausting descent, they arrived at the bottom. Belinda fought for breath, resting for a moment as her rescuer pushed open the rear fire exit.

"I think this is it, if I calculated it right," he said. Ahead, in the alleyway, was a white van. "It is."

"What is?"

"Our way out."

He took her hand and ran into the alley toward the van. Immediately, they were startled by a barrage of police sirens coming toward them.

"Get in the van," he said.

She ran around to the passenger's side and climbed in.

He started up the engine and raced away as the police cars reached them.

"What are you doing?" Belinda said. "They're the police. They can help us."

"What gives you that idea?"

Frustrated, the pitch of her voice rose to a screech. "We've just been involved in a terrorist attack. Who better to go to than the authorities?"

"You don't get it, do you?" he said.

"Get what?"

He turned his shielded face to her again. "Those killers were the authorities."

Just the sound of that comment caused Belinda to shiver, though she didn't understand it.

The chase continued. Pedestrians stopped to watch the convoy of police cars, blue lights flashing, and the ear-piercing squall of sirens.

The van turned a corner and was immediately halted by a police roadblock. The police cars behind them screeched to a stop, blocking them in.

Officers in front and behind them emerged from their vehicles, firearms trained on the van.

The stranger turned to Belinda. "Get in the back of the van."

"What?"

"Get. In. The. Back. Of. The. Van."

Moving as though she was on autopilot, she was clueless as to what she was doing. Nevertheless, she climbed over the seat.

Captain Lewis Jordan, the Denver Police Department's Chief of Police, studied the scene. With twenty years' experience in crisis situations, he knew the suspects before him were cornered with no opportunity for flight.

He smiled smugly, wiped his graying moustache with his right forefinger, and raised the bullhorn to his mouth. "You are surrounded. You have no chance of escape. Come out with your hands raised over your heads."

Jordan waited for sixty seconds and issued the order again. No response came, prompting him to take the initiative. "On my mark, gentlemen—"

The van exploded. Police and onlookers recoiled instinctively with the shock of the blast. Momentarily blinded by the brightness of the fire, they cautiously turned back to the sight of the blaze.

"Terrorists!" somebody yelled.

Suddenly—*something*— emerged from the flames. It was so fast their eyes didn't have the chance to fully register it. At first glance, it appeared to be a type of low-flying aircraft that bore a passing resemblance to a metallic-blue sports car.

Transfixed onlookers clicked on their mobile phone cameras as the craft launched itself across the police barricade. In the blink of an eye, it disappeared in the direction of Highway 70.

Inside the aircraft, Belinda found herself sitting in a reclining position with a crisscross safety harness secured around her chest and torso. Screens and digital readouts on the inside of the roof were spread out before her. The city became an indecipherable blur through the small tinted door window.

Piloting the craft from her left, the stranger typed something into a touch-sensitive panel built into the dashboard.

"All right, all right." She tapped the palm of her right hand on the fingertips of her left. "Time out, please."

He adjusted the throttle and the craft turned onto its side, maneuvering around a line of traffic on the highway, flying vertically between them. "Hang in there. Everything's under control." He straightened the vehicle and the jets launched them forward at astonishing speed.

Belinda yelled, "Stop it, please! We're gonna crash."

"No, we're not. I've typed in our coordinates. It has a satellite link to all traffic between here and where we're going so it'll maneuver around every vehicle."

Questioning her own sanity, she said, "What is this thing?"

"It's a test aircraft. A radar-invisible one-of-a-kind. We're safe. Nobody's going to find us."

"Why did you blow up the van?"

18

"I had to erase as much forensic evidence as possible. It could have led them to where I bought it from, and that was pretty close to where we're headed."

"Where are we headed?"

"Not far from Aspen. We should be there in about twenty-five minutes."

Her mind in turmoil, Belinda dared not imagine what speed they were flying at if they could reach Aspen in that time. But there was another bewildering question she felt compelled to ask. "Why didn't *we* blow up with the van?"

"Oh, the shell on this is made from an experimental, concussion-resistant alloy. The detonation of two grenades is its limit."

"That's pretty amazing."

"How about a little music?" he said. "Do you like rock?"

She barely heard him and didn't respond. It wasn't long before snow became visible through the side window. She lay back in stunned silence.

Three

The Cabin

The aircraft landed outside a wooden cabin deep within the snow-covered mountains.

Belinda's safety harness automatically detached itself and retracted into the seat. The side door slid upward, and she noticed they'd landed directly against the porch of the cabin.

"I didn't want you to be knee-deep in snow," he said.

Shaking, she reached out and eased herself onto the porch.

"It's dryer this way." The stranger climbed across the passenger's side to join her. She assumed he was trying to put her at ease by acting nonchalant.

He walked across the porch and inserted a key into the cabin door. Belinda considered the sight somewhat bizarre—a tall, muscular man in black combat fatigues, and a sleek helmet with a reflective visor, acting so normal.

She was instantly drawn to the vision before her. The moonlight shone down onto a valley of snow, creating a calming, hypnotic, purple-blue effect. It was a contender for the most beautiful sight she had ever seen, and such a dramatic contrast to that which had led her to it.

He pushed the door open and stepped inside. "You'd better come in or you're gonna freeze."

She turned around and cautiously followed him into the living room. Nothing about the interior registered with her. "Excuse me?"

"Yes?"

"Do you think you could take that helmet off now, please?"

"I'm sorry. I forgot about that."

He removed the helmet and she gazed upon him fully. He looked to be in his mid-twenties, and he was dashingly attractive. Mid-brown hair fell to the base of his neck, just below his square jaw. She had already seen his striking green eyes on the rooftop.

She couldn't quite place his looks. They seemed to be a combination of rugged, yet wholesome. Despite a small, star-shaped scar in the middle of his forehead, he didn't appear villainous or dishonest in any way. He placed the helmet down on a black leather sofa beside him.

"Why'd you wear that?" she said.

"The helmet?"

"Yes."

"Because a bullet to the head can be fatal. It's made of a bullet-resistant alloy, and has a built-in gas and smoke filter. That's how I got to you without choking on the smoke."

"I see." Belinda finally looked around her and noticed how cozy the cabin was. It was obviously being lived in. The small kitchen through a door at the end of the living room prompted a smile. He clearly wasn't partial to washing dishes. *Typical guy.* Looking down, she saw a thick beige carpet. *That looks expensive.*

As she surveyed the room, she noticed a stereo system, a high definition television, and what appeared to be three DVD, or possibly Blu-ray players. There was also a fine-quality leather sofa and recliner set, a mahogany drinks cabinet, and two paintings on the wall. One showed a lavish

Caribbean coastline in the sunset, and the other, a sailboat on a lake or maybe an ocean. It wasn't clear. Nevertheless, it was apparent that whoever her mysterious rescuer was, he was doing quite well for himself.

"I'd better get the fire started. It's going to be a cold one tonight," he said.

Despite having just been through the most terrifying experience of her life, there was something about him that made her feel safe. She tried to speak, but the shock of the night finally took its toll. "W-what is . . . ? What . . . ?" Her lips quivered and she broke down.

He hurried across to her and held her tightly. "It's all right. Just let it go."

She quivered as she tried to get her words out. "What is y . . . ?"

"Excuse me?"

She looked up at him again. As he wiped the tears from her eyes, she held his gaze for a painfully uncomfortable moment. She felt drawn to him, even though he was a stranger, and she had no reason to trust him. Her hands were still trembling with residual fear, and her heart ached for the comfort of an embrace.

Caution was no longer a factor. She took the initiative, grasped the back of his head, and touched her lips to his. But he was unexpectedly hesitant. Surprised by how *surprised* he was, she slowly drew away.

She was momentarily caught in an ambivalence of disappointment and relief. The way he drew away caused her to feel more secure with him than ever. His resistance did, at least, prove he wasn't a sexual predator or an opportunist. "What is your name?" she finally managed, realizing she'd been too rattled to ask him earlier.

He smiled warmly. "Brandon. Brandon Drake."

"But . . . who are you?"

"There'll be time for all that tomorrow. For now, I just want . . . no, I *need* you to know you're going to be safe here. Please, trust me."

She nodded. The last time he'd said those words to her, he'd followed by saving her life. Why wouldn't he have just left her on the roof, or even pushed her off if she couldn't trust him?

He made his way over to the liquor cabinet, took out a bottle of vodka and a crystal-cut glass, and handed her the glass. It was as though he was doing everything he could to make her feel comfortable.

"Thank you," she said.

After unscrewing the bottle, he poured her a shot. "Would you like some tonic with that?"

"No, but I wouldn't mind another shot. Or two."

He gave her a rather generous splash. The glass was almost half full by the time he'd finished. She consumed the entire contents in one mouthful.

He walked into the bedroom, returned with a pillow and a blanket, and laid them out across the leather couch.

"Is that for me?" she said.

"No, this is for me. You take the bed. You look like you need some serious rest."

She looked at him, bemused. His kindness and generosity were beyond what she'd been used to. "Why are you doing this for me?"

"Couldn't very well have left you out in the snow, now could I?"

She felt sleepy. The vodka had affected her rapidly.

"Look, I think you need to get some sleep," he said, as though noticing her weary eyes.

She needed no further prompting. He took the empty glass from her and led her to the bedroom door, but didn't go in with her.

"Try to get some rest." He closed the door.

Belinda looked around the bedroom. It had a bathroom in the far left corner. There was also the faint hint of a man's antiperspirant, but she couldn't tell which brand. The bedroom was warm and snug and the bed looked delicious—but terribly empty. A part of her still wished he hadn't been such a gentleman.

She stripped down to her bra and panties, switched off the light, and climbed into bed. Emotionally exhausted and slightly drunk, she couldn't stop the questions from flooding her mind. Maybe in the morning she'd learn some answers.

Brandon gazed at the bedroom door with uncertainty. Why had he brought her to the cabin? His life depended upon it remaining a secret. What was he going to do about his beautiful guest?

He removed his combat attire and picked up his jeans and a shirt from beside the sofa. As the minutes ticked by, he realized how much he wanted Belinda to stay with him, but he was uncomfortable with it. He stood to lose so much if she was to betray him. But why would she?

Ultimately, he had to face a cold, hard truth about himself that made him extremely vulnerable.

He was lonely.

Four

Exile

Brandon awoke with a start at 4:12 a.m. coated with perspiration. Every time he slipped into sleep he awoke again, his mind preoccupied with his failure to get to Carringby Tower before the attack. Yet he'd acted precisely according to the information he had. It was the second time in a month he'd screwed up and it was weighing heavily on his mind.

And then there was the matter of his guest in the next room. *My God. What was I thinking?*

He leaped off the sofa and took a t-shirt and jeans that were resting on the back of the leather recliner. Quickly, he dressed himself.

He slipped his sneakers on, made his way over to the corner of the living room, and stopped at a break in the carpet. At first glance it appeared to be nothing more than lackluster workmanship by the carpet installer. He knelt down and scurried around until he found a hook buried in the carpet bed. Pulling on it, he brought up a trap door leading to a wooden basement stairwell. Just underneath the doorframe he found the light switch and flipped it on. With one hand holding the trap door, he descended the steps and closed himself in.

Arriving at the bottom, he looked around the well-insulated basement. There a door to the outside in the far right hand corner, a boiler, and an electrical generator to his immediate left. A sizeable leather sack rested beneath the generator. He crouched down, unzipped it, and briefly checked a bulging collection of cash.

Satisfied, he zipped it up again, and with considerable effort, hooked the strap across his shoulder. The one-hundred-pound weight of more than one-million dollars in old twenty-dollar bills, was taxing.

He scaled the steps and pushed open the trap door with his back. With difficulty, he managed to rest the sack on the top step and gradually eased it onto the living room carpet. His breathing was labored, his toil enhanced by a gnawing sense of loss brought on only by his own weakness and stupidity. *Why did I bring her here?*

After climbing up, he pushed the sack farther into the living room. As he did so, the trap door slipped from his back and closed again with an almighty crash. His heart almost stopped with the fear it might have woken her.

He took the sack to the front door and dropped it on the porch. He then reached out and touched the door handle of the test aircraft. The door instantly unlocked and rose upwards as the internal electronics display illuminated the porch.

Leaning inside the craft, he touched a sensor and the seats folded forward with almost-silent motion. Once they were flattened forward, he pushed the sack across the porch and into the back of the craft beside two sophisticated-looking chrome attaché cases. Satisfied everything was in place, he activated the seats again, and closed the door.

The incredible spectacle of the snow canyon caught his attention, and a stab of sadness pierced his heart. The cabin was so perfect. It was isolated and safe. But now he was going to have to abandon it and brave the outside world where danger awaited him around every corner. It took all of his strength not to weep. *Why did I have to be so stupid? If only I hadn't brought her back.*

The hairs on the back of his neck stood on end with the eerie sense that someone was behind him. He turned with a start to see Belinda standing in the living room, wearing one of his t-shirts that ended at her knees. Even slightly hung-over and having just awoken in the middle of the night, her appeal hadn't faded. He gazed upon her flowing, soft auburn hair, fulsome lips, and soulful brown eyes. Her lightly tanned skin had a flawless complexion, and he couldn't deny how captivating he found her.

"Hi," she said.

"I thought you were asleep. How long have you been standing there?"

"Just for a second. I heard a noise and it woke me up."

"You should go back to bed. You need your rest after what you've been through."

"Do you honestly think I'm going to get much sleep after all that's happened?"

He rubbed his bare arms realizing how cold it was. "Come on. Let's get back inside." He walked past her, closed the door, and faced the back window. As desirable as she was, he became extremely uncomfortable with her standing in his living room wearing no pants. "I'd really appreciate it if you'd put some clothes on."

He glanced behind him as the bedroom door clicked shut.

Belinda tried to get back to sleep, but it was futile. Her mind was permeated with questions, and she knew her brooding host wasn't likely to be forthcoming with any answers. She didn't know what to make of him. She'd known, and been intimate with many men, including total strangers. But she'd never encountered one who had a problem with seeing her in various states of undress. Was it because he didn't find her attractive? Surely someone as handsome and athletic-looking as he was wouldn't have been the shy type.

Then she realized she was being irrational. She didn't even know him. He might be a psychopath for all she knew. In her heart, she didn't believe that.

At 8 a.m. she dressed herself properly and stepped out into the living room. She heard him scurrying around in the kitchen.

"Hi," he said. "I'm just making some coffee. Would you like some breakfast."

"That'd be great. Thank you."

She continued to be mystified by him. He'd saved her life, and was tall, attractive and heroic. But who the hell was he? And where were they? All he'd told her was 'somewhere near Aspen.' That could mean anywhere in a vast, snowy, mountainous wilderness such as this.

She gingerly entered the small kitchen and saw the view through the window. The ground was covered with perfect, untouched snow, decorated with a spattering of aspen trees within a spacious clearing the size of a tennis court. The way in which the snow had fallen upon the trees formed shapes like alien creatures.

Behind the clearing was a forest of aspen trees with only hints of green from the branches visible through their snow coating. The tip of the mountains behind it on the far horizon reached up to a rich blue skyline. It was a vision from a fairy tale, reminiscent of a classic Christmas postcard.

In Belinda's opinion, she had found herself in the most perfect place on earth. However, the experience was dampened by the circumstances. She couldn't imagine where it was all going to lead.

She became aware of the delicious scent of heated bread, and then Brandon handed her a tray of croissants and coffee. "Make yourself comfortable and relax in the living room."

"Sure. Thank you," she said, and took the tray.

"After breakfast, I'll go into Aspen to get a more . . . *conventional* vehicle, and then I'll take you back to Denver, all right?"

She knew she should have felt relieved he was going to take her home. He clearly had no ill intentions toward her. But she couldn't deny a touch of disappointment. "Why did you bring me here? You got me off of that roof, and I can't tell you how grateful I am. But why didn't you just leave me in Denver?"

He looked at her sadly. "I made a mistake."

Brandon flew the proto-type aircraft to the bottom of the canyon and hid it in a dense wooded lot, almost forty miles from the cabin. From there, he made the remaining, laborious, three mile journey on foot into Aspen.

Belinda's words echoed in his mind. Why couldn't he have just left her in Denver? He had no excuse or reason for bringing her back with him, except for . . . what? The maddening solitude of living in the cabin alone for so long? The natural need he felt to be with a woman? Every time he looked at her, his heart fluttered with the undeniable pull of attraction. Ruefulness for what he was about to do consumed him.

His circumstances dictated he couldn't afford to be recognized in public. If the situation arose in which a photograph of him was made public by the authorities, witnesses might identify him as having made frequent appearances in the area. He was determined that nobody would ever discover his safe haven. He knew he was going to have to abandon it for the time being, although he was hopeful the day would come when he might return to it.

Having to disguise himself whenever he went into town, applying facial prosthetics in the small aircraft, was always a painstaking procedure.

The hurried cash purchase of a van, specially adapted for driving through snow with the appropriate tires, was the essential purpose of the visit. He drove an eight-thousand dollar, used, white Dodge Sprinter into the forest where he'd concealed the aircraft. With precision flying, he hovered it facing away from the open rear of the van, and gradually reversed it inside.

With everything secured to his satisfaction, he made his way back. With only thirty-seven miles of raw, snow-covered ground, there were no roads to the cabin. Fortunately, the surface wasn't extreme, but it was always a rough ride, despite the modifications to the van.

Brandon hurried inside the cabin and headed straight for the bedroom without acknowledging his guest.

Belinda stood from the couch and moved to the bedroom doorway. He took two suitcases from the bedroom closet and rummaged through his drawers. She watched as he stuffed the suitcases with clothes. "Why are you doing this?" she said.

"I'm taking you back to Denver. Isn't that enough?"

30

"You thinking of moving to the city too?"

"No."

"Then why pack so much?"

He threw a pair of jeans into the case and didn't answer.

But to Belinda it was obvious. "You're leaving because of me, aren't you? You're running."

Still, no response came.

"I won't tell anyone about this place, I swear."

He paused with a look of anguish.

Sadness came over her along with the pangs of guilt. This courageous man was about to embark upon a self-imposed exile because he dared not trust her. What was he running from that could be so terrible he would do this to himself?

After collecting a few bathroom essentials, he clasped the two suitcases shut and carried them to the front door. He took his laptop from the living room table, placed it into its carrying case, and returned to the door.

"Please, don't do this," she said. "I appreciate you taking me back, but . . ."

He exhaled as though he was sorely tempted, but still didn't speak. Without looking back, he picked up the suitcases again. "Let's get going."

She followed him out and climbed into the van while he concealed his suitcases and laptop in the back of strange aircraft.

The rear doors closed, and within seconds, he was sitting in the driver's seat. She wanted to ease his anxiety, but she knew there was nothing she could say. "I'm so sorry" was the best she could offer.

Five

Trust

Belinda gazed out of the window as Brandon drove the van through Glenwood Springs. It was past one o'clock in the afternoon, and it would be at least two and a half hours before they reached Denver. The silence was oppressive. She wished he would give her some answers, or at least say something. He drove on as though she wasn't even there. He'd been so warm toward her only the night before. Why had he become so cold? Nothing made any sense. She questioned whether she would ever learn who he was, what he was all about, or who had been responsible for attacking Carringby Industries.

She felt ambivalent about him taking her back to Denver. He'd saved her life, and was now willing to sacrifice his home in order to get her back to hers. She didn't know what he was running from, but it was obviously something extremely threatening to him. The sadness in his eyes was clear. She wondered what kind of a man would do something so selfless for a stranger.

She had fallen in love with his cabin almost immediately. She'd never forget the view from the kitchen window at daybreak, or the spectacular sight of the snow canyon in the moonlight. It was a secret paradise; a sanctuary so far removed from the stresses, strains, and misery of the city. Only the night before, those factors had intensified to the most horrific level she'd ever experienced.

The sight of her colleagues being massacred played over in her mind incessantly. It was a miracle she was still alive, and only by virtue of the guy who was driving her back to that same world. All that waited for her in Denver was loneliness, unemployment, and dreams of an amazing haven somewhere in the mountains.

Although she'd been planning to go into Denver with her friends from college the night before, she hadn't been in contact with any of them for almost a year. She'd been estranged from her family for eleven years, and wasn't close to anybody. That was the empty existence to which he was returning her.

"What's wrong?" he said finally.

"Nothing," she replied. "And . . . *everything*."

"You're going to be fine. In a few hours you'll be back in your own home, and you can get on with the rest of your life." He kept his eyes forward as the road sped by. "I'm sorry for everything you've been through."

She felt slightly encouraged he was talking again. "That's just the point. I have no idea what I've been through, and it's driving me crazy."

"Believe me, it's better that you don't know. If I explained it all to you, anything could slip out in conversation, or even in your sleep. You could tell a secret to someone you trust and tell them not to tell anyone. They could then go and tell someone else *they* trust and tell *them* not to tell anyone. Before you know it, the whole damn world's going to be in on it, and that wouldn't be good for you, I can assure you."

"You're making a lot of assumptions."

"Like what?"

"You're presuming I have people in my life I trust and that I'm close to."

"Don't you?"

"No."

He seemed to become slightly easier about the situation, as though he was relieved she was so alone. "Don't you have family?" he said. "Friends? What about boyfriends?"

"Nobody at the moment."

"OK. What about family? Do you have a mother or father?"

She shrugged her shoulders. "I never knew my father. I was a one-night-stand baby. My mother held it against me ever since."

"Why? She can't blame you for that."

"She's Catholic and they're real big on guilt. I couldn't take the dogma anymore so I ran away from home when I was sixteen."

"When did you see your mother last?" His tone seemed filled with an intense urgency to learn more about her.

"Four years ago, and that was after seven years of no contact. It was a disaster. She disowned me after I told her to go to hell."

A combination of guilt and relief showed in his eyes. "I'm sorry to hear that. What about your friends? Surely you must have some friends."

"Acquaintances. I was planning on going out with some of my old colleagues from college last night. I hadn't seen any of them in over a year. I watched the people I knew best get gunned down before my eyes, but I'd never been tight with any of them either. I keep to myself. Life's a lot easier that way."

He glanced at her empathetically. "You don't really believe that, do you?"

She reached across and turned on the radio in an attempt to lift the bleak atmosphere. The news came on:

"Removal of the dead from Carringby Industries by the Denver Fire Department has ended this afternoon," the female reporter began. "Sixty-two fatalities have been recorded, although not all have been identified. The reason for the attack and the identities of the assailants are still not known."

"You know who did this, don't you?" she said.

He didn't answer.

The newscaster continued. "Fifty-one of the victims were located on the floor of the office of CEO, Barton Carringby, who was also killed during the shootings. However, this tragic incident has brought with it another mystery. Belinda Carolyn Reese, Barton Carringby's personal secretary, is currently listed as missing. It has now been confirmed she was not among the dead."

Brandon's head snapped toward the radio.

"Personal items belonging to Ms. Reese were discovered in one of the restrooms, leaving the possibility she may have accidentally left it behind and was out of the building at the time of the attack.

"However, Molly Rigsby, a member of Carringby's cleaning staff, swears she left the building minutes before the attack, and that Ms. Reese was at her desk at that time.

"According to Stan Winger, a former college friend of Ms. Reese's, they were due to meet up last night for a college reunion, but they were unable to reach her, and received no contact from her. At this time, her disappearance is under investigation."

"I've got to let somebody know I'm OK," Belinda said. "I can't believe it. Now I'm all over the damn radio."

Brandon shook his head. "What did they find of yours in that restroom?"

"Just my purse. I was putting my lipstick on when it happened."

"Was there a photograph of you in there?"

"I don't think so. I use public transportation, and don't carry my driver's license with me. Why?"

He paused for a moment, and then said, "All right, I need to buy a newspaper from somewhere. This just got real complicated."

"Complicated? In what way?"

They were approaching a town up ahead. "I'm going to stop at a store. I need to see how far this has gone, and then try to figure it out."

He drove through the town slowly until he came to a convenience store and pulled over. "I'll be back in a minute. Stay in the van." He switched off the engine and climbed out.

Brandon returned within minutes and handed Belinda a copy of *The Denver Post*. The Carringby story on the front page showed a picture of a burned-out office floor with firefighters in the background. She scanned along the sidebar and quickly spotted her name, but there wasn't a photograph of her.

"It's going to be just a matter of time before they track down a photo of you," he said. "If I keep moving and take you to Denver, I could be placing you in serious danger. I'm not going to force you to come back to the cabin with me. It's entirely up to you. But I'm telling you, it's the safest place you could be right now. I'm asking you to trust me."

"Oh, like you trusted me?" she shot back at him.

He nodded, as though he knew he deserved a response like that.

Caught in a maelstrom of confusion, she held his gaze, afraid, uncertain, and not knowing where to turn. Finally she said, "What serious danger would you be placing me in by taking me back to Denver?"

"It's very complicated."

"So you said."

What he was advising was what her heart truly desired, reckless though it may be. She no longer had anything back in Denver, and what reason had he given her not to trust him? No man had ever saved her life before, and none had ever intrigued her like Brandon. Aside from his annoying secrecy, he'd been kind and hadn't asked anything of her, even though she'd as much as offered herself to him. She'd been in shock, terribly shaken, and desperately in need of comfort. She'd literally been his for the taking, and yet he'd walked away and taken the couch.

And she couldn't remember the last time she'd laid eyes on a guy who was so damn handsome either—that difficult-to-place ruggedness with the defined square jaw and gentle green eyes.

After a long, tense silence, she made up her mind. "Take me back to the cabin with you."

With a sigh of relief, he turned the van around.

Belinda gazed into the ether as he drove her away into a world of the unknown.

Six

The Heart of a Hero

Brandon allowed himself a moment of relief and a liberating calm came over him. He knew Belinda would be safe in the cabin, and there would be no reason for him to keep running. For the first time in two months, he'd have someone to talk to. He would finally be spared the soul-destroying isolation, which could have been compared to perpetual solitary confinement.

It was three in the afternoon when they arrived back at the cabin, and it had become particularly chilly since they left. He walked over to the log fire and lit it.

Once the flames were spreading, he turned to Belinda. "I can't even begin to imagine how you're feeling right now."

"It's . . . OK," she said. "Or, at least it might be, if I can get some answers."

"Yeah, I can understand that. I'll go make us some coffee, and then we'll talk, all right?"

She smiled approvingly.

He entered the kitchen and picked up the kettle from the counter. As he took it over to the faucet, he noticed, through the window, a bear cub coming toward the cabin from the forest. It left a line of tiny footprints in the snow, and then stopped as it noticed him through the window.

Brandon beamed. Setting the kettle aside, he turned back to one of the kitchen cupboards. After taking out a jar of honey and a large ceramic bowl, he collected a packet of nuts, berries, and an apple. He filled up the bowl, took the honey jar, and returned to the living room.

Belinda looked at him, puzzled. "Is everything all right?"

With a glow of enthusiasm, he said, "Would you just excuse me for a moment?" He moved over to his snow boots by the door and briskly slipped them on. "I've got a little friend and I think he's hungry. I'll be right back, I promise."

He closed the door behind him, walked around to the back of the cabin, and carefully sat on a small bench positioned just beneath the kitchen window. The bear kept its distance until he was completely still.

Slowly, he placed the bowl of fruit and nuts and the opened jar of honey, approximately two feet before him. The bear immediately trotted toward them. "Hey there, little guy. Are you hungry?" Brandon said in a soft, child-like voice. "How've you been?"

The cub began to eagerly devour the offering. Brandon sat back and watched with a stab of conscience. "You almost missed out on this today, bud."

Belinda looked around the place trying to imagine it might become her home for the foreseeable future. It was absurd. All she knew was that the life she'd had twenty-four hours ago was no longer. It was as though an invisible hand had picked her up, taken her out of reality, and placed her . . . *where?*

She stepped into the kitchen and moved closer to the window. The bear was so engrossed in its feast that it didn't see her. She watched Brandon slowly outstretch his arm until his fingertips were a mere inches away from the bear's forehead. It looked up finally and sniffed his hand. She could see he was extremely cautious not to frighten it. He gently petted the soft, light-brown fur, and the bear edged closer to him.

A lump formed in her throat as she watched the scene unfold before her. It was such a heart-warming sight, complemented by the beauty of the surroundings. She was more convinced than ever that this man, who had brought her back to his secret home, was, in no way, a bad guy. Only a person with a most caring nature would become so enthusiastic about feeding a little furry creature. It was most probably lost.

She'd heard animals had an instinct that enabled them to be repelled by an aggressor or a predator. Clearly, this lone, wild, bear cub sensed nothing of the kind in Brandon. *Who are you, Brandon Drake?*

Empathy came over her. She had no idea how long Brandon had been alone, but she could understand how he would have been drawn to the cub. Not only was it an irresistibly beautiful creature, it would have easily struck a chord with him: two lonely souls who had connected in a vast, isolated wilderness.

She remembered when she'd told him that her living alone and not getting involved with people made her life so much easier. He'd questioned whether she truly believed it and she hadn't replied.

But he was right. She didn't believe it. She was just being stoical, putting up a barrier. Her life had been almost as lonely as his.

Transfixed, she continued to watch the exchange between Brandon and the cub.

The bear decided it'd had its fill, turned, and walked away. Brandon picked up the bowl and the honey jar, and waited until his little friend disappeared through the trees.

He returned to the porch, opened the front door, and removed his snow boots.

"That is one gorgeous little bear cub."

He looked up, surprised to see Belinda standing in the kitchen doorway. "You saw that?"

"Yes."

"Yeah, he's a cutie, but he's not going to be for too long, that's for sure." He paused for a moment. "Actually I don't know if it's a he or a she. It's been coming around here for about four weeks. I figured it'd either been abandoned by its mother, or the mother may have died. Maybe she got shot by hunters."

"Yeah, I guess so."

"OK, I'll go make us that coffee." His tone was far more cheerful than it had been. It was clear that being back home had removed the dark cloud that had been hovering over him.

"Thank you so much, Brandon. I can't tell you how much I appreciate everything you've done for me."

"Hey, don't mention it. At least now we're back, we can chill, maybe watch some TV. There's a home-made satellite receiver I've got fixed up on the roof, so it's not a part of any subscription." He winked at her mischievously.

She smiled heartily. "That'd be great."

A few minutes later, he came out of the kitchen, handed her a coffee, and moved toward the leather couch. "Come and take a seat. We can talk for a while, and then I'll start preparing dinner. "

"You cook?" she said.

"Enough to get by, but I'm not very good at it."

"Would you like some help?"

"Sure, but only if you want to." He couldn't be sure if it was gentlemanly to have his guest toiling in the kitchen with him. Neither could he shake the feeling that he should be taking care of her, and not the other way around.

"Actually, I love to cook," she said jovially.

"OK. In that case, thank you. Should be fun." Nervously, he sat down. "So, where do I start?"

She sat beside him, fidgeting. "How about you tell me who you are, Brandon? Does this cabin belong to you?"

"The cabin used to belong to my grandfather," he said. "It has a fairly sordid history."

"Sordid?"

"My father told me about the cabin before he died. My grandfather was somewhat unscrupulous, you might say."

"How so?"

"He had women who he used to bring here in secret, behind my grandmother's back." His mind momentarily flashed back to when he was a small boy, no older than four or five. He was standing with his father and grandfather in the front yard of the home where he'd grown up in New Mexico. It was his last memory of his grandfather, but he distinctly recalled him being tall and broad-shouldered—a giant to his infantile eyes. He recalled how hard and cold the man's face had been. There hadn't been a hint of warmth in him, and his eyes . . . Brandon tried to bring to mind the word that described them. *What was it about gramps' eyes?*

And then it came to him, sending a shudder coursing along his spine: *cruel.*

"Are you OK?" Belinda said.

He smiled apologetically. "I'm sorry. I just spaced out for a minute."

"I can see that." She made a move to place a supportive hand on his shoulder, but immediately held back. "Please go on. So, you inherited the cabin from your grandfather. But who are you? What do you do? You know . . . for a living?"

"I am . . . I mean, I *was,* a soldier."

"So, what happened? Did you resign from the army?"

"Not exactly. I went absent without leave. But it's not what you think. I'm not a deserter. I got injured in Afghanistan and was reassigned to a research facility in Washington. I was happy there."

"Research facility? What kind of research?"

"Weapons and tech development. I've always loved working with engines and gadgets. Guess that's why they posted me there. Two months ago, I accidentally uncovered something at the lab I was assigned to and everything went to hell."

Her eyebrows rose. "Tech development? Like that flying car thing?"

Brandon chuckled at how understandably wrong she was. "It's not a car. It's called the Turbo Swan. It's a Vertical Take-off and Landing turbo-jet aircraft."

"A what?"

"Well, it's like a jet aircraft, but smaller than the size of a sports car. We just put it together to test the miniaturized engines, the alloy shell material, and some of the internal electronics."

"Why'd you call it 'Turbo Swan'?"

He laughed. "Because it's like a turbo-charged, low-flying bird."

"Did you steal it? Is that why you're running?"

"It's a little more complicated than that. What I'm actually running from is the reason I had to go AWOL. It's just difficult to explain, and I'm still really concerned about you knowing too much, for your own safety. If you were to insist, I'd take you back to Denver. But I'm much more comfortable knowing you're here where it's safe."

She shuddered.

"What's wrong?" he said.

"Just when you said 'where it's safe'. It brought back the sound of the machine gun fire."

He looked at her sympathetically. "I'm here working on this because another attack is going to happen soon. I just haven't figured out where or when yet."

"If you know who did it, and who's going to do it again, isn't there some way you could tell the authorities?"

He closed his eyes despairingly at her impossible question. How was he going to explain it? When he first found out what was happening, it had frightened him almost as much as the battlefield had. He knew he had to look at it objectively and consider how a civilian would react. Would Belinda cope with knowing? Or would she panic? "I . . . I need you to give me some time to figure this out. Please, could you just hang in there for a while? Let's just take things one step at a time."

Reluctantly, she agreed. "OK."

Seven

Conspiracy

As night fell once more, Brandon prepared a meal of spaghetti bolognaise and he and Belinda dined with a bottle of wine. It hadn't required much effort on Belinda's part. Boiling spaghetti and heating up a can of pre-prepared bolognaise on the stove was as basic as it could get. She found it rather amusing and somewhat endearing. The simplicity of the way he lived had a certain charm that she couldn't define.

Afterward, they sat on the sofa sipping chardonnay. The heat from the log fire, the crackling, and the aroma of the burning logs, seemed to create the perfect atmosphere. The cabin and Brandon's kindness enabled her to relax in the aftermath of her traumatic experience. But occasionally, when she looked into his eyes, she could see fear. There was so much about him for her to uncover.

Her desire to rush into an intimate connection with him was strong, far more so than her dates with the suits. She'd meet a visiting executive or representative at work and he'd give her the eye. They would go out for dinner that night, then to bed. In the morning, it would all be over. Usually, she would never see them again. She knew it wasn't healthy. "So, what was life like in the army?" she said, distracting her train of thought.

"I'd been serving for eight years," he replied pensively. "I was pushed into it by my father when I was nineteen, and I always hated it. My dad, Major Howard Drake, was a stiff-upper-lip soldier, but his values and mine were always at odds. He was just like my grandfather, and so were my fellow troopers."

"It sounds like you were like a fish out of water."

"I was. But I got through it knowing I was fighting for the one thing that's the most important to me."

"What's that?"

"Freedom," he said with conviction. "I was absolutely committed on the field. It was the social side of army life that didn't sit well with me, like the way the guys used to treat women."

Belinda frowned. "How did they treat them?"

"They'd pick up ladies in bars, coldly take them to bed, and then bid them adios the next day. People have feelings, and they were total jerks."

Belinda finally gave in to the urge to place her arm around his rock-solid shoulders. He tapped her fingers affectionately, although his anxiety was apparent. She knew he was being gracious, but she could sense his discomfort and took her hand away.

"You said that you were injured," she said. "What happened?"

He gazed into space. "It happened just outside Helmand. We went in to take out an enemy cell in the desert. A buddy of mine was on foot ahead of me when we were headed toward the cave where they were holed up. One of them hurled out a grenade and it landed just ahead of him. I ran forward and pushed him out of the way. The grenade blew and a shard of shrapnel caught me in the head. Next thing I remember, I was waking up in a hospital back in DC."

She touched the scar on his forehead. "Is that it?" Their eyes locked. She could see he was uncomfortable and took her hand away again. "I'm sorry, Brandon. This is personal stuff. I know it's none of my business."

"No, really. It's OK. It healed up and I'm fine now. Guess I got real lucky."

To Belinda, it was yet another story of his unrelenting heroism, and his self-deprecating attitude toward it made him all the more endearing.

The more she listened, the more intrigued she became. For a soldier who'd seen battlefield action, he seemed like such a gentle and sensitive soul. Wouldn't his persona have been harder-edged than this, and not so thoughtful? Or could his nervous and pensive nature be the result of battlefield trauma? It was confusing and impossible for her to assess. She couldn't imagine he was lying to her, especially after experiencing his performance on the Carringby rooftop.

Their gazes lingered upon one another for a prolonged moment, neither of them daring to make the first move.

Awkwardly, he cut the moment short and reached for the bottle of chardonnay beside his feet. "Would you like some more wine?"

***

"Come in."

Upon hearing the cold invitation, Agent Martyn McKay entered the spacious, opulent office—the domain of his new commander. The aroma of stale cigars was instantly recognizable.

At thirty years of age, McKay, a relatively new recruit to Homeland Security, had difficulty containing his apprehension. Having been assigned to Capitol Hill for over a month, the presence of his superior, Senator Garrison Treadwell, still caused him some angst.

Attired in a dark blue suit, Treadwell wore a full head of thick silver hair like a narcissistic crown.

McKay considered the circumstances under which he'd been assigned to his position, and it didn't sit well with him. Treadwell's previous assistant had died of a brain aneurysm. McKay had been assigned to him as a matter of urgency. He'd known from the beginning Treadwell didn't appreciate his presence. The senator preferred to make his own selections, but was, perhaps wary of making too much of an issue with the intelligence community. The current situation they were dealing with was particularly delicate. As such, McKay felt nothing more than tolerated.

Treadwell looked up from his desk. "Well?"

The agent swallowed hard. "We've had a report from the Denver Police Department, sir. There was a sighting of the Turbo Swan after the attack on Carringby Industries last night."

"Anything else?"

"Yes, sir. The police recovered a mark-four spider cable and an abandoned EG-Nine wire-glider unit from the adjacent tower. They've been identified by Mach Industries as theirs."

"Drake," Treadwell mumbled, and slammed the side of his fist onto his oak desk.

McKay's lips pursed in frustration. He'd been transferred from Langley to assist the senator after another attack, similar to Carringby, four weeks earlier. He'd never been told directly what it was about, and was vexed further by Treadwell's persistent mumbling and talking in riddles.

Treadwell stroked his chin as though in contemplation. After a few moments, he turned back to McKay. "This is going to require a more direct approach."

"What would you like me to do, sir?"

The senator stood and moved closer to his subordinate in an intimidating fashion. "Contact the Delta Unit and tell them to accelerate the agenda by one hour. They'll know what you mean."

It was obvious to McKay that Treadwell knew much more about the situation than he was letting on, but that didn't help him in the least.

"Tell them to be prepared, and if the worst should happen . . ."

"*The worst,* sir? What do you mean?"

"Tell them to execute."

"Execute?"

Treadwell sighed impatiently. "Kill Brandon Drake."

Eight

The Code

"Good morning," Brandon said as he stepped out of the shower with a towel around his waist.

Belinda paused for a moment, having difficulty looking away from his cut abdominals and protruding chest. "Hi. Would you like breakfast?" she said finally.

"Are you kidding? I'm famished."

She made her way out of the bedroom toward the kitchen, and heard him following her.

"So, what would you like?" he said. "I'm out of croissants, but there're corn flakes and chocolate crispies in the cupboard."

"The chocolate crispies sound great."

"How did you sleep?"

"Better. I was so tired, you wouldn't believe it."

"Oh, yes I would. What you've been through would be enough to exhaust the world's toughest."

She turned to him with understanding. "You went through it too, remember?" A question came to her. They were deep into a remote, alpine region, way beyond Aspen, and probably thirty or more miles away from their nearest neighbor. Yet the cabin was so warm. "How is this place heated, Brandon?"

"Oh, there's a generator in the basement. I'm always fixing it 'cause it's old and worn, but it'll do for now. The log fire helps too."

It surprised her how such things were of interest to her. Subconsciously, she'd already decided this is where she wanted her home to be more than anywhere else. "What do you do here all day?"

He took out two cereal bowls and two large coffee mugs, and said, "You'd be surprised how busy I find myself. Currently, I'm working on when the next you-know-what is going to happen. I've only got the code for information about one more incident, so this is going to be my last chance not to mess it up."

She held him by the shoulders and shook him lightly. "You didn't mess up. Please believe that. I'd be dead if it wasn't for you."

He smiled sadly. "There were sixty-two others who didn't fare so well because I was late. I just wanted to warn everybody to get out of the building before it happened. I thought I had everything, right down to the last detail. I even arrived all tooled up just in case I ran into the bastards, but my timing was wrong."

"Is there anything I can do to help?"

He shrugged his shoulders. "I doubt it. I'm working with a complicated crypto-numeric code. I have a program in the laptop that'll figure it out, but I'm no longer sure it's accurate."

"What code is that?"

"It's the plans for the attacks. It's how I'm finding out when and where they're happening."

"But . . . where did you get it?"

He looked at her uneasily, but didn't answer. "Come on. Let's have some breakfast."

After breakfast, Brandon stood up from the kitchen table. "You're going to need some supplies while you're here."

Belinda cringed. "I know. It's just that . . ."

"Just what?"

"I don't have any money. The police have it all. I had around sixty dollars in my purse and a couple of credit cards."

"Hey, believe me, that's not even an issue. I've got more than enough."

"But I can't expect you to keep me." Since she was sixteen, she'd learned the value of being self-sufficient, in nobody's debt, and answerable to as few as possible. It was a way of life she didn't feel comfortable changing.

"It's not a problem, I promise," he said with the most easy-going manner. "Put it down to extenuating circumstances."

"All right, but I'll pay you back. Agreed?"

"Hey, hey. It's fine, believe me."

She was rendered speechless by how incredibly generous he was. Despite her discomfort toward his magnanimity, she couldn't deny the state her life was in. In that moment, the thought of spending the rest of her days simply sitting at the kitchen table, with that incredible view of the snow, trees, and mountains through the window, seemed like paradise.

He stood up from the table, made his way into the bedroom, and threw on some clothes. As he was putting his leather jacket on, he said, "What's your shoe size?"

Belinda sat on the sofa watching daytime talk shows on Brandon's high-definition television screen. It was so relaxing, like she was on vacation from her life.

Her mind wandered, trying to imagine what she would've been doing had the attack not happened. What tasks would Mr. Carringby have set for her? How would she have been feeling? Would it have been another tedious day at the office? Or would he have given her something challenging to do for once?

Whatever an alternate universe might have offered, it wouldn't have compared to where she found herself. She felt a stab of guilt at becoming contented by virtue of an incident that had cost the lives of sixty-two others. *Please forgive me*, she silently petitioned her lost colleagues.

A powerful desire came over her for Brandon to find her something she could help him with. She was overcome with a personal need to assist in preventing the terror she had suffered from happening to anyone else. She needed something to give her life a sense of purpose. Perhaps she could help him decipher the mysterious code he'd been so cagey about. *Why the hell does he have to be so secretive?*

Brandon returned soon after midday and stepped into the cabin with two large bags of provisions, and a dozen red roses, ill-concealed under the armpit of his jacket.

Belinda had been on his mind constantly since he left. It was eerie how insightful she was. When she'd acknowledged he'd been through the Carringby attack with her, it was as though she knew his trauma. He remembered how rattled he'd been before setting off for Denver to intercept the attack. He couldn't forget how he'd been so terrified he almost couldn't bring himself to walk out the door. On the battlefield he had the back up of his unit, but at Carringby, he was alone. And Belinda seemed to know.

His entrance startled her out of her reverie. But the moment she saw the flowers, she shot him a beaming smile. "Oh, my God. Did you buy those for me?"

He grinned playfully. "No, I got them for my little bear friend. It really loves the taste of roses."

She giggled. "No, you didn't."

"I thought you'd like them, so I figured . . ."

"You were right. I do."

He dropped the bags beside the door and handed her the flowers. His gesture had warmed her heart, as was obvious from the look in her eyes. He couldn't disguise his elation that it had affected her so profoundly. Knowing most ladies were particularly fond of flowers, he'd bought them for her in his eagerness to make her feel as 'at home' as possible. He was constantly mindful that he was in a familiar place, but she was not.

She pointed to his right cheek. "You've got something on your face."

He touched his skin, realizing there were remnants of the adhesive he'd used to fix his disguise, and brushed it off. "Thanks."

Belinda immersed herself in an endorphin high so compelling she couldn't bring herself to acknowledge caution or hypothetical negatives.

She looked fondly at her flowers as she took them into the kitchen. Placing them in a vase of water, she questioned why he would have done something like that for her. He was the most caring and thoughtful person she'd ever known. He seemed to be made up of every quality she'd never dared wish for—strong, heroic, selfless and compassionate, deeply caring, good-looking, and with a physique that could have gained him acceptance into Chippendales. He was too good to be true. At any other time, it would've been cause for alarm. A lifetime of frustration and disappointment had caused her to become pessimistic.

"OK," he said. "I got you some snow boots and a few new clothes. Just casual stuff. I think they're the right size."

She shook her head, overwhelmed by how special he was making her feel. She was about to speak when she noticed the bear cub coming through the trees. "Brandon?"

"Yeah."

"Your little friend's back."

He hurried into the kitchen and looked at the bear through the window. "Hey, would you like to come out with me?"

She turned to him with uncertainty. "Are you sure? I mean, what if I scare it?"

"It was unsure of me to begin with, but I won him over. You'll need to put your snow boots on, though."

Excitedly, she returned to the living room.

Nine

A Hero's Secret

Wearing a gray hooded, insulated snow jacket Brandon had bought for her, Belinda slowly followed him around the cabin. She inhaled the cool, unique fragrance of the wilderness as she waited out-of-sight, just before the clearing. Brandon eased himself onto the bench and placed the bowl of nuts in the snow.

The bear seemed confident enough and hurried over to its food.

Brandon whispered, "I think it's OK. Just take it slowly."

Belinda gingerly-but-excitedly stepped forward and sat down beside him. The bear looked up at her, and then resumed eating, completely unconcerned.

"Hey, it looks like he's OK with you." Brandon handed her half of an apple. "Try to give him this. He loves apples."

She took the apple and eased it toward the bear. It looked up again and there was a glint of recognition in its eyes. Hungrily, it stood on its hind legs and grasped the fruit, enabling her to make an observation. "There's your answer."

"What?"

"He's a boy."

Brandon looked back at the bear. "So he is. He's never stood up like that for me. He must really like you."

"He's beautiful," she said.

"Yeah, he sure is. Wanna try and pet him?"

"Sure." She gently reached out and touched the bear's nose. It responded fearlessly.

Brandon joined her and stroked its head. "This little guy just about saved my sanity over the last few weeks."

Sympathy came over her at the thought of Brandon's lonely plight. She struggled to imagine what such isolation must have done to his mind.

She turned back to the bear. "Maybe you should give him a name."

"Um, never thought about that. How about *Snooky*?"

She chuckled. "Snooky? That's a silly name."

With a light-hearted, juvenile tone, he said, "I *am* silly."

As they continued to pet the bear, their fingers touched, and Brandon froze. She looked into his eyes longingly, and swallowed hard. She drew closer to him, but he eased away. It was the same reluctance he'd shown on the night he'd rescued her, and it confused her. "What is it, Brandon?"

He turned away. To Belinda, it looked as though he was turning away in shame. "I don't mean to pry, and please tell me if it's none of my business, but . . ." She paused as she summoned the courage to ask the desperately personal question. After all, he wasn't wearing a ring, so what else could it be? "Are you gay? Or . . . is there someone else?"

He slowly turned back to her. "No. It's nothing like that."

She sighed of relief, but she could see he was painfully distressed. "Is it me? Something's wrong, isn't it? Please tell me."

"I don't know if you'll understand. It's really rather difficult to explain."

"Just say it." She noticed perspiration on his brow. He was becoming such a contrast to the courageous hero of the night before last. She wondered how a man could stare death in the face, and act with such tremendous efficiency, only to suddenly collapse under the weight of a simple question.

She also noticed something about him that seemed to occur only when he was distressed. She'd seen it the day before when he was preparing to abandon the cabin to take her back to Denver. The star-shaped scar on his forehead seemed to become deeper and more pronounced as the blood pounded in his temples.

"I've never . . ." He closed his eyes, his cheeks flushing a bright shade of crimson. "I've never been with a woman like *that* before." As the final word fell from his mouth, he lowered his head.

She looked at him dumbfounded. He wasn't joking. His perspiration, flushed cheeks, and agonized expression were evidence enough for her. But how could it be? He was so handsome, so fit—so astonishingly attractive. "OK. I don't really know how to respond to that."

"I guess the circumstances for me to meet the right girl just never happened. I sure didn't wanna wind up acting like my army buddies, or my dad and grandfather. It's been bugging me for a long time, but it's just down to a set of circumstances. I don't know what else to say."

She took her hand away from the bear and placed her arm around his shoulders. It was difficult to know what to say, but she knew she should try to ease his distress. "You don't have to do anything with me that you don't want to, and I have no expectations of you, all right?"

He exhaled, clearly relieved.

She decided to see how far she could take the moment. Their lips touched and she attempted to guide him through the experience. First the passionate tasting of him, and then slowly, she inserted the tip of her tongue between his lips. Cautiously, he followed her lead. She extended her tongue deeper into his mouth and he awkwardly reciprocated, their respiration increasing in unison.

However, he broke away from her abruptly.

"It's all right," she said, trying to disguise her disappointment.

"I'm not ready. Not yet. Please, just give me some time. I know this must seem strange, but it isn't because of you, I swear. I'm dealing with a lot right now."

She took a deep breath in an attempt to calm her gnawing passion, and gently caressed his cheek. "I think I understand."

They looked across to see the bear staring at them. After a few moments, it turned away toward the trees.

"Come on. Let's get back inside," Brandon said.

Belinda walked ahead of him and stopped in her tracks, sincerely wanting to assuage his distress. "Brandon, it's all right, really."

He simply nodded, clearly unconvinced. She was aware that no matter how valiantly she was trying to brush off her disappointment, desire still burned in her eyes.

He closed the cabin door behind them and returned to the kitchen. Belinda followed, blown away by his revelation, and was struggling to process it. "Seriously? You've never been with a woman?"

"Nope. Never."

"But how do you feel about that? I mean, it's such a natural part of life, I just can't imagine."

"There's a saying that you never miss what you've never had," he said, blushing. "But you know what? It's not true. I miss this like hell. I'm just afraid of . . ."

She rested her hand upon his shoulder supportively. "Afraid of what?"

"Afraid I'll mess it up."

She shot him an understanding smile. "Everybody messes it up sometimes, even the most experienced. Messing it up can be part of the fun."

He laughed nervously. "Well, maybe someday. Who knows? I just don't think my head's in the right place at the moment, with what I've got to do and all."

"I understand. If there's anything I can do to help, just let me know. OK?"

"You got it." He moved over to his leather recliner, sat down, and resumed his task with a highly-sophisticated-looking laptop. A sequence of numbers filled the screen.

Belinda came up behind him, her mind blank at what she saw. "Wow. Is this the code you were talking about?"

"This is it, and it's an absolute nightmare. The program I've got installed to decode it isn't the best. I didn't have time to update it at the lab. Because of that, it takes days. All it's going to show at the end is a date, a time, and a location." He scrolled down the screen to show her that the code extended for page after endless page.

She gasped. "Oh, boy."

"It's a complex new type of crypto-numeric," he said. "They clearly didn't want anybody figuring it out, but lives are at stake. I really have no choice but to keep working on it."

She leaned over and kissed his cheek. This time, he smiled comfortably. "Well, I'm here if you need me," she said.

"Belinda?"

"Yes."

He smiled at her. "Thank you. I can't tell you how much better it is being here with you."

She didn't say anything, but knew the affection in her eyes spoke for her. It was remarkable to her that *he* was thankful to *her* after everything he'd done. He was introducing her to feelings she'd never known before. No man had ever actually cared about her in the past. They might have slept with her, but that wasn't caring. It was an exercise in mutual taking. Despite the gnawing questions she still had, she knew she was developing a deep tenderness for Brandon, and, somehow, a sense of sadness. He seemed to have the weight of the world on his shoulders. But why? Who, or *what*, was he fighting that was causing him so much anguish?

The numbers scrambled and changed on the monitor screen like a swarm of insects, faster that the eye could see. Brandon watched intently, waiting with painstaking patience.

It took hours for the first result to appear—the letter 'S.' He took a pen and a sheet of paper from the desk, and wrote it down. It was nothing. Just one letter. But it was the beginning of the answer to his last chance to stop the attacks, once and for all. *Where is it going to happen? Who's gonna be next?*

Ten

Tonight

Brandon continued to sleep on the couch. He occupied himself with his work spending hour after hour focused on his laptop, and left it running around the clock.

Waking at 7 a.m. every morning, he threw on his warm, water-proof clothing and rubber-soled boots. He scaled the steep, two mile-high ridge behind the cabin, pushing himself to the limit. He'd resumed his morning training routine after a three day break. The door closing upon his return was always Belinda's wake-up call.

She immersed herself in the experience of the cabin—its serenity, beauty, and the departure it offered from the frustrating life she'd left behind. She was living a utopian fantasy that she didn't want to end.

The decoder in Brandon's laptop produced an average of two letters per day. Belinda found her calling by studying them intently to see if she could glean anything from the location it was slowly spelling out. So far, there wasn't enough to identify, but helping with something so vital gave her a feeling of self-worth.

Brandon often found himself watching her as she studied the letters. Even the way she chewed her hair when she was concentrating gave him a warm feeling inside. He'd never seen anybody do that before.

Their relationship grew, day by day. While the laptop processed the code, Brandon occasionally gave himself a break. They sat together watching movies, had snowball fights, fed Snooky together, and acted as free as children, enjoying their reprieve from the horrors of the world. Their lives became intertwined, sharing every facet of daily life. They worked as a team, with their only disagreement being over music. Brandon had a penchant for eighties-style arena rock, but Belinda preferred soul and blues. Unfortunately, he didn't have any soul or blues in his CD collection.

He quickly discovered what real cooking was all about when Belinda took control of the kitchen. He smiled inwardly, embarrassed by his initial offering to her. She was a fine teacher in that department, although burning the potatoes on his first attempt became a source of mutual laughter.

On their seventh night together, snow was falling again. Brandon lit the fire and continued with his task on the laptop. The sheet of paper lay next to him with the sequence of letters having grown considerably. "I'm so close now," he said. "I've got most of the location letters, but I still can't quite make it out. I've got a time and confirmation of this month. I'm just hoping it hasn't already happened."

"There's been nothing else that looked like Carringby on the news," Belinda said. "I've been keeping a close watch."

He gave her an appreciative smile. "I know you have. You've been absolutely awesome."

A beep from the laptop caught his attention. He looked down to see the number '1' with a cursor flashing beside it, awaiting the next numeral. He'd have preferred it to have been a '2' as the first digit. The anticipation of the missing second number only put him on tenterhooks. Despite Belinda having not seen anything during her days searching news channels, his paranoia of failing for a third time was compromising his rationality. His hands began to tremble.

"What's wrong?" she said.

"I don't know if it's already happened."

"I swear nothing's been on the news."

"I know, but I've got a 'one', as in ten, eleven, twelve, or thirteen."

"It could also be fourteen through nineteen," she said hopefully.

He rubbed his eyes nervously, stared at the cursor, and muttered impatiently through his teeth, "Come on, come on, you son of a bitch."

And then the missing number appeared: '4'.

His heart went into palpitations. "Oh, my God."

"What's wrong?"

He looked at her with dread in his eyes, and his forehead scar deepened again. "It's tonight."

"Tonight?"

"That's what it says. February fourteenth, at twenty-three hundred hours. Why the hell would they pick Valentine's Day? Sick bastards. But what if it's wrong?"

"How so?"

"It's like what happened at Carringby. I decoded the time, but they arrived earlier than what it said. They could've changed the plans, and I still have no idea where it's going down."

Belinda picked up the paper on the table and studied the letters: S, T, L, K, E, C, I, Y, U, T, C, O, T, N.

Brandon studied her expression as her eyes swept across the letters. He could almost see her realization dawning. "You think you know where it is?"

"I'm not sure. I feel like something's screaming at me, but I can't quite get it. It reminds me of a crossword, like trying to find the missing letters." And then the penny dropped. "Salt Lake City, Utah!" she shouted out excitedly.

Brandon leaped off the recliner. "Are you sure?"

"Positive." She pointed it out to him on the paper. "The 'A' and 'L' are missing from 'Salt,' only the 'A' from 'Lake,' and the 'A' and 'H' from 'Utah.' I have no idea what C, O, T, N, means."

"*Colton*," he said. "Oh, my God. It's a munitions factory they're gonna hit. Colton Ranch. It's just outside of Salt Lake. Thank you so much, Belinda. You don't know how much you've just helped me."

She looked at him uneasily. "What are you going to do?"

"I'm gonna suit up and get out there." He hurried over to his Kevlar attire draped across the leather sofa.

"And do what?"

He stopped in his tracks. She did have a point. Seeing no other way to answer her, he said, "Whatever I can."

Her body tensed and panic appeared in her eyes. "Please don't do this, Brandon. I'm begging you. There has to be another way."

He looked at her, sorely torn. It was even worse than on the afternoon he'd left for Denver. This time, he had more to lose than ever. Having Belinda living and working with him had given happiness he'd never known before, but he could see no other options. "Please understand, I don't want to go. I'm scared, as anyone would be, but I have no choice."

"Why?"

He picked up his combat attire. "Because there's no one else. I have to stop them. I have to help those people."

"Brandon, stop. Don't do this. Don't leave me, please."

"I have to."

"What can you possibly do if they're going to attack a weapons manufacturer? You're just one man. If they can get through that kind of security, you won't stand a chance."

He pulled on his combat pants hurriedly. "They won't have to get through any security."

"What do you mean?"

He struggled to know how he was going to explain it all. Every answer he could give would only lead to another question. "They're already inside the base."

"Then call Colton Ranch and warn them."

"I already did that in the beginning with the Everidge attack in Dallas. They treated it as a prank call. Two hundred and thirteen people died because I didn't act."

Belinda was silent for a moment. But then an idea came to her. "The press."

"What?"

"Call the press and tell them what you know. They can be deadly to any organization, believe me. My first job after college was for a government-funded communications corporation. It was shut down after the media exposed it for secretly operating a money laundering outfit."

He didn't speak. His fear of revealing himself, in any way, to the media was a constant concern.

"How about if I call them?" she suggested.

"You?"

"Yes, *me*. Now please, Brandon, don't go. Let me help you."

He put his combat jacket back on the sofa and looked into her eyes. Every one of his instincts cried out to stay with her in his serene utopia. But what if she was wrong? Her expression showed such assured sincerity. She'd worked in the corporate sector and had knowledge of the press and its powers that he didn't. He'd grown to trust her, and was overcome with an eagerness to take her at her word. Her powers of persuasion were also enhanced by the realization that she was as reliant on him as anyone else. What would happen to her if anything went wrong? It was an unbearable thought.

Convinced of her judgment, he accepted there was an alternative to personal intervention, one that was likely going to be far more effective. "All right, let's call it in."

Belinda spoke to a reporter through Brandon's sat-scrambler phone. The conversation became increasingly heated. "The Colton Ranch Plant is going to fall under attack tonight at eleven, you have to believe me . . . No, I can't prove it. All I can tell you is that this is related to the attacks on Everidge in Dallas, and Carringby in Denver."

Brandon took the phone from her and switched it off.

"Are you sure the call wasn't traced?" she said.

"They can't trace a call from this phone. It's a one-of-a-kind sat-scrambler."

"What's that? Does it have some kind of jamming technology?"

"Not exactly. It has divertive capabilities. The NSA might try to trace the call, but their surveillance technology will pinpoint the location to a place far from here." A sly, knowing grin crept from the corner of his mouth. "Very, very far from here." He closed his eyes and exhaled, hoping intensely that they'd done the right thing.

Belinda lightly caressed his arms. "Everything's going to be fine. I can feel it."

"I sure hope you're right."

"Either way, it's over. It's not your responsibility anymore." She gestured to the sofa. "Let's chill out and, if you feel ready, you can tell me all about what's been happening."

He looked at her with extreme uncertainty. Ultimately, he knew he couldn't keep the truth from her any longer. "All right," he said. "But it's a long story."

Eleven

First Time

"OK," Brandon said. "I'd been assigned to the Mach Industries facility in Arlington after I was injured on the field. It was after about a year when I was doing some research. I discovered . . ."

"What?" Belinda said.

"The attacks are not the work of terrorists."

"They're not?"

He hesitated again, but eventually resumed. "It's the CIA, Belinda. Or, a rogue faction of it, at least. They're initiating false terrorist attacks to create excuses for wars against foreign nations."

She gasped. "Now I understand what you meant in the van on that first night."

"What's that?"

"You said 'Those killers were the authorities'. Now it makes sense. But it still doesn't explain why."

"Two months ago, I found out what they were doing and I saved the codes for the plans to a flash drive. It was a deleted file I'd stumbled across in the mainframe. Nobody could have found it even if they'd gone looking, which is why I don't think they know what I have."

"I wouldn't be so sure of that," she said.

"Well, yeah, I guess. They know I have a hell of a lot of their tech. I had to get out of there, so I loaded up the Turbo Swan and escaped in it."

"What did Carringby have to do with any of this?"

"It was on the plans, along with the dates and times. With Carringby, it was all about the XD-47."

"What is that, exactly?" she said

"What's what?"

"Those letters and numbers. XD-47. I saw them all the time, but I didn't take any notice. What do they mean?"

"It's a serial number for a component in a missile."

Belinda's jaw dropped. "Carringby was manufacturing a missile?"

"Parts for one, but those thugs didn't really want it. The army already had the XD-47. They've had it for almost a year."

"So why attack Carringby?"

"They wanted to make it look like somebody else wanted it. It's an excuse for a war."

"Why would anybody want to start a war?"

"For profit. There's phenomenal money involved. I decoded the plans from the flash drive. That's how I knew they were going to attack Carringby, and I tried to stop it."

"What did you hope to accomplish?"

"I-I had to do at least something," he said. "I couldn't just ignore it and hope it would all go away."

"Many people died, my colleagues included," she said bitterly. "I'm not saying I was close to them, but I had regard for them. Are you saying they died just for some kind of theatrical staging?"

He looked away, loathing having to give the only answer he could. "Yes. All I have is the equipment I stole. There's nothing else I can do. If I'm apprehended, I'll be charged with desertion and theft of government property. They could put me away for a very long time."

Belinda slapped the arm of the chair. "It's absurd. They could take your freedom from you because you tried to save innocent people? What kind of a world do we live in when the law could allow something so cruel and ridiculous?"

He placed his hand on hers appreciatively.

"I'm so sorry, Brandon. At least now I understand what you're all about. I wish you'd have told me this before."

"I had to know if you could handle it," he said. "I mean, this is terrifying stuff."

There was a long silence as they stared at one another. Her compassion and understanding touched him profoundly, and the moment caught him by surprise. His heart raced, but he wasn't afraid or uncertain this time.

She touched his cheek, and for once, he permitted himself the luxury of responding. Regardless of the outcome, the fact that the burden had been taken out of his hands brought a sense of liberation to him.

Their mouths met, ensnaring him in the grip of passion. His body cried out for her touch, but his sexual inexperience consumed him again. *My God, what the hell am I doing?*

Flashes came before his eyes—his experiences on the battlefield in Afghanistan, and the sight of his buddies falling to enemy fire. Every one of them had been cold in their treatment of women. He questioned if that was why? Was it because they knew they were going to die? That screwing so many women was their only chance of preserving their genes? *That can't be what this is all about.*

"It's all right," she whispered, her breath coming in short, excited bursts.

He knew there was nothing unknown about it to Belinda. But to him it was an experience both alien—and yet

71

strangely familiar. Somewhat free of his burdens, he felt he knew what to do instinctively.

He gently picked her up in his arms and lowered her gracefully onto the rug in front of the log fire. Regardless of how many times he'd visualized this moment in his mind, nothing could have prepared him for it. He removed his Kevlar armored top, discarded it, and knelt down. The situation had taken hold of them both with such spontaneity. It was a moment that had been given to them so perfectly.

Slowly easing his way forward, he cautiously removed her jeans. He noticed the skin on her thighs was smooth and flawless, with the most delectable bronze coloring.

In a dreamlike state, he brought his mouth to her groin and kissed her intimately, drawing her into a frenzy of passion. The pure, sensual scent of her gripped his senses, inducing a tempest of unbridled desire within him.

She pressed her hips downwards and moaned, revealing to him that he'd found his target. That knowledge urged him on to caress her tenderly with an intense need to please her.

After a few moments, he stood and cast off his Kevlar pants. He knelt down again and rested his elbows on either side of her, his torso inches above hers.

She cried out as they became as one for the first time. For Brandon, it was a moment of wonder. The tenderness he felt for her was so real, he had difficulty imagining they'd ever been anything other than lovers. The sensation of her body was beyond his most vivid fantasy.

He'd heard of how men usually finished far too early on their first time, but he was determined not to disgrace himself in that way. *Control. Stay in control.*

For long, exquisite minutes, they drowned in one another's eyes as he took her breath away with each gentle stroke of his pelvis. It was an agony of ecstasy for him as he repeatedly slowed down and resumed, determined to keep going for however long he needed to.

After a seeming eternity of surfing the line between sensual torment and delight, the cabin came alive as they climaxed together. Intensity appeared in her eyes, signaling her release. His own came in time with hers as he joined his mouth to hers.

Eventually, he gently rested beside her. She returned his embrace, capturing his breath with her own.

Belinda held him tightly as they lay together. A tranquil peace filled the room, with the fire blazing beside them, and the snow falling gently outside. She considered how his strength and gentleness had ignited her passions. Her emotions had taken her by surprise. This ran far deeper than what she usually felt when she was with a man. He'd made love to her in a way she'd never known before. She had an empathetic connection with Brandon, a remarkable human being who had come into her life under circumstances so unlikely they seemed almost fated.

"By the way," she said, breaking the silence. "Happy Valentine's Day."

Twelve

APB

Brandon and Belinda spent the next four hours walking the cerebral high of taking their relationship to the next level. Eventually, reality began to rear its ugly head.

Sitting with her in silence, Brandon pondered their earlier discussion about the conspiracy. He tried to figure out his place in all of the turmoil. He'd always wanted to do the right thing, but he'd never been able to decide whether it was out of honest morality, or rebellion. He remembered despising his father for being an unpleasant authoritarian, who had bullied him into serving an even darker authority. He recalled the times they'd fought over their countless differences of opinion, but he'd never been given the chance to resolve his issues with the man. His father had died of a heart attack leaving Brandon's own heart filled with resentment, further fueled by a life of being oppressed by others.

Fortunately, he'd had the nurturing, moral guidance of a loving mother who'd taught him right from wrong. His father had treated her with cold, loveless disregard, as though she'd been his servant.

Belinda enabled him to analyze his motives in a way he'd never considered before, and the true appeal of doing the right thing. She was alive only because of what he'd done on his own initiative, not under the command of others. She was reliant on him for her survival. It wasn't a desire to control her in the least. Her need for him gave him

74

a sense of worth and purpose. She validated his existence. In so doing, she held a place in his heart so precious, he would've gladly laid down his life for her. It was the feeling she had inspired in him from the outset, but he hadn't been able to positively identify it. Now he realized, and it gave him a deeper understanding of himself than ever before.

He picked up the TV remote with trepidation. It would all be over by now, and he was stricken with the paranoia that Belinda's phone call hadn't worked. After considerable procrastination, he switched the TV on and flicked through the news channels. It wasn't long before he discovered the primary news report.

". . . attack against the Colton Ranch munitions plant in Salt Lake is a mystery." The female commentator said as she stood against a backdrop of fire.

Brandon's heart came into his throat at what he saw.

Belinda lurched toward screen. "Oh, my God. Is this it?"

"Yes."

"An anonymous call to the *Salt Lake Tribune* preceded the event," the newscaster continued. "At this time, the reason behind these attacks against government facilities is unknown, and no one has, as yet, claimed responsibility. All personnel at Colton Ranch were liberated in time, but the explosive devices were detonated, nonetheless."

Brandon's hand came across his chest in an attempt to still his pounding heart. He watched Belinda chewing her hair as she watched, engrossed. *God, I love you.*

"I can't get over it," she said joyously. "I've just saved lives with a mere phone call. I mean, how do you figure that? It's like . . . I don't know. The finest moment of my life. It's the most worthwhile thing I've ever done."

He smiled. He couldn't forget his fears on the night of the Carringby attack, and the fact that so many lives had been lost. But neither could he deny the rush that had gone through him when he'd glided Belinda off the rooftop.

"What did you mean when you said the attackers were inside the munitions plant?" she said.

"Infiltration. They would have been posing as employees, setting this up for months, otherwise getting in from the outside would have been virtually impossible. It looks like they detonated the explosives from a remote location."

"It's believed," the reporter continued, "that this attack is directly related to the attacks on Carringby Industries in Denver a week ago, and the Everidge Corporation in Dallas five weeks ago. All personnel who died in the Carringby attack have now been identified, and the families of all concerned have been notified."

Brandon moved across to Belinda and held her as her head bowed, clearly in silent grieving for her deceased colleagues.

"The mystery of Belinda Carolyn Reese, the personal secretary of the late Barton Carringby, who was not found among the dead, deepens further." Belinda's college graduation photo appeared on the screen. "One week after she disappeared, the destiny of Ms. Reese has become the subject of numerous internet forums."

Belinda's jaw dropped in amazement at seeing her own face on the screen.

Brandon felt the blood draining from his face and his forehead fell into his hands. "Oh, no."

"What?"

"This is what I was afraid of," he said ominously. "I have a really bad feeling about this."

***

Agent Martyn McKay approached Senator Treadwell's office grasping a folder. He knocked on the door with his usual apprehension.

"Come in."

"Senator Treadwell?"

The senator didn't look at him, his attention fixed on his widescreen television. The image of Belinda Reese's photograph was set in freeze-frame. "What is it?"

"I have the NSA report with the details of where the call to the *Salt Lake Tribune* originated, as you requested."

Treadwell turned to his subordinate with a persistently contemptuous demeanor. "And where would that be?"

"Johannesburg, South Africa."

The senator shook his head, despondently.

"Sir?"

"Is every operative straight out of the academy these days?"

"Sir, I'm not quite sure I follow you."

Treadwell stood and made a move toward McKay. "None of you have done your homework on this one," he said angrily. "Drake stole an experimental sat-scrambler phone from the Arlington lab. That call came from nowhere near South Africa."

"I don't understand, sir. If Drake is with the terrorists, why would he be trying to stop them?"

"I didn't say he was with *those* terrorists. Drake is an interesting boy. Don't let him fool you."

"Interesting, sir?"

"He's young, virile, handsome, appealing to the majority of young ladies, I would imagine. How would you feel if you were totally innocent in such matters?"

McKay sighed with frustration. It was yet another of Treadwell's infamous riddles. "I don't follow you, sir."

"No, you wouldn't, would you." Treadwell gestured to the image on the TV screen. "A beautiful young woman unaccounted for after the Carringby attack, and a young woman's voice was recorded warning the *Salt Lake Tribune.*"

"Yes?"

"Try to imagine. Hypothetically, you have no intimate experience with women. Totally alone, you decide to interfere with a well-planned terrorist operation, and in the process, you decide to save a woman's life." The senator grinned. "Imagine the boon to your ego and sense of masculinity, knowing she is completely depending on you. Surely, you would now do anything to protect her."

McKay nodded uncertainly. What Treadwell was saying made perfect sense, but the relevance was still lost on him. "What do you want me to do, sir?"

"If we can't locate Drake, we must strive to draw him to us." He moved closer and positioned his nose inches away from McKay's. "Arrange for a nationwide APB on Belinda Reese. Top priority."

Thirteen

Goodbyes

Belinda shuddered as she sat astride Brandon. "Just try to relax," she said breathlessly.

He gazed lovingly upon her passionate expression, consumed by the experience. This time, he wasn't in control of himself. "I'm tryin', I'm tryin'." He gripped her fingers as she moved up and down upon him.

Belinda giggled as she sensed he was about to unleash himself. "You are so beautiful."

"No, stop."

"Let go."

She quivered as Brandon climaxed to the accompaniment of a tormented cry of release.

She looked at him, concerned. "Brandon? Are you all right?"

"I'm fine. Just a little disappointed."

"Excuse me?"

"My pride. I wish I could have lasted a little bit longer."

She quickly succumbed to contented laughter. "Don't worry, you were great. It takes practice."

He looked at her as though unconvinced. "But you didn't . . . *you know*."

She stroked his cheek tenderly, realizing his primary concern was still for *her* well-being. "Sometimes it's better when I don't. I feel like I'm still going through it, rather than it being all over."

She pulled herself off and lay down beside him. He held her as she rested her head on his chest. With his free hand he pulled the sheets over them. Before long, the safety and quietude of the cabin drew them into slumber.

Belinda awoke before dawn to find she was alone. Alarmed, she threw the sheets off, took one of Brandon's t-shirts from the top of the dresser, and put it on.

She entered the living room and saw him in his robe, studying his laptop screen. "What are you doing up at this hour?" she said.

"I couldn't sleep."

"You're not watching porn, are you?" she half-teased.

He gave her a sly grin. "I didn't want to waken you, so I did the next best thing."

She hadn't expected that answer, but recovered quickly. "Oh. OK. I don't really mind."

He turned the laptop around to show her. "I'm working on something for *us.*"

She saw an image of snow-covered mountains on the screen, and a promo for what looked like some kind of resort. "Where's that? Somewhere else in Aspen?"

He shook his head. "Switzerland."

"Switzerland?" she exclaimed.

"It's the best place I could think of."

"For what?"

"We need to get out of the country pretty quick."

"Wanna tell me what's on your mind?"

He placed the laptop to one side, moved toward her, and gently rested his palms on her shoulders. "If we stay here, the fun could soon wear off. It'll be like living in a prison. Every time we do anything, even shop for essentials, we'll

80

have to be in disguise, and we're not gonna be able to get away with that forever."

"Does this have something to do with my picture being all over the TV?"

"Yes. Here's what I have in mind." He turned back to the laptop. "If we can make it to Canada, we might be able to get a flight out to Switzerland."

"OK, but why Canada? And why Switzerland?"

"Take a shower and get dressed," he said with a grin. "There's something I want to show you."

Belinda climbed into the back of the van behind Brandon and waited for him to open the Turbo Swan. After a few moments, the seats folded forward with the electronic motor. He reached into the back and partially unzipped the leather sack. "Take a look."

She squeezed past him and peered inside, open-jawed at the money. "Wow. Where on earth did you get all that?"

"It was all filtered away by my grandfather from his unscrupulous dealings in the seventies. It's been hidden away in the basement since he died," he said.

"Do you know how much is there?"

"One million, two-hundred-thousand dollars. Well, minus a few grand I took out to buy the two vans and for a few living expenses."

"Oh. My. God."

"I want to try to get us to Italy," he said. "Airport security isn't quite as tight there. We should be able to get fake passports for the right price. We're fugitives, remember? My plan is to drive the cash through Lombardy and get to a Swiss bank where no questions will be asked."

She gasped, her voice muffled through her fingers. "Are you serious? We're really moving to Switzerland?"

He grinned at the excitement she exuded. "It doesn't take a genius to realize how much you love this place. I figured a Swiss bank account to invest the money and the perfect place to find another cabin in the snow, would be just what you wanted. But it'll a place where we could go out in public more freely." He then added coyly, "That is, if you're sure you really wanna do this"

She stood up, her eyes beaming with excitement, and hugged him tightly.

He knew there were risks with what he was planning. He wanted to be with her so passionately, but didn't relish the idea of endangering her. However, if what he suspected was true, she would be in even greater danger if she was to return to Denver alone.

She crouched low again, glanced back at the sack, and then pointed to the two attaché cases beside it. "What are they?"

"They're filled with some pretty sophisticated tech I took from the facility I used to work at."

"Like the stuff you used at Carringby Tower?"

"Yeah. Anyway, we'd better get packing. We've got one hell of a long drive ahead of us."

"Couldn't we just fly to Canada in the Turbo Swan?" she said. "It'd be a lot faster, surely."

"Not a chance. We've got to look as inconspicuous as possible. We're gonna be walking on dangerous ground as it is, without drawing attention to ourselves in what looks like a flying Ferrari. I just want to get near the Canadian border and then leave the Turbo Swan someplace where they won't find it until we're long gone."

"Good point," she said, and followed him back inside. "But how will we get across the border?"

"I'll rent a car, put the money and our essentials in it, and leave the Turbo Swan and the attaché cases. They're army property, so the authorities can take it from there."

Their packing was sparse at best. Belinda had the clothes she'd arrived at the cabin with and the few extras Brandon had bought for her in Aspen. He threw three pairs of jeans into a suitcase, a handful of shirts, tank-tops, bathroom essentials, and a backpack.

All the time he was packing, Brandon second-guessed himself about leaving the government property. He couldn't shake the feeling that between now and when they arrived at their destination, he was going to find himself in dire need of them.

He took a fresh bowl of fruit, nuts, and the jar of honey around to the back of the cabin for Snooky. The little bear was already waiting for him. Sadness pierced his heart, along with the feeling he was betraying the only friend he'd had before Belinda came into his life.

His history with the bear flashed before him. It had only been five weeks, but it seemed so long ago since they first met. He remembered how he'd paced the cabin living room for days after he'd cracked the code for the Everidge attack in Dallas. He'd used the sat-scrambler phone to call the corporation on the afternoon before the incident, and pleaded with the CEO's secretary to believe him. She'd responded with contempt, hostility, and threatened him with the police.

That night, he sat watching the news and learned of the death toll. It had crushed him. The guilt tore at him, rendering him unable to sleep. He tortured himself with the knowledge that he should've intervened personally, and vowed not to take the easy way out the next time. The following morning, at dawn, he'd scaled the ridge harder than ever before, punishing himself for his failure. Upon his return, he'd rested on the bench beneath the kitchen window. That was the first time he saw the bear cub. It had come toward him, lost, alone, and hungry. But it gave him just enough to keep him motivated.

It *needed* him.

He stroked the creature's forehead as it ate. "I'm so sorry I've got to go, Snooky. I really wish you could understand what I'm saying to you. I have no choice, but I'm really gonna miss you, bud."

He heard Belinda's footsteps coming up behind him, but they stopped. He knew she was watching him, although he felt she wanted him to have a last moment with his friend in private.

Snooky looked up into Brandon's eyes as he petted its brow. He had no idea how saying goodbye to his wild pet would affect him, and fought back his tears. "Who's gonna take care of you now?"

Finally, he pulled it together and turned away to join Belinda, not daring to look back. The scene had affected her too, as was apparent from her moistened eyes.

As they reached the turn to the porch, they were startled by a roar so powerful that the air itself seemed to vibrate.

Alarmed, they turned, and Brandon cautiously eased his way back along the side of the cabin, bracing his chest against the wood. Within seconds, he could see clearly from the shadows.

Snooky ran across the snow toward a huge, cinnamon-colored sow of the Black Bear species—his own kind. The sow dropped onto all fours to greet the little cub.

Brandon watched, open-jawed. Snooky's mother had finally found him.

Or had she? It was such a notable coincidence, it caused him to contemplate the possibility that it was always meant to be—that the universe had brought the cub to him in his darkest hour, only to be reunited with his mother when the time was right.

Perhaps.

With his feelings of sadness and conscience alleviated enormously, he took Belinda's hand. They grabbed their suitcases from the cabin, then walked outside and locked the door.

He approached the van and opened the passenger's side door for her.

As he walked around to the driver's side, he stopped momentarily to look back at the cabin with sadness in his heart. He didn't know if he would ever see his idyllic home again.

Finally, he climbed into the van and turned to Belinda. They were tied to one another now, for better or worse.

As the engine started, Belinda gazed with awe at the snow-caked landscape. It reminded her of how she'd seen it for the first time on that dark night. Although it was spectacular in daylight, it lacked the ethereal, supernatural quality it had in the moonlight. That was a vision she would carry with her for the rest of her life.

Her mind became awash with thoughts of the technological wonders that might be in the two attaché cases. She'd already experienced the wire glider equipment, the laser cutter, and the Turbo Swan. What else did he have in his arsenal?

Fourteen

On the Run

Belinda placed her hand on Brandon's lap as he drove. One of his rock CD's played at a low level, just enough to provide some background ambiance. "I hope Snooky's going to be all right," she said.

"He will be. I just know it," he replied. "I still can't get over what I just saw. His mother came back just as we were leaving."

"It's certainly remarkable. What family do *you* have, Brandon?"

Despite feeling somewhat uneasy, he said, "Aunts and uncles scattered here and there. I've never really been close to them."

"You said your father died. What happened to your mom?"

His eyes misted at the mention of his mother. He could almost smell her warm scent, and see her shimmering golden locks resting on her shoulders. "S-she's still alive. She lives in New Mexico in the house where I grew up. I want you to meet her, and I'm going to do everything I can to make that happen. I want to have a happy family for the first time in my life."

"Can't you call her?"

"Too dangerous. Her line will be tapped by now, the house will be bugged, and her every move will be under surveillance without her even knowing it. If they know I'm in contact with her, they'll go after her to get to me."

"Oh, my God. This is really scary stuff."

"I know."

"I can see how much you love your mom, Brandon. What's her name?"

"Annabelle," he said.

Belinda tilted her head with a smile. "That's a really beautiful name. Maybe someday, when this is all over, we can come back to America and visit her."

He nodded, even though he couldn't imagine the circumstances under which that would ever be possible. "I hope so. You know what she always used to tell me?"

"What?"

"'Treat others how you'd want them to treat you, Brandon'."

"The Golden Rule," she said approvingly. "I think I'd like your mom very much. It doesn't take a genius to figure out where you got your heart from."

He wiped his eyes with his sleeve. "What about your family?"

"None to speak of. They all think I'm 'of the Devil' since I left. I really don't miss them, or their bullshit beliefs."

"I know what you mean. My dad was at the far right of politics, and didn't agree with the separation of church and state." He recalled what she'd told him in the van en route to Denver on the day following the Carringby incident. "You said you'd left home at sixteen. How did you survive out there?"

"I got a job in a fast food joint and went to night school where I learned to type. Then I got a degree in marketing. I wanted to be a corporate exec so I could give my mom the finger, not that any of it did me any good. I only ever got as far as being a secretary."

"Wow. I can't imagine feeling that way toward my mother."

"I wish I didn't, but it wasn't my doing. She pushed me away. You're all I want now."

Overwhelmed by her endearing sentiment, he managed to ask, "Where are you from? I mean . . . originally?"

Belinda lowered her head sadly. "Boston, Massachusetts."

He noticed her somber expression. "What's wrong?"

"It's . . . difficult for me to talk about, but I think it would be unfair to keep it from you."

"What?"

"I was sexually abused by a priest when I was thirteen. I've had major resentment issues ever since."

"Are you serious?" he said. "Why didn't you tell me about this before?"

"I'm serious. I don't like to think about it. It stirs up a lot of anger. You're the first person I've trusted enough to tell about it since it happened."

Brandon struggled to know what to say. "Well, did you tell your mother what had happened?"

"Yes," she said. "She called me a wicked, sinful liar, and turned her back on me. I don't think I'll ever forgive her for that."

"I can't imagine how anyone could treat a child like that. Did anything happen to this priest?"

"No. He's still working at the diocese in Boston, like so many of the other bastards. Most of them get away with it."

Thoughts came to Brandon as he listened to her. Who were these monsters that they believed they had the right to do this to people? Priests, as with most authority figures, were often nothing other than corrupt men who existed at the appointment of other corrupt men. And yet they were mere mortal humans who would die like any other. Through a delusion fed by their own adherents, they had power, which they continued to use to commit the greatest of evils, and to violate the innocent. He sensed his anger growing, filling him with conviction. They both had the same enemy, but only he was aware of it. Belinda's story was a part of the same evil of which he was fighting to be free.

He became distracted by a song on the CD and smiled at the irony of the lyrics:

> *Driving on the highway of love, when I look in your eyes. Shaking all the fears that I know, with you here by my side . . .*

Glancing at Belinda, it was clear from her smile that she'd noticed it too.

They'd been driving for four hours. Belinda took in the breathtaking scenery of the Rockies. Moments recurred when she questioned the reality of her situation. Was she really in the van with this incredible man whom she'd known for such a short time, but for whom she felt so deeply? Was she really traveling with him into the unknown, leaving all she'd ever known behind her, potentially forever? Her gaze lingered on him as his attention was fixed on the road. Enraptured by his gentle, sensitive nature, she immersed herself in the knowledge that there was no finer man she could've found.

"I'm going to find somewhere to eat," Brandon said. "I'm hungry. How about you?"

"I'm starving."

"All right, I think there's a town up ahead."

"Do you know where we are?"

He gestured to his portable satellite navigation unit on the windshield. "According to this, we're coming up to a town called Moore, just outside of Cheyenne."

Her heart fluttered for the briefest moment as the reality of her situation was punctuated, once more. "Wyoming."

"You got it."

As they approached the town, a main street lined with stores including a supermarket and a private hardware store, showed Moore was a small community. A DVD rental store with a window display offering VHS indicated the town was behind the times.

"I'm going to pull in over beside that convenience store," Brandon said. "Are you gonna be OK in here?"

"It's getting quite late. Don't you think we should try to find a motel soon?"

He nodded although there was a hint of worry in his eyes as he stepped out of the van.

"What's wrong?" she said.

"I'm not in disguise, but I think I'll be OK. It's just a brief stop in a town we won't be coming back to. I'll be right back." He closed the door and headed down the street.

Once he was out of sight, Belinda couldn't resist the impulse to stretch her legs and stepped outside. She closed the door behind her and walked just a few steps down the path in the direction Brandon had taken.

She became immediately self-conscious. A middle-aged man and his wife walked past her, both staring in alarm.

She looked back at them to see they were looking back at her. Desperately uncomfortable, she turned away.

Across the street she saw a young couple gazing at her with the same suspicion in their eyes. Her pace quickened. She could have sworn she saw the young man take his cell phone out of his pocket.

She faced forward to see a young woman turn a corner and stop in her tracks the instant she saw Belinda. Fearfully, the woman turned back down the street she had come from.

What the hell is going on here? Eager to find Brandon, Belinda hurried on, wishing she'd paid attention to which store he'd gone into.

She turned down the sidewalk she'd seen the young woman walk down and broke into a run. She was eager to catch up with her to learn what the problem was.

Something caught her eye on the wall a few yards behind her. Slowly, she made her way back. As she came closer to it, a chill went through her. The realization of what was fixed to the brickwork caused her blood to turn to ice— her college graduation photograph on a poster:

WANTED

Belinda Carolyn Reese

Suspected of Terrorist Activity in Denver, Colorado

$100,000 Reward for Information Leading to Capture

Her hand came across her mouth as she stifled a whimper. *Oh, dear God. What is happening?*

Her attention was abruptly distracted by a strange blue light illuminating the darkening half-light of the dusk. It was immediately followed by the deafening shrill of a siren behind her. She screamed, startled, and spun around to find herself cornered by a police car parked diagonally across her path.

Two burly officers exited the vehicle training their pistols on her. Infused with terror, she froze.

"Belinda Reese. Put your hands behind your head and drop to your knees!"

Fifteen

Nightmare

Belinda trembled as the two towering officers came closer. Gripping her shoulders, they roughly pulled her to her feet. "Over to the trunk of the car, *now*. Ten fingers on the fender."

Numb with shock, she did as she was ordered. Her throat became dry and her palms were clammy. Her heart pounded as fiercely as if the poster's accusation were true. There was no distinction between the emotions of the innocent and the guilty in that moment. The sheer terror exerted by the two Herculean authority figures would have caused even the strongest to submit.

She gritted her teeth as one of them slid his hands up and down her legs, and then around her waist. Unable to contain herself, she cried, "Somebody, help me!"

"Calm down lady and this'll go easy," the first officer said. "Belinda Carolyn Reese. You have the right to remain silent. If you give up that right, anything you say can and will be used against you in a court of law. You have the right to an attorney, and for that attorney to be present during questioning. If you cannot afford an attorney, one will be provided for y—"

Belinda screamed in surprise as both officers slumped onto the trunk of the squad car. Frozen for a moment, she tried to process the bizarre. They were arresting her and then they simply fell unconscious before her eyes.

She turned around and her heart leaped. Brandon walked toward her tucking something into the rim of his jeans underneath his denim jacket. "Oh, thank God," she said, and threw herself into his arms, sobbing.

"It's all right. But sweetheart, we've got to go, like *now*."

Breaking the embrace, she took Brandon's hand, and ran with him back to the van, barely aware of the pedestrians bearing witness to their flight.

The officer who'd begun to read Belinda her rights revived and staggered away from the trunk of the police car. Dazed and disoriented, he made his way out of the side street onto the main thoroughfare. He spotted Belinda climbing into the van but didn't gain a clear view of her accomplice.

Barely able to stand, he took out his notebook and pen and awkwardly scribbled down the license plate. He captured the last digit before the vehicle sped past him.

Belinda was still shaking and hyperventilating, uncontrollably.

"Easy, baby," Brandon said, and glanced at the rear view side mirror. "They're not following us, but we need to get as far away from the Cheyenne region as we can before we stop again."

"My face was on a wanted poster," she said. "They think I'm a terrorist."

"No, they don't. They're doing all this to get to me."

"To get to *you*?"

"They don't want me taken in by the police because I know too much. They want them to take you in so that I'll go to *them*. They're trying to set a trap."

Her tears abated as exhaustion came over her. "This can't be real. They've even been in my apartment."

"What?"

"There's nowhere else they could have gotten that graduation photo."

"You disappeared after a terrorist attack. The police would've gone to your apartment as a priority first and then given it to the press. It wouldn't have been *them*."

"What did you do to those cops?"

He reached into the rim of his pants and took out a pistol-like device with a transparent screen covering the tip of the muzzle. "I was looking for you and then I heard you scream so I came running."

Belinda stared at the weapon in his hand. "What is that thing?"

"I had it on me just in case," he said nonchalantly. "It's a sonic force emitter. It knocks the hell out of you, but it doesn't cause any harm. I don't want to kill anyone. It just hits you with a concentrated wall of sound waves."

"Please, Brandon. Turn the van around and take us back to the cabin. It's not worth the risk."

"I could. But we are so close. If you can just hang in there, we'll be out of the country forty-eight hours from now. We'll be free."

She shrugged, emotionally drained. "OK, if you're sure."

He kept his eyes on the road and drove without a word.

Within three hours, night had fallen. Given the hour, Belinda knew they had to find somewhere to sleep.

"We need to find a drug store," Brandon said.

"Why?"

"Do you have any idea how much you still look like that graduation photo?"

"I hadn't given it much thought."

"Well you do. How much do you know about hairdressing?"

"Quite a bit. Why?"

He pointed to a line of stores ahead. "There's a drug store. I need you to tell me what I need to buy."

"For my hair?"

"You have shoulder-length, brunette hair. We need to make it the complete opposite."

Seized with concern, she said, "You're not going to cut my hair are you?"

"I'm sorry. I really am, baby. But we have no choice. It'll grow back, won't it?"

"Yes, it'll grow back in time. I've done it a couple of times before, but . . ." She paused before coming to terms with the idea and realized necessity took priority over her liking her hair the way it was. "You're right. We have to."

"So, what do I need to buy?"

"You're going to need to get a comb, a brush, a hair dryer, scissors, styling mousse, and a bottle of peroxide-blonde hair dye solution."

He pulled the van up outside the store. "Hide in the back."

"After what happened back there, you don't have to tell me twice." She climbed over the seat, through the linen veil separation, and crouched down next to the Turbo Swan.

"I'll be as quick as I can," he said, and closed the door behind him.

Belinda heard him walking away, her heart pounding. Being alone felt terrifying, even though Brandon would only be gone for a couple of minutes. The butterflies in the pit of her stomach wouldn't stop and her breathing came in deep, labored gasps.

As the seconds ticked by, she began to enter the first stages of panic. Her experience in Moore continued to play over in her mind. Within a few minutes of her leaving the van, she'd been staring down the barrel of a police pistol.

The van door opened and she held her breath.

"Hi, sweetheart," Brandon said. "There wasn't a line, so I just asked the assistant and she got the stuff for me."

She breathed a sigh of relief and cautiously peered through the drapes. "Is it safe to come out, do you think?"

"Everything's fine." He dropped the bag of hair products onto the passenger's floorboard. "Now, let's hit the road."

It was approaching 11 p.m. when Brandon pulled up at a motel in the remote town of Morgan, Wyoming. Located off a dirt road, which was off yet another dirt road, it seemed only the basics of life existed there.

He settled up with the owner of the run-down motel, a gruff-and-wizened old man whose breath was virtually flammable. With no new fixtures in the office, it appeared as though the place hadn't been decorated or attended to since the 70s. However, Brandon knew whatever was available would have to suffice for the night.

"Room thirty-three," the old man said, and handed him the key. "We call it the honeymoon suite."

"I'm sure it's delightful," Brandon said sardonically. "Do you mind if I park my van at the back of the motel. I'm a little paranoid about . . . thieves." His true fear was that the van had been seen evading the police in a town in that state.

"In these parts son, I don't cotton-pickin' blame ya." The proprietor took another gulp out of a bottle of Red Eye he had concealed under the desk.

"Thanks for the heads-up." Brandon turned to leave, smirking at the man's caricature nature. As he closed the door behind him, he silently marveled that it was still attached to the door frame.

He drove around to the rear of the motel, safely out of sight. Belinda remained crouched behind the veil. "Come on," he said. "I got us a double room. Let's get some sleep."

"Is it a double bed? I really need you next to me tonight."

"Yeah. The old timer called it the honeymoon suite. It'll change your life, I'm sure."

Belinda held Brandon tightly as she slept, the musty smell of damp constantly in the air. Her sleep was fitful throughout the night. In her dreams she ran through fog, unable to see anything ahead of her.

Then she awoke to find herself in the motel room totally alone. Her hands searched the bed frantically, but Brandon wasn't there. "Brandon? Brandon?" she called out repeatedly, but there was no response.

She became frantic, climbed out of bed, and ran to look in the bathroom. "Oh, my God. He's gone. He's abandoned me. *NO!*"

The front door suddenly shattered with violent force. She ran out of the bathroom and faced the silhouettes of a squad of armed police officers with their pistols trained on her. She threw her hands in the air, but it made no difference.

They opened fire—

She shot upright in bed, coated with perspiration. It took a moment for her to regain her senses.

Her sudden movement awoke Brandon. "Are you all right?" he said.

"Just a dream."

He turned over and looked at her. "Are you sure?"

She looked down into his sleepy eyes and became tearful. "Don't leave me. Don't ever leave me. Please."

He rubbed his eyes with his knuckles and sat up to hold her gently. "Of course I'm not going to leave you, baby. We're in this together."

She threw her arms around him. "I so needed to hear that, because . . . I need you to be there in the morning."

They had difficulty sleeping following Belinda's nightmare. Brandon decided they should get out of bed before seven and attend to an essential task.

After they'd taken a shower, Belinda guided Brandon through cutting lock after lock of her beautiful auburn hair. She winced as she watched in the motel room dresser's mirror. Her hair was precious to her and seeing it butchered was a disconcerting experience. As it became increasingly shorter, she became aware that now she wouldn't have anything to chew on.

Ever one step ahead of the game, Brandon was careful to capture every strand of her severed locks in a towel. A pile of auburn hair on the carpet would have provided the authorities with valuable evidence, should the motel ever be searched.

Within an hour, he'd applied peroxide and neutralizer to what was left of her hair, blow-dried mousse into it, and given her a forward fringe.

As she studied her face in the mirror, her new look reminded her of the style of a catwalk model. "I can live with that," she said with mock smugness.

"Well, they say blondes have more fun." He picked up the towel of hair and the peroxide and neutralizer bottles. "I've got to get rid of all this stuff."

"OK, I'll be out in a moment." With that, she set about gathering her belongings.

Brandon headed out to the back of the rooms and quickly found a garbage can. He spent a few moments picking up refuse bags to bury his evidence under. The rats in the can filled him with revulsion, but he knew he didn't have a choice.

He recalled, after the incident in Moore, Belinda had pleaded with him to turn around and take them back to the cabin. Was she right? He couldn't be sure. All he knew was that an irresistible force—a powerful urge for freedom—drove him onward.

As he put the lid of the can back on, he felt compelled to walk a little farther around the back of the motel. He was overcome with a profound sense of uncertainty. Were they going to make it to Switzerland? Would he actually find freedom with Belinda in a picturesque land?

He turned the corner behind the shabby rooms and felt the blood draining from his face. His footsteps slowed with the dreaded realization of what he saw. The van wasn't there.

Belinda came up behind him. "Hey, are you ready?"

Already shaken by his discovery, he was startled by her.

"Are you OK?" she said.

"The van," he replied, his voice weak and quivering.

Belinda stepped around to where he stood. "Where is it?"

"It's gone. The Turbo Swan was in the back, along with the weapons, the equipment I took, the money, our ticket out . . . It's all gone."

Sixteen

The Brothers

Miguel Gomez grinned as he drove the van along the highway into Morgan. The town was coming alive for the day, and his urgency to get out of the area caused his adrenaline to surge. As a member of a family of illegal immigrants, 'living off the land,' as they called helping themselves to whatever didn't belong to them, was their only means of survival. At this stage of their travels across the United States, the van would provide a perfect mobile storage facility for them.

At twenty-two, Miguel's skills in theft hadn't reached their full height. As such, his sense of urgency clouded his judgment, especially with regard to the speed limit.

"I wanna check out the back."

Miguel's impetuous, nineteen-year-old brother, Fausta, sat up, rested his knees on the passenger seat, and eased his head through the veil.

"What's it look like? Is it roomy?" Miguel said.

"Bro?"

"What?"

"You gotta see what's back here, bro."

Miguel, being somewhat rotund, struggled as he tried to turn around to peak through the veil, but the effort was in vain. His attempt, while driving at such a high speed, caused the van to swerve across the dusty road. "What is it?"

"I don't know, man. Looks like some kinda spaceship."

Miguel laughed. "What've you been smoking?"

"Seriously, bro. I've never seen anything like it."

Miguel noticed a police motorcycle behind them in the rear view mirror and swallowed hard. Momentarily torn between whether to accelerate or slow down, he decided upon the latter, confident he could charm his way out of the situation.

Fausta pulled his head from the veil. "Why are you slowing down?"

"We got trouble, man. Big trouble. Look." Miguel pointed to the mirror.

"Mierda," Fausta said.

The van gradually came to a halt on the side of the road and the officer pulled up behind it. Miguel and Fausta watched apprehensively as he came closer. His pistol was clearly visible on his belt holster.

As the officer arrived at the driver's side of the van, Miguel wound down the window.

"Either of you own this vehicle?" the officer said.

"No, sir." Miguel realized his anxiety was impairing his ability to sound convincing. "I-it belongs to my cousin. He let us borrow it."

"And your cousin's name would be?"

"C-Carlitos Gomez."

"I need your license and the vehicle's registration."

Miguel shot Fausta a hopeless glance.

"Turn the engine off," the officer said.

Miguel complied.

The officer took out his radio receiver and put it to his mouth. The reply came quickly. "Sheriff, this is Ranger. I've just stopped a couple of Hispanic kids in a white Dodge Sprinter doin' over seventy. They say it belongs to their cousin. My mobile computer's down. Would you run a check on the license plate?"

"Go ahead."

Miguel and Fausta watched, trembling, as Ranger read out the license number. It took all of a minute, which seemed like an hour to them. Both were tempted to make a run for it, but knew they couldn't out-race a motorcycle.

The sheriff's reply came, but the Gomez brothers couldn't hear what was being said. They only saw Ranger nodding intently and surreptitiously glancing back at them with a sinister, judgmental glare.

Something was said when Ranger snapped his head toward them and drew his pistol. "Step out of the van with your hands raised over your heads!"

Horrified, the two thieves did as they were ordered. Miguel felt perspiration dripping from his brow.

Ranger put the radio back to his mouth. "Sheriff, I need back-up. There are two of them in the van."

"It's the girl who's wanted," the sheriff said.

"There is no girl, Sheriff, just a couple of young guys."

There was an awkward pause before the sheriff's voice came through the receiver again. "I'm sending Wallace out to you. If the girl isn't with them, I'm pretty sure they'll know where she is . . . with a little persuading."

***

Sheriff Earl Gillespie, a stout man of fifty-four, scowled at Miguel and Fausta as he entered one of the Morgan police station's meager holding cells. "Who are you dirtballs, anyway?" he said.

"W-we're nobody, sir, you have to believe us," Miguel whimpered. "We don't know about no girl, honest."

"You just happened to be riding around in a van that was seen being used in the escape of a wanted terrorist outside of Cheyenne last night." Convinced of their involvement, Gillespie wasn't about to show them an ounce of mercy.

"Honestly, sir," Fausta said, "we don't know nothing 'bout no terrorist."

"Then what were you doing in that van? And don't give me any of that cousin bullshit. Don't you realize what's going down here? Do you have any idea how serious it is to be caught up in terrorist activity?"

"We stole the van," Fausta said finally, clearly unable to withstand his own fear. "We're nothing, sir, you've gotta believe us. We're not terrorists."

Gillespie was inclined to embrace that as a possibility. Their badly-worn attire and unkempt appearance certainly suggested *need*. "Stole it? Where did you steal it from?"

"Some motel, just before you get into town," Miguel said.

"Describe this motel."

"Sí, señor. It was it a really old, rundown shack."

Ranger stepped out of the office and joined the sheriff. Gillespie turned to him. "You know old Ruben's motel outside of town?"

"Sure, Sheriff."

"Well, that's where the girl is. If I were you, I'd get down there right away."

"Yes, sir."

Gillespie turned back to the Gomez brothers. There was total silence as he took their measure, ensnaring them in the grip of fear. They were no different from all the other illegals he'd dealt with. So much was at stake for them—their remaining in the USA, their future liberty, and the risk of them becoming separated from their family. Holding his cruel stare for long, agonizing moments, he relished their anguish. Finally, with a smirk, he walked away.

***

Brandon had been pacing around the seedy motel room for forty minutes while Belinda looked on, deeply concerned.

Abruptly, he stopped pacing. "I'm going to ask that old guy at the desk. See if he knows anything. Will you be OK for a minute?"

"Sure."

Although she was a wanted fugitive with no means of transportation, there was something about Brandon that made her feel safe at all times. However, she felt the stress was beginning to wear her down.

As Brandon turned the corner to the office, he noticed a police motorcycle parked outside. Stopping in his tracks, he waited a beat before making slow, calculated steps forward. He came closer and the conversation inside became more audible.

"Good morning, Ruben," the officer said in a stern-but-amenable tone.

"What can I do for ya, young fella?" The old man's voice sounded raspy, most likely from the bottle of Red Eye he'd consumed during the night.

"I'm here on official business. A white Dodge Sprinter was stolen from here last night. I want to know who it belonged to."

"A wha—"

"A van, Ruben. A white van with Colorado plates. I wanna know who it belongs to."

"Oh, yeah. The young guy in thirty . . . three, I think I put him?"

"Young guy? Not a woman?"

"Can't seem to recall seeing no woman with him."

Brandon turned around urgently, careful not to make any alerting noises. When he was in the clear, he sprinted back to the room.

He startled Belinda as he entered. "What happened?" she said.

"We have to go. I know where the van is."

"Where?"

"The police have it." He looked around the room, his gaze falling upon the backpack on the bed. Grasping it, he snaked the strap across his shoulder and took Belinda's hand. "Come on, baby. Let's get out of here."

They'd barely got themselves out of sight behind the adjacent row of rooms, when Ruben led the officer into room thirty-three.

Brandon and Belinda held themselves perfectly still with pounding hearts. Brandon noticed beads of perspiration on her brow. They waited for what seemed like an eternity until the two men finally exited the room.

The officer took out his radio. "Sheriff, it looks like the van belonged to some young guy who was here at old Ruben's motel, but he's gone now. There was no sign of any girl, apparently. What do you want me to do?"

Brandon strained to make out the sheriff's response, but all he heard was the officer replying, "Yes, sir."

After another minute, Ruben and the officer disappeared around the corner.

Brandon turned to Belinda hastily. "I have to get to that impound yard. I'm getting the van back, but there's a risk."

Belinda looked at him uncertainly. "Oh, Brandon. What are you going to do?"

"Everything is in the van except . . ."

"What?"

With a shrewd glint in his eyes, he tapped the backpack and placed it on the ground. "There's something else I took." He unzipped the backpack, and rummaged around inside until he found an electric hair clipper.

She stared at the clipper, shaking her head as though bemused. "What do you need that for?"

Seventeen

Caught

Brandon and Belinda wandered out of sight through the trees surrounding the highway. Within thirty minutes, they'd reached the outskirts of Morgan. Brandon knew it was safe for him. But even with Belinda's new look, it was too risky for her to enter the town. She was still all over the news.

"OK, baby," he said, "I'm all set. I need you to wait for me, all right?"

"OK." Her tone indicated her confidence was waning.

"There's food and drink I bought from that store last night in the backpack." He looked around at the forestry, sensing her anxiety. But he knew there wasn't a moment to lose. "I know this isn't ideal, so I'll be as quick as I can. Hang in there. I am so sorry, baby."

"Please be careful," she said.

Sorrowfully, he nodded.

He ran through the trees, stopping sporadically along the three mile trek. He reached the town remarkably quickly. Slowing his pace accordingly, he casually assimilated himself among the pedestrians.

The basic area reminded him of a town from the Old West. A few rusted parked cars and an electronics store were enough to convince him he was still in his own era.

An elderly woman turned a corner and came toward him. He smiled warmly and she reciprocated. "Excuse me. Sorry to bother you, ma'am," he said.

"Yes, dear."

"I wonder if you could help me. I'm trying to find the local sheriff's office. Would you happen to know where that is?"

"Of course." She turned and pointed straight along the dusty road. "You don't have far to walk. It's about a half mile along that road. You'll come to it on the left along the way there."

"Thank you."

After following the lady's directions for a few minutes, he saw the station ahead of him. It was a pathetic-looking shack of an outpost, and without the car storage pound he'd anticipated. He could see his van protruding from the rear of the building sheltered by a flimsy wooden horning.

His heart thundered in his chest with apprehension. He'd witnessed more than enough death on the battlefields of Afghanistan, and was no stranger to fear.

However, scurrying alongside a hick town's sheriff's office filled him with anxiety the likes of which he'd never felt before. Perhaps it was because, in the desert, he'd accepted the possibility of personal doom. This time, he'd set his heart upon the real possibility of a happy and peaceful life with his new love. Perhaps his fear was simply a manifestation of that hope. If he failed, he wouldn't only be failing himself, he would be failing Belinda, and the thought of that was unbearable.

He reached into his right side pocket and took out the keys to the van, silently praying the Turbo Swan was still in the back. Even if it wasn't, he knew he was the only one who could open it. It was constructed from an innovative, bonded-titanium alloy that was resistant to firepower and intense heat. The door locks were programmed to accept his unique fingerprints—a precaution he'd taken before he escaped from Mach Industries. But none of that would have stopped them from towing it out of the van and taking it away.

When he reached the end of the brick wall, he ran across the station's yard toward the van. "Please be in there," he quietly muttered as he came closer to his quarry—and his freedom.

He reached the driver's side door, and inserted the key into the lock, cringing at the clicking sound it made. He climbed inside, and against every iota of common sense, he wasted a moment throwing open the veil. The Turbo Swan was still there, to which he gave another sigh of relief.

"Hold it right there!"

Brandon froze. He'd been so close. Perhaps he could make a run for it—close the door, insert the key, and step on the gas. But there wasn't enough time to perform all of those tasks in less time than it would take a bullet to strike him. Out of options, he secreted the key under the upholstery and backed out of the van, keeping his hands held high.

"Put your hands behind your head. You have the right to remain silent . . ."

The officer's arrogance seemed in keeping with his position, but Brandon refused to show fear as the cuffs were placed on him.

The sheriff led Brandon by the arm into a cell. He noticed two Mexicans in the cell opposite. A powerful anger rose in him as the sheriff manhandled him, although he managed to contain himself.

"I'm gonna run your ID, dirtball," the sheriff said, "and then we'll find out who you are, what you've got in common with those two Mexican scrotums and that van."

The sheriff moved away from the cells leaving Brandon face to face with the two illegal immigrants who had stolen his van—the imbeciles who'd placed him in this predicament. Their actions had resulted in his beloved Belinda being stranded in the woods alone with meager rations. True hatred for the brothers began to fester in his heart. An overwhelming force surged through him. *They* had done this to the woman he loved.

After thirty minutes, his cell door opened and the sheriff stepped inside with the arresting officer. "Come out, kid. We're gonna print you."

Apprehensively, Brandon stood. "Look, Sheriff, you don't have to worry about anything. I'm not a criminal."

"Take his prints, Wallace. I ain't takin' his word for that."

The officer grasped Brandon's shoulder and forcibly guided him out of the cell toward the fingerprint room. Once completed, Brandon knew his fingerprints would be sent through a computerized identification system. His fear exacerbated as he was led along the corridor, uncertain of what the procedure would reveal about him.

Shortly afterward, the fingerprint results came back, and Gillespie returned to Brandon's cell. "I don't get it. There's nothing on you other than a military distinction. Battlefield injury during the rescue of one of your comrades."

Brandon was hesitant. On the one hand, he was relieved there was no record of his going AWOL. However, it raised the question of who would've hidden that information, and

113

for what purpose? "So, you have no problem with me, right?"

"On the contrary. You're stayin' with me, soldier-boy. As soon as I send this down the line, I'm going to find out once and for all what you are all about."

Brandon's initial fears resurfaced. Gillespie wasn't simply going to leave it at that. All of the possibilities occurred to him in a flood of horror. Not only might his going AWOL be discovered, but the investigation would alert those in government to the fact that he was in custody. That information, in turn, would find its way into the hands of the conspiracy's personnel, who would undoubtedly have him killed. And Belinda was stranded alone in the forest.

In that moment, he knew, at all costs, he had to escape.

***

Senator Garrison Treadwell sat in his office sifting through files when he was interrupted by a knock on his door. "Come in."

Agent Martyn McKay entered, and Treadwell noticed the levity in his eyes.

"I have a report from the police in Morgan, Wyoming, sir," McKay said eagerly.

"Where'n the hell is that?"

"It's a small town in the northeast region of Wyoming, sir."

"And?"

"It's Drake, sir."

"What about him?"

McKay caught his breath. "We've got him."

114

The senator was suddenly gripped with urgency. "Get the jet ready, and arrange for a helicopter at Cheyenne airport. I want it ready for take-off when we arrive."

"Yes, sir."

Treadwell waited for McKay to leave and hastily took out his cell phone. After two rings it was answered. "Wilmot," he said sternly, "I want you to contact Bragg and get a contingency out to a place called Morgan in Wyoming, immediately. I'm putting you in charge. If Spicer isn't overseas, I want him included. Don't screw this up."

Eighteen

The Rage

Belinda listened to the birds singing in the forest, her back braced up against the bark of the tall tree. Strangely, the sound of the birds seemed to compound her sense of loneliness. Brandon had been gone for three hours, and her angst was increasing by the minute.

Her nightmare came back to her with an ominous likening to a premonition. She was alone, and her protector was nowhere to be seen. She shuddered with the fear that the authorities would appear in the woods with their pistols trained upon her. The instinct to chew her hair was strong, but even that was no longer a possibility.

Restless, she stood and wandered around a little, never losing sight of the tree. Brandon could return at any moment. She couldn't risk getting lost in the woods.

She questioned repeatedly why he couldn't have just turned the van around after the incident in Moore. She could understand his reasons for leaving the cabin, and she'd been completely willing at the time. But not now. What had begun as an idyllic escape to a new life had become an unbearable ordeal.

She turned and saw the tree in the distance, quickly realizing she'd roamed too far. With a flutter of panic, she ran back, hoping against hope she'd see Brandon coming from behind the hill . . .

But there was still no sign of him.

Fearfully disappointed, she sat against the tree again, and resumed her endless waiting. Her mind continually wandered into thoughts of the cabin and how happy she had been there. Vulnerable and scared, her head fell into her hands, and she wept.

***

Brandon sat on the cell bunk, his concern for Belinda tormenting him. Her beauty, her supportive, gentle nature, and the way in which she filled his heart with excitement were profound. She had made him feel as though he could accomplish absolutely anything. She'd introduced him to a new side of himself and given him companionship, which had caused him to realize how loathsome his period of isolation had been. Now, he couldn't shake the feeling that he'd failed her.

He was constantly aware of the Gomez brothers' eyes on him.

"That van out there, man," Fausta said. "What is that . . . *thing* in the back?"

Voracious anger came over Brandon as the circumstances exploded in his mind again. He was sitting in that cell. Worst of all, his lover was alone in the woods, not knowing what had become of him, or what was to become of her. And it was all because of *them*. His eyes rose with hatred, causing the young immigrant to visibly shiver.

Without warning, he lurched forward with the speed of a cobra, driving the blade of his right hand into the cell bars. The Gomez brothers jerked back at his sudden movement. His eyes ablaze with fury, he bellowed, "Don't even talk to me, you son of a bitch. It's all your fault. I wanna kill you,

117

you bastards!" All of his control, his reasoning, and his composure, had given way to overpowering rage. He'd finally found someone who meant more to him than he meant to himself. If given the opportunity, he felt he would've willingly killed any man who placed Belinda's life or well-being in jeopardy.

Gillespie ran along the corridor with urgency at the sound of Brandon's outburst. "What the hell is going on down here?"

Fausta grasped the bars of his cell. "Sheriff, you gotta let us outta here. That guy over there is crazy, señor. He's one crazy mother. I saw the way his hand hit the bars. It was like karate, or kung fu, or something. He's dangerous, señor."

The sheriff turned to see Brandon's cold demeanor. Drake's face was flushed, and the scar on his forehead seemed to have become deeper. Never in his career had Gillespie stared into to such eyes of granite. Brandon's look reminded him of the Legend of Medusa. For an instant, he felt he'd been turned to stone.

It was actually comforting for him to turn back to the Gomez brothers. "You two are released on the condition that you guide my deputy to your family and we escort your sorry asses out of the state. Clear?"

"*Sí, sí*, Señor Sheriff," Miguel said submissively.

Ranger appeared from around the corner of the corridor with a set of keys in his hand. After unlocking the cell, he escorted the brothers out.

"All right, dirtballs. Get out," Gillespie said.

Gillespie knew it wasn't the most appropriate moment to confront Brandon with an ultimatum. But for the sake of his own pride, he knew he had to exert some degree of authority. He turned back to his prisoner, but Brandon's attention seemed to be focused on the Gomez brothers as they were led away. He then bowed his head as though attempting to compose himself.

"Don't do anything to ruffle my feathers, psycho boy," Gillespie said, "or you just might discover what kind of power the Department of Corrections actually does have around here."

Brandon's eyes rose again, their chilling resonance penetrating. "You have no power over me. The only power you have is that which was given to you. Study your history. Real power is something you *take*. You were given your power, which means they can take it away just as quickly. You're just a pawn."

"Don't push your luck, kid."

"Tell me, Sheriff. Did you voluntarily choose to become a police officer out of an altruistic desire to serve the community? Or because you get off on the sense of power you think that badge gives to you?"

Gillespie swallowed hard. He had never encountered the likes of this prisoner before. He'd known thugs, illegal immigrants, and drug pushers. But not enraged, articulate, mystery men. There was something about Brandon Drake that didn't fit any category, and most disturbing of all, he seemed to be fearless. "I don't know who you are. I don't know *what* you are. But I'm going to find out, kid. Nobody gets past Earl Gillespie, understand?"

Brandon shot him a contemptuous glance. "You pathetic nobody. Do your worst."

Gillespie chuckled in an attempt to conceal his discomfort, but he was far from dismissive toward

Brandon. He realized bravado was the most futile of all approaches. In response, he simply flicked a strand of his thinning, black, comb-over hair away from his eyes, and moved on.

Brandon turned to the back of his cell. A slightly rebellious smile crept from the corner of his mouth, despite the rage that filled his heart. The concept of authority figures had left a bitter taste in his mouth. He'd long since come to the conclusion that 'authority' was a bane: a falsity that man, whose ultimate destiny was the grave, could delude himself into a feeling of superiority over his fellow man. In the name of that delusion, he'd seen so much evil committed. Such was the nature of his vitriol toward Gillespie.

He studied the portal. There were three iron bars, behind which was a cracked window. Now that he was finally alone, there wasn't a moment to lose.

Upon his entry to the station, he'd been frisked for concealed weapons—his arms, legs, waist, chest, wrists, and ankles.

He carefully reached underneath the hair at the base of his neck and grasped a small package taped to his scalp. Belinda had been bewildered at first when she saw him shaving a section of hair away before he set off for the sheriff's office. Most of his weaponry was in the attaché cases. However, given the nature of his circumstances, he'd pre-empted the possibility of being arrested, and kept an emergency contingency on him at all times.

After opening the small opaque sack, he took out a cellophane package. He broke the seal and cautiously removed two pieces of putty, one white and one blue, separated by another seal in the plastic packet. His hands trembled in his awareness of the extreme hazard.

With supreme care and control, he edged his way back to the bunk bed and steadily stood upon it. From there he was at the height necessary to reach the top of the first iron bar.

He took small samples of the white and blue putty and gently pressed them together against the iron. If so much as a microbe of the substance touched his skin after it had catalyzed, it would bore through his flesh and bone within a second.

He knew that the ideal tool for this task would have been his pocket-sized laser torch. However, it was locked away in one of the attaché cases in the back of the Turbo Swan. He doubted he could've concealed it well enough to avoid detection during a frisk anyway.

As the chemicals merged, they began to eat through the bar. He then pressed the two putty solutions to the tops of the second and third bars.

He stepped off the bunk bed and repeated the procedure at the base of the bars.

Nineteen

Breakout

Treadwell's helicopter had been airborne for twenty minutes since its hurried departure from Cheyenne airport. Agent McKay sat beside the senator in the rear of the aircraft.

After receiving the information about Drake's arrest, their emergency flight in Treadwell's private, Mach One, Cessna Citation X jet began at 12:00. They were in a helicopter from Cheyenne to Morgan by 15:00.

McKay's satellite phone rang. "McKay speaking . . . OK, I'll put him on." He turned to Treadwell. "It's Wilmot, sir."

Treadwell took the phone. "Where are you, Wilmot? . . . No, don't go to the police station. Keep them all where you are. He's in a cell right now. If we can deal with this peacefully, that's how I want to play it. I don't want those boys alarming him. I just need them if the worst happens." He handed the phone back to McKay.

McKay noticed Treadwell's distressed expression. For the first time since being assigned to the case, he saw a hint of vulnerability in, what was usually, a brutally cold individual.

McKay hadn't been partial to the senator on a personal level. He'd been assigned to the Drake case and eagerly embraced the career opportunity of working with a United States senator. He never questioned the virtue of the investigation.

Whenever doubt crossed his mind, a flashback to his eighteenth birthday always quashed his reservations. Having been the lead singer of a local band in Virginia, with dreams of stardom, his mother and father had subjected him to a loving rebuke and words of wisdom. His band's drummer was killed in a car accident while intoxicated. His guitar and bass players were addicted to cocaine and still struggling to find work in bars.

The talk with his parents led him to the police academy and, through distinction, to the CIA, where he began his training in intelligence. Afterwards, he was assigned to the Homeland Security office, the Strategic Detection of Terrorism, based at Langley.

Another award for distinguished service led to his assignment to Senator Treadwell and the Drake case. But what the Drake case truly entailed continued to elude him.

He'd become uncomfortable when Treadwell ordered an all-points-bulletin against the innocent woman Drake had rescued from a terrorist attack. He still didn't know whether Drake was with the terrorists, a rival terrorist organization, or something else entirely.

His initial orders were to pursue Drake's capture without involving the police or the media. It was an impossible task, especially without knowing why. But he hadn't dared question the order.

McKay was thankful for each day he worked for Homeland Security. More than that, he thanked his parents. With gnawing disquiet, he accepted his orders.

Treadwell turned to the pilot. "How long to Morgan?"

"About another twenty-five minutes, sir. I hit a strong headwind just outside Cheyenne and it slowed us down a little. I'm sorry, sir."

Treadwell sat back and sighed. "McKay, call that sheriff's office and give me the phone."

"Sir, I thought you didn't want to alert them that we were coming."

"That was then. Now call that goddamn number."

McKay took out his cell phone again, found Gillespie's number, and pressed send. "It's ringing, sir."

"Gimme that."

Gillespie sat at his desk, his legs rested on the table. He was still shaken by the chilling look in Drake's eyes.

The phone rang, startling him out of his trance, and he picked up the handset. "Gillespie." He struggled to hear the voice on the other end over the sound of the helicopter, but could make out what was being said. "It's all right, Senator, he's safely secured in a cell here. Trust me, he ain't goin' nowhere."

"Are you absolutely sure you have Drake in custody?" Treadwell said.

"He's iron-clad. Why would you think he's not?"

"These are orders from Washington, Sheriff. This is the most dangerous prisoner you will ever have in your cells. Do *not* let him escape. Is that clear?"

Gillespie chuckled. "Now, how'n the hell is he going to escape? Can he punch out a brick-and-cement wall with his bare hands?"

"Go and check on him."

"Sure I can check. But it's stupid." Gillespie ended the call.

The last iron bar eroded away from its base, and Brandon grasped it before it could fall to the ground with a clang.

As he placed it on the bunk with the other two bars, he noticed the remnants of the corrosive putty had already burned through the bunk mattress.

From the opaque packet, he fished out a half-inch diamond-tipped blade. A flattened finger press on the back enabled the application of pressure. The blade glowed for a fleeting second as the diamond caught the light through the window.

He stood on the edge of the bunk frame and waited a few seconds for the stumps to corrode and crystalize. Once contact with the bar's remnants was safe, he pressed his thumb against the flattened back of the blade, and cut through the glass with ease.

His incision around the perimeter of the window came to an end as the final shard was severed. After easing the pane back onto his hands, he gently guided it onto the bunk.

He gripped the window ledge and leaned through the gap, aware of the razor-sharp glass remnants. Pulling himself up, he saw his van before him.

He was halfway through when the helicopter appeared above him, and his adrenaline surged once more. Lurching forward, he knew there wasn't a second to waste.

As the helicopter approached the sheriff's office, Treadwell looked out the window at the run-down outpost. His heart sank as any shred of hope that this establishment had the ability to contain the likes of Brandon Drake disintegrated.

"Sir, please. What is it about Brandon Drake that you fear him so much?" McKay said.

Treadwell turned to his underling with a look of doom. "You have no idea."

Gillespie arrived at Brandon's cell, and it took him a moment to realize his prisoner wasn't sitting on the bunk. And then he noticed the three bars and burn holes. "What the hell?" He glanced up and saw two feet clad in sneakers disappearing through the open window of what had once been a secure holding cell. "Son of a bitch," he hissed, and ran back out through the corridors.

As soon as Brandon's feet touched the ground, he sprinted toward the van. He gripped the handle of the driver's side door and pulled came open. Reaching under the upholstery of the underside to the cab, he seized the key.

Not being an accomplished car thief, he was mystified as to how the two illegal immigrants could've driven the van away. Hot-wiring wasn't an option with that particular model. If given enough time, he was confident he could have figured it out.

He heard a noise and looked behind him.

Ranger came up from behind, having just secured the Gomez brothers in a squad car. He ran toward the van and reached out for Brandon. "Hey!"

Brandon shot his foot out, striking Ranger's jaw, rendering the officer senseless.

He climbed onto the driver's seat and turned the key at the moment the helicopter landed, the whirling blades producing a dust storm across the yard. He slammed the door shut and started the engine. Pressing his toes on the accelerator, the tires screeched and he sped away.

Twenty

Race

Gillespie burst through the front doors of the police station aiming his pistol toward the van. He fired, but the bullet lodged itself harmlessly in the metallic shell. "You son of a bitch!"

Treadwell climbed out of the helicopter with urgency. "Keep this thing running," he said to the pilot. "That's him. He got away. I was right."

McKay followed behind him. "Right about what, sir?"

"I knew he'd break out."

"Is that why you set up the contingency plan?"

Ignoring him, the senator hurried over to Gillespie. "Sheriff, get after Drake. We'll track him from the air."

"Who in the hell are you supposed to be?" Gillespie said.

"I'm the US senator you've been talking to, goddammit. Now, get moving!"

Treadwell and McKay climbed back into the helicopter.

Brandon pressed the accelerator to the floor, but he'd already gained considerable distance from the station.

He checked the rear view mirror, and soon noticed Gillespie's squad car in the distance. He could also hear the helicopter overhead as he raced through Morgan.

The trees appeared ahead of him. Desperately anxious to have Belinda by his side again, he could only imagine how terrified she must have been.

Agent Andrew Wilmot sat in a Chevy Camaro alongside a military entourage. Three high-mobility Humvees accompanied him in a secluded inlet on the roadside, two miles south of Morgan.

At thirty-five, Wilmot's conservative appearance and short, neatly-groomed, dark-brown hair conveyed the desired image for his position—keen operative with meticulous adherence to professionalism. Having been flown out from Washington to Wyoming in a supersonic jet at a moment's notice, he'd never had to move this fast in his life.

His cell phone flashed and he seized it. "Yes, sir."

Treadwell's voice came through the handset. "Drake is driving a white Dodge Sprinter, and he's headed your way. No, wait . . . He's stopping. He's pulled over beside the grass verge . . . He's out of the van now and heading into the trees. The girl has to be in those woods. Move now and get to her before he does. But whatever you do, do not engage Drake. I repeat, do not engage Brandon Drake."

Wilmot darted out of the Chevy and into the woods.

His phone rang again. "Yes, sir."

"I have you all in sight. The girl is approximately two hundred yards northwest of you. You're closer to her than Drake is, so don't blow this one."

"I'm on it."

Belinda shivered as the late afternoon winter chill cut through her clothes. The helicopter hovered overhead as she involuntarily hugged the tree she'd spent hours perched against. "Oh Brandon, where are you?"

The sound of running footsteps alerted her attention. "Brandon?" She'd moved mere feet away from the tree and saw a man in a suit running toward her. He was clearly a threat. She turned to run in the opposite direction, but he was upon of her in an instant.

"Hold it!" he said, and grappled her in a bear hug.

Belinda struggled, her heart pounding in her ears. Despite her effort, her strength was no match for his. "Somebody, help me!"

Brandon appeared as she fought her captor. "No!" he cried.

She saw the scar on Brandon's forehead become a darker shade of purple. She knew it meant something sinister. But what?

The assailant's grip weakened and she broke away just as Brandon reached her. He spun her around, ensuring she was shielded by his own body, and then—

Brandon's right leg flew up with a speed that was almost impossible for Belinda to register. The flat of his sneaker struck her attacker across his left jaw. The man in the suit hadn't fallen before two more blows from Brandon's foot connected with his head. Dazed, he staggered back.

There was bloodlust in Brandon's eyes. It both comforted and chilled her. He was maniacal. Leaping into the air, he spun around, throwing his heel into her attacker's head before landing in a balanced stance. The man fell, his face bloodied and his eyes senseless.

Never before had she seen such a display of aerial, acrobatic prowess outside of a martial arts movie. It was yet another mystery added to the enigma of Brandon Drake.

Brandon moved over to the attacker's limp form. "You bastard!" he bellowed.

He's going to kill him. Belinda grasped his shoulders as he crouched down ready to pummel the man into oblivion. "Brandon, stop. I'm OK. Please. You're not a murderer."

Her words seemed to draw him out of his trance. He looked up at her, his breathing coming in short, exhausted bursts.

"We have to go."

He stood and grasped her hand. After she picked up their shoulder bag of essentials from behind the tree, they ran.

After climbing into the van, Brandon checked the wing mirror to see Gillespie almost on top of them.

Belinda followed his gaze and panicked. "Hurry."

He started up the engine and thrust his foot onto the gas pedal. The squad car almost collided with him as Gillespie attempted to block his path, but the van evaded it by a fraction of an inch. Avoiding the near impact caused Gillespie to stall the car, enabling Brandon to speed away.

Treadwell took out his cell phone again and waited as it continued to ring out. "Where the hell is Wilmot?" As soon as the words rolled off his tongue, he knew the answer. "Fool."

He punched in another number, putting his contingency plan into motion. "Spicer, this is Senator Treadwell. A white Dodge Sprinter is coming your way. I need you to create a roadblock."

Sergeant First Class David Spicer sat in one of the three military Humvees positioned beside Wilmot's Camaro.

Having been jetted out to a nearby airfield in a supersonic jet with five other troopers from Fort Bragg, he knew it was a national emergency. But this was one mission with which he was ill-at-ease for personal reasons. Nevertheless, he was compelled to obey orders. He was soon to be promoted to the rank of Master Sergeant. Regardless of his own issues, he had to remain committed to duty.

He was about to affirm receipt of Treadwell's order when the Dodge Sprinter sped past them. "He just passed us, sir."

"Get after him, soldier. That's an order."

Spicer motioned to the other two Humvees to move forward. As they were about to pull out, they were forced to brake as Gillespie cut across their path.

Once the road was clear again, they fed their way onto the road and gave chase.

Brandon spotted the entourage in his rear view mirror— the sheriff, three Humvees, and the helicopter overhead, which he could hear constantly. "Goddammit. Hold on, baby. This is gonna be a close call."

"I don't want to 'hold on' anymore, Brandon," she said. "We had it all. We had freedom in the cabin, and we threw it away."

"I know. I messed up real bad."

"And how did you do that stuff back there?"

"What stuff"?

"That Tai Wan stuff."

He shrugged, confused. "I don't know what you mean."

"The oriental stuff. The karate. You kicked that guy in the head faster than I can snap my fingers."

"I did?"

"You did."

Mystified by her words, he knew they were in a crisis situation that required his utmost focus. Keeping his foot firmly pressed to the floor, he raced through three towns. He barely noticed the townsfolk stopping in their tracks as the convoy sped through their streets.

As he came upon a bridge, he turned onto a main highway and cursed. They'd hit the five o'clock traffic.

Twenty-One

Invincible

Brandon realized their predicament. They were already on the entrance ramp, caught in the gridlock, with no means of turning back. Noticed Belinda was breathing heavily, he said, "Well, here we go again. Get in the back."

Without a second's hesitation, she threw off her seat belt and climbed into the rear of the van. Brandon switched off the engine and followed her.

His fingerprints came into contact with the Turbo Swan's door handle sensor and instantly, the door rose. After reclining into the pilot's seat, he reached across to open the passenger side for Belinda.

"You're not going to blow the van up again, are you?" she said.

"Not with this much traffic around, that'd be crazy." He activated the Turbo Swan's jets. "Ready?"

"You bet."

The MP3 sound unit came on and the shallow craft was filled with the sound of arena rock.

"Let's get out of here." He pushed the throttle forward and the Turbo Swan burst through the back doors of the van.

Belinda's hands curled around the safety harness.

Brandon noticed the stunned expressions on an elderly couple in a Buick Estate as the crystal-blue aircraft burst out of the van in front of them.

Ahead, soldiers arrived at the top of the entrance ramp, creating a barricade across the bridge. A soldier stepped out of his Humvee and grasped a stack of road cones from the back. He raised his free hand to halt all oncoming traffic, and ran approximately fifty feet across the bridge. From there, he laid the cones out and waved the helicopter down.

An older man and a younger man, both in suits, exited the helicopter, but Brandon couldn't make out their faces from this distance. As he flew toward them, five soldiers trained their rifles on the Turbo Swan.

He came closer to them on the bridge where no civilians were in immediate danger, and held the Turbo Swan hovering before them. The older man in the suit seemed to be issuing an order to the soldiers: "Fire!"

A barrage of bullets struck the Turbo Swan and bounced harmlessly off the alloy. Brandon smiled, a sense of invulnerability coming over him.

He activated the zoom sensor on the view screen and studied the face of the man who'd just given the order. "Oh, my God."

"What?" Belinda said.

"I know who that is."

"Who is it?"

"His name is Garrison Treadwell. He's a US senator. He's the man who had me taken out of the field and put me in weapons testing." Questions filled his mind. Why would this man, who had been somewhat of a benefactor to him, now be commanding a mission to take him out? "What if he's the man responsible for the fake terrorist attacks?" Brandon realized there was no other explanation. Anger, resentment, and extreme rebellion coursed through him. He wanted to taunt this man who had caused so much misery—

to *play* with him. He vengefully gloated, knowing that the US Army was confronting them, but could not touch them.

He glanced at Belinda and she returned his rebellious glee. Their exhilaration was beyond their ability to contain. He could see her terror had given way to the same feeling he had. They were invincible.

He held the Turbo Swan tauntingly before Treadwell and the soldiers while the track on the MP3 boomed through the sound-speakers:

> *I'm talkin' 'bout love . . . Talkin' 'bout things that love's gonna do . . .*

The harmony hooked them. The situation was almost unreal, like an adventure from a dream. The danger of the moment had given way to the fantasy of many possibilities.

And then, David came into sight.

Brandon's jaw dropped as horror and distress replaced the elation in his heart. "No."

David Spicer was the soldier he'd saved from the incendiary on the battlefield in Afghanistan. He felt a sudden stabbing pain striking him at the front of his skull as the memory came back. So much after the explosion was a haze.

He switched the zoom screen to the other soldiers. As their faces came into view, his eyes widened upon the realization that all personnel had been selected from his own division. "What the hell?"

"What?"

"They're from the Eighty-Second."

"The what?"

"The Eighty-Second Airborne Division. My unit."

Overcome with confusion, Brandon questioned why Treadwell would've involved his own division in this? What did he think he was going to accomplish by pitting him against his friends?

With intense focus, he kept his eyes on the screen.

Treadwell turned to David. "Spicer, bring the rocket launcher."

David looked at him with deep reluctance. "B-but, sir—"

"Bring it."

The perturbed soldier moved the back of the Humvee to collect the rocket launcher. He reasoned the Turbo Swan might have been invulnerable to bullets, and even grenades. But it was unlikely it could withstand a missile at close range—a fact, he was confident, would be well known to Drake. With a desperately heavy heart, he returned to Treadwell's side.

"Blow that son of a bitch away," the senator ordered.

Spicer was close to begging Treadwell for a show of mercy—anything to be taken away from this moment. "Sir, there's a civilian in there with him," he said in an urgent appeal to be spared the order.

"An accomplice. Brandon Drake is a traitor, a deserter, a thief of government property, and a wanted fugitive. Now you blow that bastard away, or so help me, I'll see you court-marshaled."

The weight of the rocket launcher tripled in Spicer's arms as he lifted it onto his shoulder.

Brandon and Belinda watched as David trained the lethal weapon upon them.

"Go, Brandon, please," she said desperately.

137

But Brandon was oblivious. He studied Spicer's face closely on the viewing screen and could see beads of perspiration forming on his friend's brow. His and Belinda's lives were in serious jeopardy. Yet, he was obsessed with knowing whether or not his friend, a man whose life he had risked his own for, would actually kill him. It was a moment of utter insanity, but he couldn't pull himself away from it.

"Fire!" Treadwell roared.

Brandon yelled, "Oh Christ, don't do it."

"What are you waiting for?" Belinda screamed. "Go, Brandon, go!"

Twenty-Two

Retaliation

Brandon watched the pained expression on David Spicer's face through the monitor. Was David trying to communicate with him? Treadwell stood marginally behind him. It seemed he was trying to issue a silent-mouth plea to him, away from the senator's field of vision. That could only mean David was aware of the Turbo Swan and the zoom-camera. Brandon had no idea the details of it had already been made known to the Eighty-Second. It had only ever been a test unit.

He studied Spicer's face intently, trying to lip read him. *What are you saying, buddy?*

David pronounced the movement of his lips slowly. Finally, Brandon understood. "*Drake–Go–Now–Please.*"

Brandon felt a stab of conscience. He had the answer he was looking for. David would do whatever it took not to kill him, and now it was up to him not to add to the man's distress.

He moved the throttle and the jets tilted the Turbo Swan onto its side. With the craft in a vertical position, he thrust it forward.

"Fire, I said!" Treadwell barked.

"I'm just getting used to this new sighting system, sir," Spicer said, stalling. "It's got a new configuration that's a real pain."

139

However, he timed it perfectly, and jettisoned the missile. It shot along the vertical underside of the Turbo Swan and detonated harmlessly in the forest, obliterating several trees.

Treadwell turned to Spicer with a hint of contentment in his demeanor.

David shrugged insincerely. "You know, I had Drake in my sights, and at the last minute, that machine—"

The senator laughed and tapped the soldier on his back. "You did well, my boy. You're no match for him anyway." With that, he turned and walked away.

Spicer's brow furrowed with bewilderment as he lowered the rocket-launcher. Looking out over the bridge at the stationary cars, he could see the looks of fear on the faces of the motorists and empathized with them. They'd found themselves in the middle of a military operation with missile explosions, but there was no way they could escape. They were stranded in gridlock with a war unfolding before them.

Treadwell's cell phone rang. Being otherwise involved, he was sorely tempted to ignore it. But given the circumstances, he knew it might be a matter of some importance and decided to answer. "Treadwell."

"Sir?" Wilmot's voice came through the earpiece as a groaning, weary mumble.

Treadwell rolled his eyes. "What is it, Wilmot?"

"You're not going to believe this."

"What won't I believe?"

"I-I need help. I'm in the woods and I'm injured. It was Drake. I've never seen anything like it. He's unbelievable.

I've seen martial arts people in action before, but not like—
"

Treadwell ended the call abruptly and approached McKay. "Do you have anything?"

"He was heading east, but we lost him before the satellite tracker could pinpoint him. My guess is he's heading into North Dakota."

Treadwell moved to the edge of the highway bridge and gazed in the direction the Turbo Swan had fled. He held the one-thousand-yard stare for a pensive moment before muttering, "No, he's not."

***

"Where are we going?" Belinda said.

Brandon fixed his gaze on the navigation coordinator. "Right now, were heading toward North Dakota. Once we get there we're gonna take a detour back to Aspen."

Her heart soared with relief. "The cabin?"

"Yes."

"So, why don't we go there directly?"

"We can't afford for them to ever find the cabin. I'm using a little sleight-of-hand to trick them into thinking we're going in the opposite direction. Once we reach North Dakota, we'll make a U-turn. That's the trouble with this thing. It's so damn noticeable."

A moment of despair came over Belinda. Her fear, tension, anxiety, prolonged cold, and the loneliness of being stranded behind the tree had all been in vain. They hadn't gotten anywhere near Switzerland, or even Canada. But the thought of returning to that serene, idyllic cabin in the snow was ecstatically appealing.

Brandon aimed the Turbo Swan toward the unpopulated flatlands and came to a decision. The time had come for him to stop running. Treadwell planned to ensnare him by pursuing Belinda, independent of public knowledge.

But he was just one man going up against a corrupt government faction, who could call on the army, including his own division, at any time. He didn't have a hope of succeeding if he tried to engage them hand-to-hand.

However, shrewdness was fundamental to battle strategy. The conspiracy's greatest fear was in the people of America learning what he knew. He needed a media event that would crush Treadwell in one sweeping move.

He was also aware of the tremendous personal risk in going public. He was still liable for desertion and the theft of army equipment. Stepping into the open would provide the conspirators with more reason to assassinate him.

But now he had someone more important to worry about. If there was to be any hope for his happiness with Belinda, Treadwell had to be stopped.

One hour after their escape from the highway bridge, the Turbo Swan landed beside the cabin. Brandon climbed onto the porch and held out his hand for Belinda.

Once she was standing, she stopped to inhale the cool, crisp, dusk air, comforted by the contrast of the cabin to the experience from which she'd returned.

"Let's get inside," he said.

She smiled and followed him in with a vague sense of déjà vu.

The door closed behind them and she stood with her back against it, gazing at Brandon—his stature, his striking looks, and his build. She thought of how incredible he was, maneuvering the Turbo Swan, evading and thwarting the most powerful of authority's forces, and those incredible fighting moves. He was extraordinary. He'd rescued her from so much, from the Carringby rooftop, to the Cheyenne police, and now the army.

Most intriguing of all was that he never boasted about his accomplishments. Every skill and attribute he'd revealed had been a surprise, and on each occasion, at exactly the right moment.

"Give me a minute," he said, and made a brisk move toward the bedroom.

After a few minutes, he returned with a tripod in one hand and a digital camera in the other.

"What are they for?" she said.

"I need you to help me."

"What do you mean?"

"We're not running anymore. This time, we're going after *them*."

Brandon set up the tripod and camera and aimed it toward the back wall.

She watched, intrigued, as he removed all of the paintings and ornaments from the wall, and concealed them behind the camera. "Why are you clearing everything away?"

"To remove any clues of this location. Would you come over here please, babe?" He gestured to the bare wall. "I'm going to sit over there. I need you to check this viewfinder, make sure I'm in shot, and then push this button, OK?" He pointed to a red button next to the viewfinder.

"Sure, but why?"

He smiled a half-smile. "I'm going to do the one thing they never thought I'd dare."

"What?"

"I'm going to pull the rug right out from under those bastards, and expose them to the world." He tapped the camera. "*This* is for Channel 7."

"Channel 7? No way," she said excitedly. "You mean you're going to be on TV?"

Brandon chuckled. "You're unbelievable. For everything we've been through, you still think being on TV is the most amazing thing life has to offer."

"OK, you've got a point."

He sat on a small chair in front of the camera. "Am I in shot?"

She looked at the viewfinder. "Yep, got you. But you look, somehow . . . fatter."

"It's because it's widescreen," he said slightly defensively. "Ready to go?"

"Uh, OK." She touched the red button. "It's rolling."

He glanced up at her, noticing the look of intrigue in her eyes, as though she couldn't imagine what he was going to say.

Finally, he composed himself and gazed into the camera lens. "My name is Brandon Drake, and I have information vital to the people of the United States of America."

Twenty-Three

Channel 7

Julie Beacham cringed as she approached Kevin Hobson's office, knowing that no matter what was going well, Hobson would kill it. She held a yellow envelope, delivered by a courier, addressed to the CEO of Channel 7.

Working as an investigative journalist in Los Angeles was a highly competitive vocation. At twenty-five, Julie was willing to tolerate a little awkwardness just to get ahead.

If only Mr. Hobson was a more pleasant individual. She often considered his attitude might have been the reason she'd managed to successfully gain her position with Channel 7 so easily. Few others wanted to have anything to do with him.

She came to the end of the sprawling corridor and knocked on Hobson's door. Nobody could avoid the bronze-emblazoned placard fixed at eye level on the door:

Kevin Hobson
C.E.O.

A terse reply came from within. "What is it?"
Julie took a deep breath. "It's me. I have a delivery for you."

After an awkward pause, she could hear him fumbling around inside and whispering something to someone. She rolled her eyes. *Another one.*

Within moments, the door opened. A naked blonde hurried out of the office, covering herself with her crumpled clothing. Shooting Julie a sheepish smile, she rushed past her.

Julie edged her way into the luxurious office to find Hobson virtually naked. She felt he would have been an attractive man had it not been for his obnoxious attitude. His thick black hair, paired ideally with his dark eyes, and waxed, bare-chested athletic physique, was notably remarkable for a man of his forty-eight years. But Julie had seen it all, and this particular scenario, so many times before.

"Godammit, Julie," he said as he pulled his pants back up. "I was just getting down to business with that broad. What is it?"

She moved closer to him awkwardly and handed him the envelope.

After feeding his arms into his shirt sleeves, he took the packet from her, and tore it open. A flash drive fell out onto the desk and he looked into the empty envelope. "That's it?"

"Guess so."

Angrily, he picked up the flash drive and inserted into the USB port on his desk computer. Having accessed the file, he performed an initial virus scan. Once all was clear, he opened it.

Instantly, the face of a stranger appeared on the screen through his media player: "My name is Brandon Drake, and

I have information vital to the people of the United States of America."

Hobson frowned. Julie's curiosity got the better of her, prompting her to move around to his side of the desk.

Brandon continued. "Ten weeks ago, I was a soldier stationed at a military weapons development facility close to Washington DC. While I was testing a highly-sophisticated piece of equipment, I uncovered a plot within the government to initiate hoax terrorist attacks against a number of key installations—specifically installations with military involvements. Those, so far, have been the Everidge Corporation in Dallas, Carringby Industries in Denver, and the Colton Ranch Munitions Plant in Utah."

"Jesus H. Christ, Julie," Hobson said. "You interrupted my goddamn screw to bring me a film of some rambling crackpot?"

"Just hang in there and give it a chance. You never know."

"I went absent without leave with a considerable quantity of military hardware. It was with the use of that hardware that I was able to enter the Carringby Industries building and facilitate the rescue of this woman . . ." Brandon motioned toward the camera. After a moment, a woman came into frame.

Julie noticed Hobson's sudden interest. He moved closer to the screen as though the face of the young woman was familiar to him.

"This is Belinda Carolyn Reese," Brandon said. "Her face is on wanted posters all across America, but she is an innocent victim being used by a corrupt politician in order to ensnare me. That politician's name is *Senator* Garrison Treadwell. He's responsible for the attacks. I believe his agenda is to create justifications for wars that will result in financial gain."

Hobson turned to Julie with an urgent demeanor. "Get me every picture we have of Belinda Reese. I wanna make sure that's her and not some look-alike."

Julie studied the face of the woman on the screen. She'd seen Belinda's graduation photograph countless times during the coverage of the Carringby attack and Belinda's subsequent vilification. The hairstyle of the woman in the recording was radically different, but there was no doubt it was her.

"What he's telling you is the truth," Belinda said. "I *am* Belinda Reese, and I've been a target of this corrupt governmental faction for the past four days. We only narrowly escaped capture in Wyoming today. We believe that if they capture Brandon, they will kill him."

"When was this sent?" Hobson said.

Julie picked up the envelope and checked the postmark date. "Two days ago, but it doesn't say from where."

"Doesn't matter. Run a search on all newsworthy incidents that occurred in Wyoming two days ago."

"We can only hope that you'll believe us, and take the necessary steps to have Garrison Treadwell investigated," Brandon said. "I am confident his financial activities will lead to the identities of his mercenaries, and to Everidge, Carringby, and Colton Ranch." He paused momentarily before concluding with, "We leave our testimony in your hands."

The screen faded to black.

"*Today* Julie," Hobson barked, slamming his palm on the desk.

Julie looked up from the screen, startled. "Belinda Reese's photograph and . . . and . . . oh, yeah, Wyoming two days ago. I'll get right on it."

Two hours had passed by the time Julie Beacham returned to Hobson's office.

"What have you got?" he said impatiently.

Julie grinned. "The woman on the screen is a perfect match for Belinda Reese, and I got a series of eyewitness reports of a—get this—flying blue Ferrari—evading a rocket launcher on a highway bridge in, guess where, two days ago?"

"Where?"

"Northeast Wyoming. And the vehicle bore a striking resemblance to descriptions witnesses made of a sports car that flew out of an explosion immediately after the Carringby terrorist attack."

Hobson's face shone as though he'd just been appointed God.

Julie continued. "I've contacted Carrie at Fox, Laurie at CNN, and Jason at Channel Thirteen."

"And?"

"None of them have received the Drake film, and I genuinely trust them, Kevin. I've been close and personal with these people since UCLA, and I only asked whether they'd received a package from Drake. I didn't tell them what was on it, if that's what you're thinking."

Hobson was silent for a moment, his chin resting upon his clenched knuckle. "Why? Why me?"

"Why not you? Fox and many of the other major networks have political connections, mostly Republican. You know that no government agency would want to be associated with you since you are so committed to . . . *tabloid* philosophy." She cringed as she made the last remark, desperately trying to word it as diplomatically as possible.

However, far from a defensive outburst, she was surprised by Hobson's spontaneous laugher.

"I'm a goddamn genius. Who says it doesn't pay to be one of the bad guys?" He raised his middle finger to the ceiling. "Screw you, Fox."

Julie shook her head, but couldn't help chuckling at the sight of the world's greatest jerk so ecstatically happy.

"Cancel every story tonight. We're putting out a special. My new best friend, Mr. Drake, is, this night, going to become a star."

"Are you crazy?" she said. "The White House itself will have you closed down."

"On what grounds?"

"Libel? Treason?"

"Don't be ridiculous. How is it libel or treason if he's stating an opinion? Hell, what if it's the truth?"

From Julie's perspective, her job was at stake and she couldn't shake her feeling of discomfort.

"Don't worry about a thing," he said. "We're just reporting the news as it comes to us. If it isn't true, we're just presenting the viewpoint of another. Constitutionally, were in the clear. Freedom of the press. Now just run it."

"As you wish," she said, mildly exasperated. "But why? Just tell me that at least. Why are you doing this?"

Kevin's expression darkened, replacing the jovial, irresponsible corporate magnate he prided himself on being. "Because . . . I believe it."

Twenty-Four

Exposé

Brandon's recording appeared in homes all across America at 18:00 hours, in all time zones.

Brandon and Belinda sat on the leather recliner in the cabin watching the broadcast.

Belinda grinned excitedly at seeing herself on television for the first time, although her sense of glee was hampered by one single factor. "Why do I look like I've put on about ten pounds?"

Brandon said, "It's like I told you. It's the widescreen aspect ratio. It does it to everybody, which is why those movie star people are always dieting like crazy."

Quickly realizing her sense of personal insecurity was not appropriate in that moment, she focused on the seriousness of the matter at hand. "What do you think is going to happen now?"

"We wait for a few days to see what the reaction is, and what the CIA's next move will be. You must understand, this isn't the actual CIA doing these things. I believe it's a splinter cell within their ranks."

"Yes, but what are *your* plans?"

"Hopefully, I won't have to do anything. I need to keep an eye on the TV to see what transpires. This should be the end of it, but if it isn't . . ."

"And if it isn't, then what?"

Fear filled his eyes as it had on the evening he was preparing to set off for Utah. "Then we go to the next phase."

***

Garrison Treadwell stepped into his opulent home in Spring Valley, Washington, and switched on the lights. After placing his briefcase beside the bureau, he removed his suit jacket and draped it over his arm. Sullenness came over him every evening when he returned home after work. It was so empty and quiet.

Routinely, he entered his living room, placed his jacket over the arm of the couch, and made his way to the liquor cabinet. Sitting on top of it was a framed photograph of his wife, son and daughter. All of them were long gone from his life.

His wife, Janice, had passed away almost ten years earlier at the age of forty-nine. A history of high blood pressure eventually led to a massive heart attack.

His son, a successful antitrust lawyer, lived in California. His estranged daughter lived in England with her husband and two children. Treadwell knew they held him responsible for their mother's death. In his heart, he was aware his domineering, uncompromising, and abrasive attitude had made her life a living hell. The photograph served as a constant reminder of what he'd lost, but could never forget.

His career and his country had become an obsession for him since the loss of his family. They were all he had left to live for, and neither were living up to his expectations. He never committed any action he believed to be unjustified. In his own mind, he was always right, but that same trait had ultimately cost him his family.

He poured himself a brandy and switched on his fifty-inch widescreen television with the remote control. After a brief search through the channels, he stopped at a Channel 7 news broadcast. Settling on the couch, he sipped his brandy.

Brandon's recording began, and Treadwell felt as though his heart had come into his throat. The glass of brandy fell from his hand as Drake spoke his name.

***

Agent Martyn McKay opened the door to his apartment in Washington DC with his cell phone held against his ear. "Yeah, I'd love to see you again, Becky. I apologize for not calling you. I've been working on a really important case . . . No, I can't really talk about it. It's classified . . . It's nothing personal, it's just extremely complicated . . . Yes, tomorrow would be great. What time would you like me to pick you up? All right, I'll be there."

He ended the call and smiled, somewhat exhilarated. Deeply attracted to Becky, a stunning fashion model, he was determined not to lose her favor.

He entered his living room and turned on the television set. Brandon and Belinda's speeches had already begun. His head snapped toward the screen. Potential answers about what the Drake case entailed were finally coming to light.

As horrifying as the revelation was, everything he was hearing fit exactly with his personal experience of Garrison

Treadwell—the secrecy, the riddles, the nonsensical orders, and the senator's defensive aggression.

But now, the soldier he'd been ordered to hunt down was answering the questions that had plagued his mind for weeks. If a word of it was true, where did he stand? Would he be implicated as an accessory? How many others were involved?

Uneasily, he sat down in cold contemplation.

***

In his quarters at Fort Bragg, David Spicer prepared for a period of rest and recreation, having just been given an unexpected and indefinite leave. His portable television set provided mild background noise.

At loose ends, he'd recently split with his girlfriend after only three weeks. He found it virtually impossible to find a woman to commit to him given the hazardous nature of his occupation. Curiously, several of his fellow troopers had somehow managed to balance a life of combat with healthy relationships. He wished endlessly he could learn the secret of their success.

He turned to the screen sharply as he heard Brandon's voice. Held transfixed for a moment, he finally sat on the edge of his bed. The recent wave of attacks had been a subject of considerable interest to him. It was all the more frustrating that nobody knew who was responsible.

Was Drake telling the truth? Treadwell was a particularly despicable man, and David hadn't fully recovered from what the senator had almost forced him to do in Wyoming. But would Treadwell have gone as far as to commit the crimes of which Drake was accusing him?

Aside from the gnawing questions, something else was wrong. To David's mind, the man on the television *wasn't* Brandon Drake. The physical appearance was that of Drake, but it was his words and the way in which he was speaking that simply didn't make any sense. It sounded as though he'd become some kind of born-again Christian, or a reincarnation of John-Boy Walton. Even the inflections in his words weren't those of the Brandon Drake he knew.

To the best of Spicer's knowledge, Drake never had any experience as an actor. In fact, Drake would have shunned such a trade as a practice of males who weren't *real* men.

"What the hell are you playing at, Drake?" he muttered in suspicious bewilderment.

Twenty-Five

The Letter

Agent Andrew Wilmot knocked on Director Elias Wolfe's office door in Langley with apprehension. His face was still badly bruised from Brandon Drake's attack. Now, he was being summoned to the director's office with a list of serious implications against him. With what Drake had revealed on national television, and his own involvement with Treadwell, he feared this was going to be his day of reckoning.

"Come in."

He entered the spotless office and saw Agent Martyn McKay sitting opposite Wolfe at the desk.

Wolfe's position as director of Strategic Detection of Terrorism, or *SDT*, a separate intelligence-gathering department, operating from CIA headquarters, called for a leader of the utmost commitment and experience. He stood up from behind his desk. At six-feet-four, with a powerful, masculine jaw-line, and commando-style short, gray hair, his authoritative demeanor was undeniable. "Take a seat, Wilmot."

"Thank you, sir." Wilmot stepped forward and sat nervously beside McKay.

"I'll get right to the point," Wolfe said. "I called you two in here because I need your help."

Wilmot felt a little easier. 'I need your help' was a long way from an accusation.

"You were both involved with Senator Treadwell on some investigation into this Brandon Drake character, correct?"

"Yes, sir," the two agents said in unison.

"I'm sure you're both aware of last night's broadcast?"

"Yes, sir."

Wolfe moved over to his drinks cabinet and took out a bottle of diet soda. "What can either of you tell me about Brandon Drake?"

McKay coughed, as though embarrassed. "Not much, sir. Senator Treadwell always seemed to talk in riddles when it came to Drake. Until last night, I had no idea what this was all about. I merely followed my orders."

"Same goes for me, sir," Wilmot said.

"So, you have no knowledge of these supposed mercenaries Drake alluded to?"

Both agents shrugged as Wolfe's eyes moved from one to the other.

Wilmot knew it didn't add up and hoped Wolfe understood he was innocent. The fact that McKay was also in the dark must have seemed strange to Wolfe.

Wolfe turned to McKay. "You mentioned orders. What were those orders?"

"I knew Drake had stolen some military hardware and the Turbo Swan test unit. That was all Senator Treadwell told me. After the Carringby incident, he ordered me to contact what he called the Delta Unit to give them the order to neutralize Drake."

"*Neutralize* Drake? What do you suppose he meant by that?"

McKay shook his head. "Senator Treadwell wouldn't tell me anything, so I presumed Drake was with a rival terrorist

157

group. Might I ask why you're not talking to the senator about this?"

Wolfe poured his soda and turned back to the two agents. "We can't ask Treadwell anything. He's disappeared."

Wilmot and McKay glanced at one another with mutual concern.

Wolfe contemplated his dilemma. The man he was asking about had been his close friend and confidante for twenty-five years. Treadwell had been well-respected in the senate, recognized for his charitable contributions to the 9/11 commission. He was also the founder of a benevolent fund for the families of active servicemen. From his early days as an honor student of law at Stanford University, to an illustrious career as a prosecuting attorney, and his rise to congress, Treadwell had led a life committed to justice. There had never been any question about Wolfe assigning agents to the senator for his anti-terrorism investigations. Treadwell had proven to be a far greater boon to the intelligence community than his position demanded.

However, the moment a disgruntled AWOL soldier began hurling accusations against him, he simply vanished without a trace.

"Had it not been for Senator Treadwell's suspicious disappearance, we would be laughing at that film Drake made." Wolfe leaned forward, closing in on McKay's face. "This 'Delta Unit' you mentioned?"

"Yes, sir."

"What is it?"

McKay took out his cell phone and scanned through his contacts. He quickly came to a number identified only by the letter D. "This is all I had, sir."

Wolfe took the phone and looked at the screen. "What happened when you called this number?"

"A man answered and I relayed whatever message Senator Treadwell wanted me to. I never understood the messages, but he always told me that *they* would."

"And?"

"They hung up and that was it."

"Couldn't he have done that himself?" Wolfe continued to study the number in his hand. There was something familiar about it. Without looking up, he gestured to Wilmot. "What about you?"

"I was assigned by Senator Treadwell to lead an operation to apprehend, who I was told, was a dangerous, wanted fugitive and his accomplice in Wyoming. I came off a little worse for wear and Drake escaped."

"So I see."

Wolfe's eyes widened as something about the number on McKay's cell phone finally made sense to him. It was certainly not a contact number for any band of mercenaries. The number was preceded by a high-level security SDT prefix code. He knew, in that moment, that the enemy was truly inside the gate.

***

Agent Gary Payne stepped into his apartment in Central Washington DC, immaculately attired in a dark suit with a leather briefcase firmly in his grasp. He switched on the light.

Having been out of the state for the past week investigating a potential terrorist threat, he'd only heard rumors of Brandon Drake's broadcast. Without having actually seen it, his concern was tempered only by the high probability that it would be received as a disgruntled AWOL soldier spinning a crackpot conspiracy theory. Nevertheless, he couldn't shake his gnawing sense of angst.

At forty-two, he'd risen through the ranks of SDT admirably, collecting a number of distinctions along the way. Obsessively ambitious, he'd never married, his career superseding any desire for intimacy other than a string of one night stands.

Senator Garrison Treadwell had scrutinized him and probed his mindset for months until he was finally certain of inviting him into his clandestine movement. On that day, Payne's dreams finally came true. Treadwell's vision for the future of America was identical to his own—a nation of prosperity and a formidable force that no other nation could make war with.

Although there had always been friction between Treadwell and himself, the sense of power he felt from being appointed commander of the senator's secret operation, had been euphoric. It was tainted only by his suspicion that Treadwell had another operative waiting to take his place. If that suspicion was true, the identity of the other had been concealed beyond detection.

He closed the door behind him and knelt down to pick up his mail. After discarding the junk mail onto the living room's coffee table, he came to a letter sent two days earlier. The handwriting on the envelope was unmistakable.

He hurriedly tore it open and drew out a handwritten letter. Within moments, distress took hold of him as he read:

Payne

I have had no choice but to disappear. Drake's broadcast has hampered the operation considerably. I have the situation well in hand, but I suggest that you and every operative involved disappear also. I don't believe your cover will withstand a thorough, official investigation. Our greatest ally was always ignorance. We no longer have that.

You have performed admirably, but Drake has become a serious problem for us all. I don't have time to go into the details now, but what you are looking for is in Drake's hands. I suggest you track him and take what's yours. I'm sure you don't need me to tell you how to do your job. Just do what you have to do.

Consumed with rage, Payne crumpled the letter in a furious grip. What Treadwell had said about Drake made no sense whatsoever, but that did nothing to change the facts. If the situation was as serious as the senator made out, he would have to disappear.

But not before taking what was his.

Twenty-Six

Cloak and Dagger

One week following the broadcast of Brandon Drake's testimony, Kevin Hobson was still pondering his position on the matter. Far from being the career-elevating event he'd hoped it would be, it had been met with unexpected silence. He was, at the very least, expecting the FBI, the police, or somebody in authority to come crawling out of the woodwork with threats of arrests, injunctions and the like. Such would have given him added credibility and further inflammatory accounts to broadcast. Many witnesses to Drake's activities had come forward to give their testimonies. All of them sounded utterly outrageous.

The only story that was noteworthy-but-related, was the disappearance of Senator Garrison Treadwell coinciding with the broadcast of Brandon's message.

Hobson heard commotion outside. "What the hell?"

Julie Beacham burst into the office. A tall man followed her, his spectacles and graying beard complementing his conventionally short-cropped hair and dark suit. A middle-aged female followed him into the room wearing a matching dark jacket and skirt.

"I'm sorry, Kevin," Julie said, clearly distressed. "They said they have a warrant."

Instantly, Hobson's face brightened. "Took your time, didn't you? So, which department are you from? CIA? FBI? Tea Party?" He laughed at his last remark as a demonstration of, not only his contempt for Republican politics, but his lack of concern.

"FBI. I'm Special Agent Dreyfus." The man gestured to his female companion, and they flashed their shields. "This is Special Agent Rossini."

"Feds, eh?" Hobson beamed. "Can I get you guys a drink?"

"No, thank you. We'd like to talk to you about the transmission you made last week."

Hobson casually walked over to the coffee percolator. "Of that, I have no doubt. The only thing I'm wondering is—what took you so long?"

The two visitors helped themselves to chairs.

"To be honest," the man said, "we've been trying to work out the best method of approach. Since Senator Treadwell disappeared, Drake's comments bear a little more credibility."

"So, you're covering your asses, is that it?" Hobson relished the moment, knowing he could be as offensive as he wished.

The agent smiled, as though refusing to rise to the bait. "In a manner of speaking. Have you had any further contact from Drake?"

"No."

"What would you do if he ever walked into this office?"

"I'd like to think I could persuade him to go on the air with me so that I could ask him . . ."

"What?"

"What's true and what's bullshit. I mean these wild reports of flying cars, and something about a stun gun that doesn't leave a mark on the victim, jailbreaks, and superhero-style rescue gigs. It is a little hard to swallow."

"Drake didn't say any of that in his video."

"No. The public did. It all came out after the broadcast."

The woman finally spoke. "Well, you might get your wish."

Hobson finally noticed her. Her silence had made her almost invisible for the most part. *Oh, if only she was a few years younger,* he thought lustfully. But the flicks of gray in her hair and the lines around her eyes deterred his interest. "What makes you so sure?"

The woman slipped her fingers beneath her hairpiece to reveal a short blonde fringe underneath. She placed the wig into her inside jacket pocket. She then peeled away false wrinkles and the orange-peel skin effect from around her eyes and cheeks, before discarding them in her pocket.

Hobson's gaze moved across to the male as he tore away his beard and removed his spectacles. More latex wrinkles came away from his face.

Finally, the 'agent' stood up and extended his hand for Hobson. "Brandon Drake. Hi, how're you doin'?"

Hobson took Brandon's hand and glanced at the young blonde sitting next to him. Mockingly seductive, Belinda winked at him.

"OK, I get it," he said, disguising his surprise. Revealing he wasn't expecting what he had just seen—that he had fallen for a trick—would have surely compromised his narcissism. "Now, what the hell are you guys doing here?"

"We're here to give you your story, live, on the air tonight," Brandon said.

"Why?"

"Surprise is the best form of attack."

"Then what's with all this cloak and dagger shit?"

Brandon leaned forward forcefully, tugging at the remnants of latex flesh clinging to his face. "I know how these scumbags operate. I suspect the reason you haven't heard anything from them since the broadcast is because they could be staking this place out."

Hobson became nervous.

"They might have been waiting for Belinda and me to come here, which means if we go on the air tonight, it can't be announced beforehand. You understand?"

"If they're staking the place out, how do you think you're going to get away after we film the interview?"

"I've got it all worked out," Brandon said. "Keep the interview short and we'll get out of here before the police arrive. We just want the chance to put our case on the air personally. The more we expose them, the more they'll need to watch their steps."

Hobson moved from behind his desk. "I've heard some wild reports about you, Mr. Drake. If you want me to run this, I want some answers."

"Shoot."

"The flying car?"

"What about it?"

"Gimme your version."

"The Turbo Swan is what I escaped from Mach Industries with. It enabled—"

"Whoa, whoa," Hobson interrupted. "The Turbo what?"

Brandon sighed impatiently. "In case you doubt, it *is* real. But it's not a car. It's a low-level-flight, stealth VTOL aircraft. It was only put together for us to test some experimental hardware on. There's nothing magical about it."

"The reports from Denver said that it flew out of an exploding van. Can you explain that to me?"

"The Turbo Swan is made from a molecular-bonded titanium alloy. It's resistant to impacts as extreme as machine gun fire, and it can absorb the concussive force of up to two grenades detonating simultaneously . . . which is actually what I did."

Hobson's expression shifted from serious and attentive to mocking laughter. "What kind of an ass-hat do you take me for?"

Anger appeared in Brandon's eyes. "Look, man, I know you might still be stuck in the Dark Ages. In the eighties. But I'm not."

Hobson reined in his sardonic attitude and decided to give Brandon a chance. "OK, in that case, perhaps you'd care to explain it to me."

Brandon paused to collect himself, and said in a calmer tone, "The Turbo Swan *is* real. As I said it's a low-level VTOL aircraft."

"OK, I got that, but how does it work at such a small size?"

"The Swan is relatively new technology combined with old technology. It isn't entirely unique. It's a Vertical Take-Off and Landing aircraft with twin high-bypass fanjets delivering thrust to four independent vectored nozzles. It uses a fly-by-wire multi-channel flight control system. High speed maneuverability is achieved with the use of forward canards in conjunction with vectored thrust nozzles. It's Gyro stabilized and silenced by an active noise reduction system delivering an electronic signal, one hundred eighty degrees out of phase to the input—"

"All right, already," Hobson cut him off again. "OK, you know your shit. So, it's as you said in the first place, some kind of VTOL technology, right?"

"Right, but combined with unique miniature engines that give it kick-ass propulsion."

Hobson noticed the surprised look in Belinda's eyes as Drake's astonishing technical explanations unfolded. He'd delivered all of that jargon as proficiently as a scientist would have. Clearly, she didn't know her boyfriend as well as she thought she did. "So where is it?"

"I can't tell you that," Brandon said.

"Oh? Why not?"

"There was no possibility of us bringing the Turbo Swan to Los Angeles. We would've risked exposure and theft, especially considering the reputation of some of L.A.'s suburbs. It would have found its way onto the back of some hoodlum's tow truck the minute our backs were turned."

Hobson assumed a faux-offended expression. "Nice to know you think so highly of our city."

"It was stolen in Wyoming, which is what led to us almost being captured. It was quite a wake-up call. I couldn't risk bringing it here."

Suspicion crossed Hobson's face. "I smell bullshit."

Brandon threw his hands in the air, exasperated. "Look, do you want this exclusive, or do we just get out of here this minute, and you can sit on your precious hope of a big story 'til kingdom come?"

There was an excruciating pause as Brandon and Kevin stared at one another in a moment of masculine, primal contest.

"Wait a second," Hobson said. "Putting you guys on the air, I'd be admitting to harboring fugitives, surely."

"Putting us on the air live and saying to world, 'Hey, here they are,' is hardly harboring."

"So, what are you going to do if they race over to arrest you?"

"Like I said. Keep it short, and we'll just get the hell out of here."

"But . . . why are you doing this? You sent the film, so why are you putting yourselves in the firing line like this?"

"Nothing has been done about the situation since the broadcast," Brandon said angrily. "We didn't want it to come to this, but maniacs are out there killing innocent people. Treadwell fled, but there have been no arrests, and no sign of an investigation. They need another kick in the ass."

"But why you? What makes it all fall on *your* shoulders?"

"Because . . ." Brandon lowered his gaze to the floor. "Because there's no one else."

There was another awkward pause. Kevin was gripped with uncertainty, but he ultimately conceded. "OK, let's run it."

***

Hiding out in a rundown motel room on the outskirts of Los Angeles, Gary Payne listened intently to the conversation between Drake and Hobson. After receiving Treadwell's letter, he'd initiated a plan to ensnare Brandon. He knew the CIA and SDT would deal with Drake's original recording with as much discretion as possible, due to the sensitive and damning nature of his claims. The silence, in turn, was likely to draw Drake out of the woodwork.

Several days earlier, he'd infiltrated Channel 7 as a member of the cleaning staff in order to gain access to Hobson's office. Once inside, he'd planted a bug underneath Hobson's desk.

He took out his cell phone, punched in a number, and the response came almost instantly. "The bird has landed," he said. "I want the two of you to meet me there in thirty. We're only going to get one chance at this. We go in, grab the son of a bitch, and get out."

Twenty-Seven

Prime Time

Hobson paced up and down behind Brandon and Belinda while the make-up girl powdered their faces.

Brandon's masculine looks appeared bizarrely feminine. "Is this really necessary?"

Hobson stopped pacing. "Is what really necessary?"

"This sissy make-up crap."

"You're going before studio lights, which means you're going to look washed out without it. Believe me, the more appealing you look to the people, the more they'll be willing to listen to you."

"More appealing? How can looking like a girl make me more appealing?"

"You won't look like a girl. It interacts with the lighting. On screen you'll look perfectly normal."

Lightening the mood, Belinda said, "I think it looks great, especially now my hair is shorter. I've never had a makeover like this before."

Brandon scowled in frustration. "Are you taking this seriously? Do you have any idea what we're up against?"

"OK, you guys are done in here," Hobson said. "Follow me."

Brandon and Belinda stood, removed their makeup gowns, and she whispered into his ear, "Now, run it by me again, just to be on the safe side."

"We have five minutes once the broadcast begins. The nearest police patrol should have four minutes to get the call from the police department and get to the building. They'll then have another two to get into the studio. That's our window. We stay on camera for five minutes, not a second more."

Hobson glanced back at them. "What are you two whispering about?"

"Who's doing the dishes tonight," Brandon said sardonically.

They followed Hobson through the corridors until they arrived at a door marked *Studio 5*.

Hobson looked at his watch. "You're on in three minutes. I've got to set this up, so just gimme a moment."

Brandon nodded impatiently.

The media mogul walked into the studio and approached an extremely attractive blonde. He handed her a piece of paper and she took it with a look of mild discomfort.

Belinda's eyes lit up with excited glee. "Oh, my God. That's Tara Willoughby."

Brandon shrugged. "So?"

"She's on TV."

"Oh, for Chrissakes."

Belinda was becoming increasingly aware of the shift in Brandon's persona. He was becoming objectionable and arrogant, and seemed all too ready to engage in arguments. Tentatively, she put it down to stress and anxiety.

As though sensing her thoughts, Brandon whispered, "I'm worried about you, is all. This is so damn dangerous."

"I know, but I'm the only one who can validate what you're saying." She held him by the shoulders. "It's my choice. I need this."

"Yeah, but—"

Hobson waved them over to him. "Brandon and Belinda, this is—"

"Tara Willoughby," Belinda finished.

"I . . . I don't know what to say," Tara said, surprised. "Please remember, I've had no time to prepare for this, so we're going to have to ad lib a little."

Hobson pointed to the sheet in Tara's hand. "The main questions are on the paper. Give it to me and I'll tape it to the front of camera two."

Tara handed it to him and glanced at her watch. "OK, let's get to it."

Belinda gazed, overawed by the spectacle of TV cameras, lights, and all of the technical apparatus hanging from the studio ceiling. They seemed to extend far higher than the cozy image of the news desk that would be caught in frame. Television, she realized, was a most deceptive illusion.

They sat behind the desk while Tara prepared herself. Her eyes darted between the paper fixed to the camera and her cue from a young, first assistant director. He showed the five digits of his opened right hand, and then there were four–three–two–one.

On cue, Tara fixed her gaze into the camera. "Good evening America. Tonight, *Seven* has an exclusive story. In an unprecedented move, we are joined by two special guests who have come to us at great personal risk."

The camera moved around to Brandon and Belinda.

Tara continued. "You may recognize these people from a privately made tape we broadcast last week—Brandon Drake and Belinda Reese."

Belinda noticed, out of the corner of her eye, Brandon secretly pressing a button on the side of his wristwatch, and felt a little more secure. She knew he was monitoring a timer so that they wouldn't accidentally exceed five minutes in front of the camera. Subtly adjusting his position, he shielded her from the direction of the door.

"Belinda, could you tell us how this ordeal began for you?" Tara said.

Still a little shaken and star-struck, Belinda attempted to respond. "I was in the restroom at Carringby Industries when it happened. I'd never been so scared in my entire life."

"What happened?"

She closed her eyes momentarily as she cast her mind back to that terrible night. "They burst into the building with machine guns, killing everyone in sight. I could see them through a crack in the restroom door, and one of them was coming closer, kicking in every door along the way. It was terrifying."

The timer on Brandon's watch continued: 0:46—0:47—0:48—

In a cleaning storage room on the floor below, Agent Gary Payne discarded his cleaner's overalls and put on black field attire. His two fellow SDT operatives, Timothy Ogilsby and John Woodford, finished putting on their own.

Payne opened the door and checked the corridor was clear. They then stepped out and made their way to the top of the stairwell.

Payne's eagerness to get to Drake before official sources did was palpable. There was so much at stake—that which would facilitate his freedom. Drake had already cost him, Ogilsby, and Woodford their careers and forced them into hiding. "We have to take him from the studio before they finish filming," he said. "There's no way of knowing which way he's going to come out and we won't have time to go looking. The police are going to be here any minute."

They looked at one another in concurrence.

"OK, let's go get him."

Putting on black ski masks, they hurried up the stairwell and through the entrance to the third floor, following Payne's lead.

Julie Beacham exited the conference room and instantly recoiled. Three masked gunmen appeared before her. The one who appeared to be the leader placed his hand against her chest. "W-what's going on? Who are you?" she stammered.

A pistol appeared before her eyes, paralyzing her with fear.

"Make one sound and I *will* kill you," the leader said with professionally calm coldness. The tone of his voice assured her he wouldn't hesitate to blow her brains out without a second thought.

Trembling, she nodded, and he led her by the arm through the corridors. Within moments they arrived at the studio door.

Brandon looked at his watch again: 1:56—1:57—1:58—

Belinda continued to relate her harrowing tale to the camera. "When I fell out of the ventilation shaft into that store cupboard, I thought I was safe. But when I stepped out, all I could see was fire and smoke. I was sure I was going to die."

The door burst open. Brandon's head snapped to the left and back to Belinda. Adrenaline surged through him.

Belinda's mouth fell open in stunned terror. "Oh, my God. They're here."

"Everybody down!" Brandon leaped up. In one swift move, he grappled Belinda and Tara off their seats and thrust them onto the floor.

Two henchmen drew their pistols, but Brandon uppercut-punched a small desk into their masked faces. They seemed distracted long enough for Brandon to get to his feet again.

Something was wrong. He was expecting either the police or the FBI to arrive to take him in. But sending armed mercenaries into a TV studio live on the air was utterly insane.

All personnel in the room panicked, creating a stampede in a desperate bid to escape the gunmen. Camera two was unmanned.

Executing a forward roll, Brandon dove across to the leader of the trio and swept his legs from under him with a single, graceful move of his right heel. The attacker fell to the floor and his mask came loose. Brandon seized the opportunity to pull it away from his head.

Belinda looked into the man's eyes from across the floor. She struggled not to lose control of her bladder as she almost had done the last time she'd seen him through Carringby's air-vent grill. His was a face that would haunt her nightmares, likely for the rest of her life.

From the wings, Hobson watched exhilarated, with an opportunistic, victoriously-clenched fist.

The blond gunman raised his pistol only to be met with a blow from the blade of Brandon's right hand. The gun flew across the studio floor giving Brandon the time necessary to run across to camera two. Gripping the camera, he moved it around onto the man's face. "Welcome to prime time, asshole."

The gunmen trained their pistols on Belinda and Tara. "Give it up or the bitches get it!" Payne bellowed.

With startling speed, Brandon drew out the sonic force emitter from the rim of his pants, and opened fire upon the three assailants. They instantly fell backward, temporarily paralyzed.

Hobson snapped his palm across his mouth, almost weeping with joy.

Brandon ran back over to Belinda and helped her to her feet. "Come on, baby. We have to get out of here."

Shaking, she took his hand and followed him behind the cameras.

Hobson noticed the leader rising from the trio of bodies. After struggling to get to his feet, he staggered across the studio floor to retrieve his pistol, and headed toward the fire exit.

After waiting for the attacker to disappear through the door, Hobson emerged from behind the wings and over to camera two. Relieved, he noticed the small red digital recording light. "We got it. Goddamn, we got it."

Brandon led Belinda down the fire escape, his hand clinging to hers fiercely. He felt her palms were clammy, and her breathing was coming in short, rapid bursts. He could almost feel her terror and anguish.

"I calculated it from the time it would take them to get inside the building," he said breathlessly. "Two minutes means they were already inside. I don't think they were acting under anyone's orders . . . No way real officials would've pulled a stunt like that on air."

"S-so . . . who were they?"

"I don't know."

"I saw the guy's face," she said. "He's the one . . . He was the one who was kicking the doors in at Carringby. I saw him take his mask off."

Brandon quickened his pace, almost causing Belinda to lose her footing. "Brandon, please slow down . . . I can't keep up."

"You have to. If those assholes were working for Treadwell we can't trust anyone. Almost anybody could be in on this."

He heard footsteps above him and looked up to see Payne coming toward them.

"Son of a bitch!" Payne spat.

"It's him!" Belinda screamed.

Brandon aimed the sonic force emitter and fired in the assailant's direction, but the shot missed.

Payne trained his pistol on them. "Drake, stop. I swear I'll kill her."

Belinda froze, but Brandon fired a second jolt, this time successfully. Payne crumpled in a heap down the steps. However, it caused a delay they could not afford.

Within a minute, they reached the bottom floor. Brandon picked up their backpack of essentials from where he'd concealed it under the stairwell earlier.

He threw open the fire exit door and stepped out into a side street. The sound of sirens was all around them.

"What are we going to do?" Belinda said desperately.

He looked at the LCD on the top of the sonic force emitter. It showed a reading of zero, indicating its power cell was depleted. "I don't know. I had everything planned and timed to the micro-second, believe me. This is like they know what I'm thinking ahead of time." Exhausted, he lowered his head despairingly. The now-familiar combination of guilt and sense of failure clouded his mind. Belinda had insisted she come with him to the studio, but he knew he shouldn't have permitted it. "I'm so sorry. I made a fatal mistake. I thought I could get us out of this, but I was wrong."

"But we haven't done anything," she said. "Once they find that out, they'll let us go."

"We're dealing with psychopathic, corrupt officials. If the police take us in, they'll come for us and we'll be killed."

Belinda shuddered. Seeing nowhere to run, they remained where they stood, unarmed and helpless, with the sound of the sirens growing ever closer.

Twenty-Eight

Labyrinth

"Oh, my God, Brandon, they're coming!" Belinda shrieked.

He looked around him, listening intently, but the sirens were coming from all directions. He realized he'd made the right decision using public transportation to get them to L.A. If they'd used the van, it might have been spotted by the police. Even if they'd got away, the license plate could have identified the location from which it had been purchased. That would've been two vans they'd know about that came from Aspen.

However, without transportation, he had no idea how they were going to escape from the side street. It was a no-win situation.

Taking Belinda's hand, he chanced heading toward his immediate right where the sirens sounded marginally quieter. "Come on," he said, and hurried toward another side street.

Belinda struggled to keep up with him, but she managed to keep a tight grip on his hand as he led her toward a labyrinth of side streets.

"We've got to lose ourselves and lay low," he said. "We need to look different, so we've got to find somewhere to change clothes."

They found themselves in a remote suburb that showed a sudden rift between the corporate areas and an off-beat impoverished zone. Their desperate flight continued, propelling them into the shadows.

Payne's eyes opened. He found himself slumped on the hard concrete landing of the fire exit's first floor. It took him several moments to realize what had happened. Unaware of how long he'd been unconscious, the fear of capture caused his adrenaline to surge.

He stood as quickly as he could manage. The blood drained from his head, and his disorientation caused him to stagger.

He picked up his pistol from the floor, and made his way down the last flight of steps using the railing to brace himself. Regardless of his condition, his obsessive need to catch Drake overcame his reason.

He edged out of the exit. Carefully peering along either side of the street, he saw that all was clear, save for the persistent sound of the sirens.

He turned to the right and moved toward a lane. He conjectured Drake and Reese wouldn't have dared to risk exposure on the main thoroughfare with so many police around. As he entered the inlet, he inhaled in an attempt to clear his head. Once he'd regained his senses, he moved forward, his pistol grasped firmly.

***

A team of ten police officers from the Los Angeles Police Department, attired in riot gear, approached Kevin Hobson in Studio 5. Tara had concluded the broadcast in a hurry, her delivery notably impaired by the trauma of the events.

Hobson struggled to process what had happened. He pondered his public statement, although he was finding it difficult to focus.

LAPD's Chief of Police, Jared Tepper, gestured for his men to apprehend the two remaining, disoriented gunmen as a priority.

A seasoned veteran of the police force in his late forties, Tepper's eyes possessed a long-since-honed, penetrating stare. His past dealings with Hobson had resulted in a strained relationship. Discussions regarding countless crime reports, newsworthy stories, and what incidents should be kept under wraps, had led to numerous disagreements.

Within moments, the two remaining assassins were pulled to their feet, handcuffed, and read their rights.

Tepper turned to Hobson. "I wanna talk to you. What the hell did you think you were doing?"

"We exercised our First Amendment rights, that's what. I'm in the clear, Jared," Hobson said.

"You were harboring a fugitive wanted by the FBI, and an AWOL soldier. In so doing, you recklessly endangered the lives of every man and woman in this room."

"They were going to give themselves up right after the broadcast. And would you mind telling me how the hell putting them on the air live can be considered harboring them? You're walking into a legal gray zone here. Freedom of the press is constitutionally sacrosanct."

Tepper exhaled, realizing he had no case, although he didn't buy the line about Drake and Reese planning to give themselves up. "Just look around you. It's only by a goddamn miracle nobody was killed."

"We gave them a chance to give us an honest interview about what's really going on, and this is what we got." Hobson gestured to the carnage around him. "How the hell could anyone know this was going to happen?"

Tepper conceded reluctantly, but knew he was wasting time. "Where did they go?"

Hobson glanced at the exit door. "I think they headed out down the fire escape. If you ask me, they didn't have any choice. That third psycho went right out after them with a loaded gun in his hand."

"How long ago?"

Hobson shrugged. "I don't know . . . four, maybe five minutes ago."

Tepper turned to his subordinates. "All right, men, they can't have gotten far. I want all of you out of the studio and down that fire escape. Cover every street, side lane, back yard, and garage. And set up roadblocks within a two mile radius."

The officers ran across to the exit, climbed down the fire escape, and split up in the street. Three headed out to the left. Four took to the right to join up with their colleagues outside the front of the building. The remaining three took the side lane.

***

Payne revived to the extent he could walk with a brisker motion and continued through the maze of streets. He listened intently for any sound or the barest hint of footsteps, but he could hear anything. Drake could have lost

182

himself anywhere in a sprawling, urban environment such as this.

He paused for a moment to catch his breath, and heard footsteps running behind him.

Bracing himself behind the wall, he peered around to see three police officers running in his direction a considerable distance away.

He took another side lane, broke into a slow run, and managed to turn into another street at the moment the officers passed the exit. He held his pistol next to his chest with the unhesitant intention of killing any who might discover him.

Deep into the backstreets, Brandon and Belinda knew they were lost. That gave Brandon a moderate advantage. If they didn't know where they were, there was more of a chance nobody else knew where they were, either.

They stopped in the shadows of a warehouse alcove to catch their breath. "We can't rest for long, baby," he said.

"I know."

"First, we need to find somewhere to change into casual clothes. If those assholes hadn't burst in and screwed everything up, we could've caught a cab and we'd be at Union Station by now. We're losing time."

She looked at him perturbed. "What do you mean?"

"We're in deep. Every second that ticks by is a second that makes us more recognizable than ever. Our second appearance on TV creates even more people who know what we look like. We've got to grab the first opportunity to change our appearance again. I can't tell you how much of a priority that is."

"Then we're wasting time. Come on."

He was relieved by her insistence. He'd stopped purely for her sake, but her eagerness had clearly superseded her weariness. "So glad you said that."

They continued running, the dusk sky providing an increasingly effective cover. However, they both knew the police could be around any corner.

In the distance, almost two miles from where they'd started, they saw an old, derelict building.

"We could change clothes in there," Brandon said. "It'll be dark inside, but that'll help as a cover."

"What if the police are waiting for us inside?"

"I'll check it out first. We have to take the chance. Just keep behind me."

She reached forward, held onto his back-stretched hand, and continued.

As they came within two hundred yards of the building, they stopped. The surrounding area resembled a war zone. There were two burned out cars and litter scattered all around. The building showed signs of fire scorching and almost every window had been vandalized. The location offered an aura of menace, and Brandon had no idea where they'd stumbled into.

They made two steps farther forward, and Belinda screamed. A line of switchblades appeared before their eyes. Shining, silver edges of death were ejected, one by one, from their hand grips.

Twenty-Nine

Gangland

Belinda gasped as six hard-looking gang members stood before them. Their cold, unflinching gazes conveyed the message they intended to slice them to shreds.

"Get behind me!" Brandon bellowed to her.

A tall black man thrust his switchblade toward them. "Drop the bag!"

Brandon experienced a surge of panic. The police were pursuing them from behind. Ahead was a street gang threatening to kill them unless they surrendered the equipment they needed to escape from Los Angeles. The situation was hopeless, but he couldn't allow anything to happen to Belinda. The thought of harm coming to her was beyond his capacity to even contemplate.

An instinct came over him and he stepped back with the speed of a cheetah, his left foot falling into a perfectly-balanced stance. Casting the backpack behind him, his consciousness gave way to something akin to autopilot. His right leg flew into the air and curved inwardly. The edge of his foot flashed across the line of switchblades causing each one to fly from the hands of their assailants. The knives landed ten feet away.

The six thugs were momentarily startled, their weapons out of reach. They turned their attention back to Brandon. The black male lunged for him first.

Brandon sidestepped him with ease and threw the blade of his right hand into his attacker's throat. The man fell to the ground gasping for air. Brandon thought the oxygen must have left his brain because he fell unconscious within moments.

A Caucasian youth displaying a moderately muscular physique was almost upon Brandon. An explosive kick to the chest sent the kid crashing onto the hood of a burned out BMW.

Through her terror, Belinda noticed the scar on Brandon's forehead throbbing. His eyes once again assumed their chilling glare of unbridled hatred.

He leaped into the air as he had done in Wyoming, and executed that same dazzling, acrobatic spin-kick into the jaws of two gang members. With shattered teeth, they fell to the ground senselessly.

She couldn't help her amazement at how he'd managed to take down four of them already, and all within a few fleeting seconds. He moved so quickly. If she hadn't seen it with her own eyes, she wouldn't have thought such feats were humanly possible.

She saw a Hispanic gang member drawing a pistol from underneath his jacket. "Brandon, he's got a gun!"

But Brandon was upon the man before he could even aim. He wrapped his arm around his opponent's, locking the firearm past the back of him, completely beyond the range of his body. As Brandon grasped the gunman's throat, the shock caused his finger to accidentally depress the trigger. The bullet struck his friend behind them squarely in the chest.

Belinda covered her ears against the deafening sound of the gunshot. The young man fell to the floor grasping his wound with crimson spurts coating his fingertips. He glanced at the blood for a moment before slipping away.

Brandon pressed the palm of his hand against his opponent's chin, forcing his head backward, and hurled him to the ground. The impact caused the thug to loosen his grip on the gun. Brandon took it from him and cast it aside. He pummeled his fists into the man's face repeatedly, leaving his nose broken, his jaw disfigured, and his face bloodied.

Despite the fact that the man was unconscious, Brandon seized the pistol beside him, and trained it toward the assailant's forehead.

"Brandon, no!" Belinda cried.

A flash came before Brandon's eyes. He appeared to be in some kind of warehouse, or aircraft hangar. There was a bare-chested man ahead of him, with his arms above his head, suspended by ropes. Brandon recognized him as a captured operative for an al Qaida-Taliban hybrid group. Brandon's unit had been interrogating him in Afghanistan for information regarding the whereabouts of a terrorist cell in the desert. The incident had taken place on the day before the explosion, which had caused his head injury and re-assignment to Mach Industries.

But the events had not transpired as he was now seeing them. He sensed a cruel rage possessing him. A bloodlust. He felt as though he was laughing at the unbridled terror in the eyes of the captive, and sensed the gun in his hand was no longer a gun. It was a blow torch.

187

His friends, including David Spicer, were in the hangar with him. They were pleading with him to stop. He could barely make out the echo of their voices behind him:

Drake, this isn't the way. Don't do this. We're not like them.
We've got to stop him.
How? You know what he can do.
We can't afford to be under an Abu Ghraib inquest, Spicer. We've got to do something.

There was also someone else in the room. Brandon could feel it. It felt like his grandfather, but that was impossible. His grandfather had died when he was a boy. The entire scene was impossible. It wasn't Brandon in the hangar either, but he could see himself and feel it as though it was.

In the vision, he came closer to the captured terrorist with the blow torch. He could feel the heat radiating from the blue flame. The man before him screamed even before he touched him, but nothing was going to deter him. He continued forward as the captive braced himself for the searing pain.

Brandon came back to reality, the vision of the restrained prisoner replaced by the unconscious hoodlum on the ground. Disturbed and disoriented, he dropped the gun and shook his head.

"A-are you all right?" Belinda said as she approached him with the backpack.

Shaken, he tried to explain to himself what he'd seen in his mind. "I-I don't know. I just saw . . . something. I don't know what it was."

"What? What did you see?"

He pinched the bridge of his nose, desperately trying to assimilate the vision. "It was me . . . But it wasn't *me*. I don't know how else to describe it."

"Brandon, there's no time for this. We've got to get out of here."

"You're right. I'm going to check out that building."

She followed him as he carefully edged along the side of the deserted factory. It was growing darker by the minute. The aura of menace in this place was oppressive.

They looked inside through a broken window. There was no sign of life, and no sounds they could hear, other than the wail of sirens in the distance.

"I think it's OK," he whispered. "Let's just get in there and change out of this smart gear."

"OK."

Hurriedly, they made their way around to the side of the building and stepped inside the dark, foreboding interior.

Having heard the gunfire earlier from two streets behind, Payne headed in the direction it had come from with his pistol drawn. He came to an abrupt halt at the sight of six unconscious thugs on the ground, and then carefully made his way forward. He picked up a gun which lay beside an unconscious man and slipped it into his pants. He wasn't about to risk the guy coming around and taking a shot at him.

The young hoodlum groaned insensibly. Payne knelt down beside him and grasped him by the lapels with one hand. With the other, he held his own gun against the kid's jaw. "What happened? Who did this to you?"

"D-don't kill me, man," the kid stammered weakly.

"I'm not going to kill you. Just tell me who did this."

"Some guy. N-not . . . human."

"Not human? What the hell are you talking about? Was he alone?"

The punk shook his head slowly.

"Who was with him?"

"Some blonde girl."

Payne was momentarily silent. It was obvious these thugs had tried to roll Drake, who, in turn, had literally wiped the floor with all six of them, single-handedly. This was far beyond Payne's own combat capabilities, or those of any other man he knew. It raised an alarming question. Why would Treadwell have put him up against someone as lethal as this? "Did you see where they went?"

The kid shook his head again. Payne coldly cast him back down and made his way across to the building.

Brandon and Belinda drew their casual wear out of the backpack, shivering with the cold interior of the dilapidated structure. Their feeling of vulnerability, being almost naked in such a dangerous environment with the authorities on their trail, hastened their pace.

The building was damp and dusty, and even the slightest move echoed throughout the vast, empty space. Rows of pillars lined the reception areas, with rusted tools and mechanical equipment scattered around. Brandon assumed it was part of an old car manufacturing plant, but it was difficult to be sure in the darkness.

Two offices in the main area, and the remains of a restroom had long-since been vandalized.

They re-dressed themselves, replaced their business shoes with sneakers, and then crudely crammed their suits into the backpack.

He handed her a baseball cap and her dark wig. "There's no way I can do the prosthetics in here, so we're gonna have to keep our heads down."

"OK."

Images of what he'd seen in the vision persistently haunted him, but he knew his priority was getting Belinda to safety.

He took up the backpack and strapped it over his shoulder. "All right, let's get outta this place." Putting his baseball cap on, he made a move toward the opposite side of the building.

The sound of footsteps could be heard in the distance. He stopped Belinda with his arm and ushered her back into the shadows. He felt her muscles tense and knew she was ready to fight.

They crouched down behind a pillar and peered around. Payne walked into a shard of moonlight coming through an empty window frame.

Brandon slipped his hand over Belinda's and gave it a comforting squeeze while they waited to see what the killer was going to do.

Glancing to his left, he spotted three police officers outside through a broken window. The first officer drew his firearm when they discovered the unconscious thugs. His two colleagues followed and drew their pistols.

The first officer took out his radio. Brandon heard him say, "This is Blaine. I'm with Cooper and Hayes. We need back up and an ambulance."

The reply came through. "What's your location? And what's the situation?"

"You know the old Newman car parts factory behind the corner of Main and Alameda?"

"Yes."

"Well, somethin' real weird's going on here. We've just found six members of Richie Sanchez' gang and they've all been beaten to a pulp." He glanced to his right. "It also looks like there's been a fatality. Gunshot wound by the looks of it."

"Is there any sign of the suspects?"

"Not yet. They might be holed up in the factory. We're going in."

Payne had clearly heard it too. Brandon noticed him bracing his back against the wall, most likely trying to figure a way out.

He was aware Belinda was struggling not to weep and swallowed hard. They were trapped inside the most hellish building imaginable, with a squad of cops about to enter. They couldn't move an inch in any direction without being seen by either the police or a merciless assassin.

Thirty

Into the Night

Brandon's gaze flitted between Payne and the entrance. Payne braced himself behind the wall of the building's restroom area. The three police officers entered less than two feet away from him.

Hopelessness, the sense of feeling trapped, and worst of all—the thought that he'd failed Belinda, tormented him. He was becoming aware that panic triggered the mysterious rage within him, wiping out his conscious awareness. *No, not now. Keep it together.* He subconsciously knew that whatever his condition was, it would destroy any chance of them getting out of this situation alive.

Through the shadows, he noticed how close Payne was to the three officers, and a calculated idea came to him. If he could startle Payne, he would alert the police to him and create a distraction. Then he could slip out of the back of the building with Belinda, cloaked by the darkness.

He picked up an old, rusted wrench from beside his feet and gently eased himself into position. He could sense Belinda's fear, but she remained composed. The risk of the two of them being exposed was considerable.

Without a sound, he drew the wrench backward and hurled it toward Payne. It lost its velocity two feet away from the killer's right leg and collided with his shin bone, producing an involuntary cry of agony.

One of the officers darted forward to seize the gunman, but Payne spun around and bludgeoned his fist into the man's jaw. The punch gave him the moment necessary to run, although he was visibly impeded by the throbbing pain in his leg.

The two other officers drew their pistols and gave chase.

With the distraction in place, Brandon ushered Belinda back through the shadows toward the rear exit.

"Stop!" one of the officers called.

Brandon glanced behind him and saw Payne turn to face the officers. It was obvious Payne couldn't outrace them with his injury slowing him down.

At close range, Payne shot the officer in the abdomen—a precise shot to the one inch gap between the bottom of the officer's bullet proof vest and the belt around his pants. The force of the impact knocked the officer several feet back before he collapsed to the ground.

The other two officers instantly gave up the chase and turned back to help their fallen colleague. Payne ran with a limp toward the end of the building and out into the night.

The second officer took out his radio. "Officer down! This is Cooper at the old Newman parts factory. I'm with Hayes. We need an ambulance immediately. Blaine's been shot." He ran across to his partner and knelt with him to help Blaine. "Easy, man. Everything's going to be fine. Help's comin'."

"N-no . . . leave me. I . . . I'll b-be fine," Blaine said. "G-get that s-son of a b-bitch."

Hayes shook his head. "Man, we can't leave you here."

"H-help's c-comin'. Just go."

The two officers looked at one another uncertainly. "Cooper, I can hear the ambulance. I'll go out and flag them down. You start after the perp, and I'll join up with you once the ambulance is here."

"D-do it . . . for me, both of you," Blaine said. "It's what I want."

Hayes glanced at his partner. "Go, Coop."

Cooper ran after Payne as sirens shrieked close by. Hayes waited with Blaine for a moment.

"Go," Blaine said.

Hayes was hesitant, but then he took off to join Cooper.

Brandon stepped out from behind a pillar and made a move toward Blaine.

Belinda gripped his shoulder, but he wasn't about to take another step toward the rear exit. The instant the two officers were out of the building, she said, "Please, baby. We've got to go."

"I can't leave him." Brandon ran across to Blaine and dropped the backpack next to him. He pulled the bullet proof vest out of the way and tore open the uniform shirt. "We've got to get some pressure on that wound."

Blaine looked up at him with a pained smile. "So . . . you were . . . in here . . . after all."

Brandon smiled at him compassionately. "Yeah, we were." He turned back to Belinda. "Baby, you've got to run. I'll catch up to you. Keep your head down and stay in the shadows."

"But . . ."

"Run!"

He glanced in the direction she'd taken as she fled, silently praying he'd be able to find her.

He reached into the backpack and took out his suit pants, folded them four times, and pulled out the leather belt. After placing the pants onto Blaine's wound, he fed the belt under his back, and pulled it around to thread the leather through the buckle.

Blaine gasped as Brandon tightened the belt over his injury. "Why . . . are you doing this . . . for me?"

"I'm ex-army. I won't leave one of my own countrymen to die in the mud if I can help it. Your buddies called for help, so just hang in there. What's your name?"

"J-Jack," Blaine replied.

They heard a siren close by.

"T-they're here," Blaine said. "P-please, go. Run, now. G-get away . . . while . . . you can."

Brandon smiled appreciatively, and felt an emotional need to comfort the fallen officer, beyond his own needs. "Thank you, Jack. But they're not coming to get *me*. They're coming to help *you*."

"T-thank you. I don't get you, but thank you."

"The belt I put around you will keep the pressure on the wound until the paramedics take care of it. Good luck, my friend." Brandon picked up the backpack.

Even through his shock and the agony in his stomach, Blaine couldn't help but marvel at Drake's sense of courage and honor. What kind of a man would risk his own life to save his enemy? In a heartbeat, he knew that, despite orders, turning Drake in would be the most immoral act he could commit. What was he to do? Follow the law? Or do what was right? There was no way a true villain would've done something like that.

He turned his head slightly and watched as the noble hero sprinted out of the building in the direction his woman had taken. He knew he was experiencing the most profound and extraordinary event of his life.

Within seconds, a convoy of squad cars and the paramedics arrived at the scene. The factory was filled and surrounded by police in riot gear. One unit took the back of the building to attend to the fallen gang members. The paramedics hurried over to Blaine and prepared a stretcher.

Tepper skirted around them and knelt down beside the injured officer. "Blaine, hang in there. What happened?"

"J-just one man . . . he shot me. C-Cooper and Hayes . . . went after him."

"Was it Drake?"

With his teeth chattering from shock, Blaine looked away. "No."

The paramedics eased him onto the stretcher and carefully removed the pants strapped to his midsection. They then proceeded to administer the appropriate emergency treatment.

Tepper stepped forward and harshly took the suit pants and belt from the paramedics while they erected the stretcher. Tepper followed them with more than a little concern. "Where did you get these?" he said, holding up the pants.

"They'd b-been d-dumped. U-used them . . . to bind up . . . the g-gunshot," Blaine said.

Tepper studied the blood-stained fabric with suspicion. "A pair of Armani pants and a brand new leather belt dumped inside *this* shithole?"

One of the paramedics interjected as they lifted Blaine into the ambulance, and shot Tepper an assertive stare. "Sir, this man is in critical condition. We'll take it from here, all right?"

Tepper realized he was acting out of line, but couldn't shake the feeling that something wasn't right. However, three fugitives were still on the loose, and one of his own had taken a bullet in his attempt to apprehend one of them.

He turned back to his men. "Gentlemen, we have three fugitives running loose in the city. Nobody goes home until they are apprehended."

After giving his instructions on combing the city, Tepper made his way around to the rear of the building.

His first view of the carnage was startling. Four men staggered as they regained their senses. One was barely conscious and being attended to by paramedics. Another was deceased, and six switchblades were scattered across the street. Tepper tried to process the scene, unable to comprehend what it would've taken to put down six armed men.

He walked over to the corpse and recognized him immediately.

A sergeant came up beside him. "You know who that is, sir?"

"Yeah," Tepper said sadly. "Wayne Meissner. He was busted on possession of heroin a couple of years back. He was from the Valley. Geeky kinda boy. He came from a good family, but got hooked up with the wrong crowd trying to fit in."

"I'll get him bagged."

Tepper nodded.

"Sir, these men said just one man did this to them. I don't buy it."

"It does seem a little out there, but he clearly had no intention of killing them." He looked across at the barely-conscious man on the ground. Two men were attending to him. One held his gun in a clear plastic bag. "And I don't think Meissner was shot with any gun other than that one."

He moved across to the three men and immediately identified the fallen criminal. "Richie Sanchez."

Sanchez looked up at Tepper wearily. "The g-guy attacked us . . . We . . . didn't do . . . nothing."

"Yeah, I'll bet. You tried to roll a guy who wandered into this shithole by mistake, only this time you picked the wrong man. A trained fighter. A soldier." Tepper chuckled at the irony. "If anything, Sanchez, I hope this has taught you clowns a valuable lesson." He caught the attention of the attending officers. "I want all these guys taken in for questioning. If they need to go to the hospital, we'll question them there. And I want forensics to run a ballistics check on that gun and Meissner's wound."

"Yes, sir."

A call came through on Tepper's radio, distracting him. "Hayes? Where are you?"

"We were pursuing one of the suspects and got as far as Main, but there's no sign of him. I have a bad feeling about this, Chief. The guy seems to have disappeared into thin air. Any luck your end?"

"No. Just stay where you are. I'm sending a squad car to pick you up. This is gonna be an all-nighter."

Tepper ended the call and looked across the activity-ridden street, overcome with confusion. He was hunting three suspects, but was no longer certain who the good guys were, and who was the enemy.

***

Brandon had been running through the back streets for ten minutes hoping Belinda had followed his instruction to stay in the shadows. There was no sign of her anywhere.

He came to a main road and chanced running along the length of it. Glancing down every side street as he passed them, there was still no sign of her.

Coming to the end of the road, a chill went through him as reality sank in. With the police and a trained assassin combing the streets for them, he'd lost Belinda.

Thirty-One

The Darkness

Belinda crouched low behind an old, black SUV parked in an open, annexed garage—one of many along the lane. None of the vehicles appeared to be prestigious. Nobody would dare park a vehicle of high value in such a place.

Stress and anxiety were exhausting her. It had only been five minutes since she'd left Brandon. She'd done as he'd asked and remained in the shadows.

The events of the night played over in her mind. Brandon had been an enigma from the start. She reminded herself of his characteristics—heroic, incredibly handsome, the ripped physique, and extraordinary fighting skills. He was sensitive, adventurous and mysterious. There was the high-tech equipment, and, of course, the cabin, and the $1.2 million.

Yet, for all of that, he'd been a virgin? And *a soldier*? On reflection, it was absurd. So, how could he be so sincere if it wasn't true? Nothing seemed to fit.

She listened intently, expecting to hear noises of cars or police sirens, but there was only silence. Even if she heard footsteps, she wouldn't dare stand up from behind the SUV to see if it was Brandon. What if it was the gunman? Or a cop?

She recalled her other, similar ordeal when she'd been stranded behind the tree in the Wyoming forest. The same torturous emotions went through her again. The desire to move on and get out of where she was overwhelmed her.

But she was restricted by the mercilessness of not knowing. Silence, she realized, was one of the world's cruelest offerings. Fleetingly, she experienced bouts of temptation to give herself up so that she'd know where she stood. If only it could finally be over. Hope was becoming more of a torment than a boon.

In an effort to conceal herself from potential threats, she'd trapped herself with no conceivable way out. Constantly mindful that Brandon wouldn't be able to find her, she remained where she was, alone in the darkness.

***

Payne came to the end of another street and darted into the alcove of an office doorway. A police car passed by slowly, and one of the officers aimed his flashlight into the street. Satisfied that nobody was there, they moved on.

Payne waited for the car to disappear into the distance, and then attempted to run across the highway, his injured leg slowing him down.

Brandon turned into the same street on the opposite side and froze. Facing one another, Payne could see Drake's eyes on his gun. "Drake!" he shouted, and aimed the pistol toward him.

The sound of sirens pierced the air. The police were virtually upon them. Brandon darted behind the wall, and Payne braced himself behind the other side of the office building. Both managed to remove themselves from sight at the moment two squad cars entered the street.

Payne noticed a cab coming toward him on the street below. Limping as fast as he could down a flight of stone steps, he managed to flag it down and climbed in. "The

Palm Dale Motel," he said, and dropped five, rolled, hundred dollar bills over the driver's shoulder. "I need to make a pick-up, and then go straight to Union Station."

The cabbie picked up the money from his lap, and a sudden enthusiasm came over him. "Jesus, man. I guess it's an emergency, right?"

"Look, do you want the five hundred, or do I give it to another cabbie?"

"I'll get you there as soon as I can, but we may have to take the side roads to get to the Palm Dale. I just got word the police are setting up road blocks on the main highways."

Payne closed his eyes and exhaled his fears. "Just do what you have to."

Brandon peered from behind the wall and watched as the cab disappeared along the highway. With the assassin out of the picture, he now had only the police to avoid.

He ran across the street again and spun around in an attempt to catch a sign of Belinda. He spotted a gas station with a public restroom approximately a quarter of a mile in the distance. His gaze lingered on his destination, but he had to find Belinda first.

After running back along the street, and then along another, he found himself back in Skid Row. Despite his unfamiliarity with Los Angeles, he was convinced he'd stumbled into a vicinity somewhere near Main and Alameda Street. That meant he couldn't be too far from Union Station. The presence of law-enforcement had most likely driven the punks into temporary hiding given how deserted the street appeared to be.

Belinda had heard Payne cry out Brandon's name in the distance. Trembling, she came out from behind the SUV, and cautiously crept along the sidewalk in the direction she thought she'd heard the bellow. Stepping out onto the street, she couldn't see anything. Fear took hold of her and she ran back to the safety of the SUV.

As she was about to step back inside the garage, she froze as a human figure appeared in silhouette at the top of the street. After a moment, she sank to her knees and gave in to her need to surrender. She simply couldn't bear it any longer. Ironically, she smiled. Finally, it was over.

And then came the most beautiful word she had ever heard.

"Baby?" Brandon hurried down the street and into the light.

Her heart leaped and she ran to him, throwing herself into his arms with an all-consuming need for comfort. "Oh, thank God. I thought I'd lost you."

"Oh, baby. I'm so sorry I left you," he said.

"You did what you had to do. I am so proud of you."

"Baby, we have to get out of here, and I know exactly where we're heading."

She looked up at him sharply. "Where?"

"About a quarter mile from here is a gas station with a restroom. If we can get to it, I can reapply our disguises, and then it'll be safer to try to get to Union Station."

"OK. Let's get going."

She clung to his arm, and Brandon kept his head bowed, his face concealed by the peak of his cap. With trepidation, she moved forward with him, away from the darkness.

They approached a more civilized area and quickened their pace in order to lose themselves among the pedestrians.

The silence that had befallen the tough part of town was quickly replaced by a chorus of voices, sounds of traffic, and the ambiance of bustling city night life. Belinda kept her bowed and eagerly strode toward the gas station.

As they stepped onto the asphalt, Brandon noticed a closed circuit TV security camera perched high on a pole. It was trained on the gas pumps, the store, and the restroom.

Before taking another step, he turned to Belinda. "We need to walk in line with that camera with our backs to it. Don't turn around. Whoever is looking at the monitor can't be aware that we looked different going in to what we'll look like when we come out."

"Got it."

Facing away from the camera, they walked hand in hand into the camera's range.

Brandon's immediate concern was that the restroom might be occupied, but upon turning the door handle, he saw it was clear. They quickly entered, closed the door behind them, and bolted the latch.

They held one another in a brief moment of respite. Brandon had no choice but to cut it short, and threw the backpack from his shoulders. "We can't reuse the old prosthetics. They'll be useless now. We have to start with fresh appliances. Let's get to work."

The facility was somewhat grimy. The toilet wasn't well-maintained, and neither was it particularly clean. However, the sink offered a bar of soap, and there was a paper towel dispenser fixed to the wall.

With frantic speed, Belinda washed the studio make-up off her face while Brandon sifted through the backpack for the prosthetics.

The instant she'd cleansed her face, he set about washing his own. He knew it was imperative that all foreign substances were removed from their skin in order for the prosthetics to adhere.

Once their faces were dry, he proceeded with the painstaking procedure of making them both look middle-aged again.

He considered how vital his ability to do this had been to his survival since his flight began. Having stolen a generous supply of skin-friendly, silicone prosthetics from Mach Industries, he'd customized the procedure from a skill he'd learned in the army. Disguise techniques were intended for soldiers to assimilate themselves as citizens of the enemy, either for infiltration, or escape purposes—not for evading the law on home soil. He smiled, rebelliously, at the irony.

The applications took almost an hour, during which time they suffered numerous starts with people trying the door handle. They were spared no tension and anxiety.

Finally, they appeared to be a middle-aged couple again, and Brandon's facial features were concealed by an extremely convincing, thin beard. He checked their appearance in the mirror, satisfied they would now have passed for their own parents.

He took out two false identity cards and handed Belinda hers. They'd taken photographs of one another in disguise to use in creating the fake IDs before leaving for L.A.—a precaution in case they were stopped.

She looked at her own ID card and frowned at the fake name he'd given her. "Jaime Branigan? Where did you get that name from?"

"I got the 'Jaime' from Jaime Sommers—The Bionic Woman. Thought you'd like it." He managed a slight smirk.

"And the 'Branigan'?"

"The late Laura Branigan. One of my favorite singers."

"I see."

She looked over his shoulder and noticed his fake name. "Kyle Summers? Sounds cool. Where did that name come from?"

"A magician I met once. He's the only guy who's ever fooled me. I figured since the point of disguise is fooling people, I'd use his name as a good luck charm."

After strapping the backpack across his shoulder, he unlocked the restroom door, casually peered through the gap, and all seemed to be clear. "OK, let's go for it. Just hold my hand, look as normal as you can, and smile like we've been in here . . . you know? *Doing* stuff."

She assumed a suggestive smile and stepped outside with him.

As they turned the corner to walk parallel to the store, a police car pulled up on the asphalt, causing their hearts to pound. At all costs, they couldn't afford to show fear.

"Just keep walking," Brandon whispered. "Feel it inside you that it isn't about us. If you believe it, they'll believe it."

Belinda focused on her own act, but shuddered as two cops stepped out of the squad car. The officers casually continued toward the store. They might have been looking for them. On the other hand, they could've been stopping for donuts.

They walked across to the sidewalk of the main highway and waited for a cab. One appeared within a few moments, and Brandon flagged it down. "This is it."

The cab stopped and they climbed inside.

"Union Station," Brandon said.

"You got it."

In the back seat, Belinda was barely aware of how tightly she was gripping Brandon's hand.

It was brief ride across to the northeast part of downtown Los Angeles, avoiding the roadblocks.

Brandon settled up with the cab driver, and they climbed out. "It's all right, baby," he said. "We made it."

She forced a smile and walked with him past the palm trees into the ticket court. Her mouth was persistently dry and her palms were damp. Despite her wig, cap, and the fact that she looked twenty years older than she really was, her sense of doom would not abate.

There were only two people in the line to the ticket window. The first took his ticket and made his way to the platform.

The second man's turn came. His breathing seemed labored as though he'd been running. Belinda wished he'd hurry and get his ticket. She sensed Brandon was getting angry having to wait.

The man purchased his ticket and turned toward them. In an instant, they were face to face with one another.

It was Payne.

Thirty-Two

Welcome Home

Brandon and Belinda held themselves perfectly still, trying not to attract Payne's notice.

Caught in a vacuum, Brandon knew he was in a position to apprehend him. But at what cost? The man facing him was a killer. He was one of the men responsible for the attack on Carringby Industries and the deaths of many. However, the killer didn't recognize them and appeared to be more concerned with catching his train. Unable to do anything, they watched as he ran from the ticket office and down the stairwell to the platform.

With another sigh of relief, they approached the ticket window.

"How're you doing, sir?" Brandon said, feigning an ultra-friendly persona. "We're trying to get to Aspen, Colorado."

The vendor said, "Quite a trek. From here, you need to go to San Francisco. From there, you'll take the California Zephyr to Glenwood Springs, and then a bus to Aspen. It'll take a couple of days."

"I know. When does it leave?"

"There's been a delay due to a technical problem. The next one leaves at seven a.m."

Brandon looked at his watch. It was almost midnight. "That's over seven hours."

"I know. I'm sorry, sir."

Knowing he had no choice, Brandon conceded. "OK. Is there anywhere around here where we can rest while we wait?"

"Sure. You can use the waiting room. You can also buy coffee and food in there."

"Thanks."

The vendor calculated the cost of their journey and Brandon handed him the cash.

The waiting area seemed to have a church-like quality, with tiled flooring, and rows of brown, leather-cushioned seats. Brandon and Belinda found two in the far corner and sank into them.

Belinda sat in stony silence.

Brandon draped his arm around her shoulder. "It's all over, baby. We've done everything we can. Once we get back to the cabin, that's where we'll stay. I'll drop the Turbo Swan off someplace where the army can find it, and then we'll stay put."

"It's not just that, Brandon," she said. "It's you."

He frowned, confused. "I don't know what you mean."

"What happened to you when those guys pulled knives on us?"

He looked away, trying to picture the moment. They'd arrived at the end of the street to find themselves facing a gang. The next thing he remembered was the disturbing vision of himself in Afghanistan. Then he was looking down at the leader of the gang with a gun in his hand. But what had happened in between? And why hadn't he thought about that until Belinda just prompted him? "What did happen?" he said.

"The same thing that happened in Wyoming. You moved like lightning. You knocked the knives out of their hands with one kick, and then you beat the crap out of every one of them. One guy pulled a gun on you, and you caught his arm. The gun went off and he shot his friend behind you. You laid waste to them all within seconds. I've never seen anything like it."

He shook his head as he tried to process what she was telling him. It sounded utterly absurd.

"You get this weird look in your eyes, like you're somebody else. And when it happens, that scar on your forehead becomes deeper. It's really creepy."

He touched the scar, almost without thinking. Belinda's words were profoundly disturbing. He truly had no answer for her, neither did he have any understanding of what it all meant. He was aware of 'something' that came over him in a heated moment. He'd managed to pull it back and stay focused when they were in the deserted factory. But what did it all mean? "I was in the army. We were trained in armed and unarmed combat, and—"

"No way, Brandon. This wasn't army combat training. This was expert martial arts and acrobatics. Do they teach you *that* in the army?"

He held her tightly, shaking his head. "I . . . don't know what to say. Honestly, baby. I don't."

She looked into his eyes, and then rested her head on his shoulders. "Just hold me."

There was a considerable police presence in the station throughout the night. Photographs of Brandon, Belinda, and Payne were handed out around the building. One officer actually asked Brandon if he had seen himself, his disguise was so convincing.

The hours rolled on, and Belinda eventually fell asleep in his arms. He remained awake all night, his thoughts in turmoil.

Brandon and Belinda stood on the platform the following morning. Despite their disguises, they both struggled to avoid appearing apprehensive. Even the station attendants caused them to feel anxious, as though their uniforms suggested 'authority.'

A middle-aged lady holding a Burberry purse stood beside them. She smiled politely and they reciprocated.

To their relief, they heard their train coming and turned to see it in the distance growing larger by the second.

"Here we go," Brandon said.

Belinda gripped his hand and instinctively walked toward the train, as though the few steps would get them to their destination faster.

Without warning, a scream came from behind them. They turned with a start to see two young thugs charging toward them. Brandon noticed one of them holding the Burberry purse. Then he saw the look of horror on the face of the lady who had smiled at them.

Belinda instinctively backed away when the muggers were almost on top of them.

Brandon spun around, his left arm shooting out with perfect timing to collide with their solar plexuses. The Burberry purse fell from the attacker's hand as he fell to the platform in a fetal position with his partner. They writhed in agony, and three station guards hurried over to them. The commuters scurried away from the scene with sounds of distress all around.

The train pulled up and the doors opened.

Brandon grasped Belinda's hand again and ushered her into the crowd of boarding commuters. "Come on. Keep your head down and get inside."

Once inside the train car, they watched the commotion and unrest outside through the window. The lady retrieved her purse and two police officers arrived to assist the station attendants with the two muggers.

"What happened?" the first officer said.

"T-these men took my purse," the lady stammered, "and then a man stopped them."

"What man? Can you point him out?"

She looked around. "I don't see him."

"What'd he look like?"

"I-I wasn't paying too much attention, but I think he was about mid-forties, brown hair, and he had a neatly-trimmed beard."

"What was he wearing?"

"I'm sorry. I don't remember."

The officer looked into the train through the carriage window, but he could only see a swarm of people inside scurrying to find places to sit. With only himself and one colleague to arrest the two thugs, he decided his priorities lay somewhere other than questioning a passing hero.

Brandon and Belinda took the last two seats facing the entrance.

After a few minutes, all was finally clear, and Brandon chanced glancing across at the platform. All of the travelers had boarded, but he could see the station attendants helping the police to escort the muggers away in handcuffs.

Another attendant appeared to be lending a sympathetic ear to the lady with the purse.

As the train started up, he sat back and tried to relax. Glancing at Belinda, he noticed her eyes were closed as though in relief.

It gradually came to him that he'd just taken down two men, and vaguely recalled the way in which he'd struck them. It had happened so quickly it was a haze to him. But it seemed to fit with what Belinda had told him about him seeming to display martial arts skills. He remembered her telling him in Wyoming that he'd beaten the man who'd accosted her with karate. He'd never practiced martial arts, and yet he'd just taken down two muggers without even thinking about it. It didn't make any sense.

He considered the particulars of what had happened. His self-imposed mission to expose Treadwell's conspiracy on national television had almost ended in disaster, and he always knew his credibility was challenged. For years, government conspiracy theories had been circulating in Western culture, never more so than since 9/11. Most people dismissed such ideas as the ravings of the disenfranchised and socially outcast, and they would have been correct—*then.*

But this time, it was for real. As he thought about it, he became certain such public doubt had played right into Treadwell's hands. It would've encouraged his confidence that any accusations the attacks had come from within would be dismissed as ridiculous. This was another obstacle Brandon's story had to overcome.

The train built up speed and the farther it took them away from Los Angeles, the easier they felt.

Exhausted from being awake all night, the mild hum of the train's engine and the rumble of the track gradually lulled him to sleep.

***

The two lovers braved their way uphill through the snow after their long train journey and a bus ride from Glenwood Springs. It had taken mere minutes for them to feed themselves into their pre-packed snow boots. It was then a three mile trek to the wooded lot.

Driven to despair by the itching of her disguise, Belinda hadn't been able to bear it any longer. Out of sight, she and Brandon finally managed to remove the prosthetics.

"Let me know when . . . we . . . get there . . . Brandon. 'Cause then . . . I'm gonna . . . throw . . . up," she said, gasping for air.

"It's not much farther. I don't know why, but I can't see the Swan."

Night was falling as the exhausting ascent up the snowy mountain continued. The moon provided them with illumination, but it was becoming darker by the moment.

They arrived at the trees, but the Turbo Swan was nowhere to be seen. Brandon pointed to the area where he'd left it and noticed the snow was extremely dense. "It looks like it's been almost submerged by a snowfall. Hang in there, babe. We're nearly there."

Out of breath, she didn't respond. *So, this is love,* is all that went through her mind.

They plowed through a forest of aspen trees and fourteen inches of snow until they reached the aircraft.

"Do you think it'll still fly?" Belinda said.

"It'll be fine. Get in." He opened up the doors and snow fell off them.

After climbing into their seats, they braced themselves for flight.

"OK, sweetheart. It's over," he said with a hopeful note of finality in his voice. "Let's go home."

She sank exhausted into the seat, and the Turbo Swan came to life. As it lifted off, a joyous smile spread across her face. There was nothing and nobody around who could possibly harm, or even find them. Her mind relaxed in anticipation of the wonderful, serene life they were returning to, once and for all.

They were finally free.

Brandon unlocked the cabin door and stepped inside, bewildered by a candle burning on the mantelpiece. He quickly detected a familiar scent. "Belinda? Do you smell smoke?"

She followed him in, and the unmistakable smell struck her. "Cigars?"

"Hello, Brandon."

The disembodied voice startled Belinda as was evidenced by her chilling scream.

Brandon turned toward the sound of the voice. It seemed to come from the far side of the living room. He could make out a shock of thick white hair above the top of his leather recliner by the moonlight.

And then the face leaned forward, emerging from the shadows.

Brandon's jaw dropped with horror and mystification. "N-no, it can't be."

Garrison Treadwell grinned cruelly, illuminated eerily by the candlelight and the cold, lunar reflection emanating through the rear window. With a glass of brandy in his hand, he took another draw upon his Cuban cigar before offering his sinister greeting: "Welcome home."

Thirty-Three

Shadows of the Night

"How did you find this place?"

Brandon's first question upon finding his enemy sitting in his safe haven spilled out of him uncontrollably. It was the place nobody else could have possibly known about. His grandfather had built it to bring his mistresses back to, and to hide his loot. His grandfather had told his father about it. His father had told Brandon about it on his deathbed. Even his mother didn't know about the cabin. Belinda was the first non-Drake to learn of its existence.

And yet there sat Treadwell.

The crooked politician placed his brandy glass on a small table beside him and drew a pistol from underneath his jacket. "I'm only using this gun to talk to you, Brandon. After all, I know what you can become when you lose your temper."

"How did you get in here?"

"In a helicopter. It's parked just over the ridge on the north plateau. I assumed you'd be coming up from the south so I wasn't about to leave a snow trail. I wanted to surprise you. I used the basement entrance to get in when I arrived this afternoon." His glance swept the room approvingly. "It's quite comfortable isn't it? I have a similar cabin in . . . another state. As you know, a home in a remote, isolated location with self-contained electricity is perfect when you need to lay low."

Brandon moved steadily toward him. "How do you know about the basement entrance?"

Treadwell trained the gun on him, halting him in his tracks. "Young man, I know far more about you than you know about yourself. In the beginning, I had no idea why you'd fled from Mach Industries, until you intervened at Carringby. I always knew where you were hiding out, but I had to be cautious. I'm just as protective about this cabin as you are. Secrecy from the world is its purpose. "

Belinda came up behind Brandon and held him tightly. He knew, with everything they'd been through, Treadwell was thoroughly unnerving her with his creepy manner.

Treadwell extinguished the cigar in an ashtray next to the brandy glass. "Ms. Reese, don't think he can protect you. He can't even protect himself. Surely my being here is proof of that."

His dignity compromised, Brandon's rage began to rise and his voice emerged as that of a guttural beast. "What do you want, Treadwell?"

"Ah, there you are. I suspected there would be a little of the *old you* remaining." The senator grinned, intentionally goading Brandon while hiding behind the protection of his loaded pistol. "You must understand, my boy. I created you. I trained you, tested you, put you through the most rigorous of ordeals, until I knew, beyond any shadow of a doubt, that I had my man."

"I barely even know you," Brandon said. "You put me into the weapons testing program after I got hit on the field. I met you once in the hospital, and again at Mach Industries. That was it."

"That's only what you remember."

"So, what? You're saying I'm brainwashed, is that it?"

"Brandon, almost everybody is brainwashed to some degree, even if they believe they're truly free. For example, parents allow their children to play video games full of gratuitous violence. But they become horrified if the child simply hears a profane term. Their sense of priority is completely reversed."

"Point taken. Now, what do you want?"

Treadwell reached across with his free hand, picked up his brandy again, and sipped it tauntingly. That complacency caused a chill to surge through Brandon. Belinda tightened her grip on his shoulder.

"I don't want anything anymore, Brandon," Treadwell said with an uncharacteristically sad tone. "My life is over. You won, my boy. You destroyed me."

"What did you expect? You used members of my own division to try to kill me."

"Merely a test. It was doubtful I was going to be able to reacquire you in Wyoming, so I used the incident to see if you would kill one of your own in order to survive. Even before that, I'd decided to use your cheap heroics as a means of testing your abilities."

"Testing my abilities?"

"Yes. I ordered a team of my most highly-trained operatives to kill you at Colton Ranch just to see if you could thwart them—and you did. Just not in the way I expected." The senator paused for a moment to allow his words to register before resuming. "In Wyoming, I saw that your former savagery had been dominated by your intellect. I gave you that blessing."

Brandon's brow crumpled under the weight of what he was hearing. "What are you talking about? What 'former savagery'?"

"You received a head injury when you rescued David Spicer in Afghanistan from a grenade."

Brandon touched the scar on his forehead. "It healed. So what?"

"The trauma to your head induced amnesia, and so . . . we gave you new memories."

Brandon was barely aware of Belinda coming around to face him, but he knew she was looking into his eyes. "New memories?" he murmured, trancelike.

Treadwell stood and made his way toward him, his left arm outstretched, and his right brandishing the pistol. "Kid, I did what I could to protect this country. You were a test case for a new breed of operative."

"What are you talking about?"

"You *were* in Afghanistan and you did save Spicer. Your head injury gave us an opportunity to rid you of your past."

Brandon felt the scar on his forehead throbbing. "W-what are you saying? What past?"

Carefully, Treadwell stepped closer. "You have an IQ of one hundred forty-four, Brandon. You're far brighter than most. You were also a martial arts champion, an extremely talented athlete, and a killer of the highest caliber. They used to call you The Scorpion. You would strike fearlessly and without hesitation, which is far more lethal than mere skill. Willingness overshadows training every time, and you, my boy, have both."

"But . . . ?" The fighting skills, the spin-kicks, and aerial acrobatics Belinda had told him about finally made sense. It also explained how he didn't understand it when she'd told him what he'd done. Now it was all clear. He was a trained martial artist, but—why didn't he remember?

Treadwell continued. "After the explosion in Afghanistan, we treated you with electro-chemical appliances and subliminal induction in order to give you a new memory. A new persona. I didn't want to lose you, you were so useful. But you were also very dangerous and uncontrollable. Nobody ever liked you, Brandon. In fact, you were hated. I gave you a kind and sensitive personality to make you more manageable.

"You were the ideal test case for memory revision. If the operation was successful and you believed your false history, I knew you'd be the perfect operative. A trained combatant, a brilliant engineer, and one who would be easy to control. I only failed on the last point, it seems."

"What kind of operative?" Brandon said. "And why put me in Mach Industries?"

"You were a different person. I had a medical report written up saying you were no longer fit for combat. I had to get you far away from anyone who knew you. I put you to work at a place where your non-combat skills could be utilized, and where I could keep a close eye on how your mind was responding to your new self."

"Putting me there was your big mistake."

"Indeed it was. Clever boy that you are, you discovered my other plans somehow, and then everything I'd worked for came apart."

Brandon swallowed hard as the cold grip of shock took hold of him. "Why, Treadwell? Why?"

"Our country needs to be great. Our economy is disastrous. I needed to create problems. I needed to make us look like we were under attack again. I would then arrange for a scapegoat nation, retaliate, and the war profits alone would have revived our economy."

"At the expense of how many innocent people?"

"Collateral damage," Treadwell said flippantly. "I have only myself to blame for your moral attitude toward all this. There was a time when you wouldn't have batted an eyelid. The national image alone would have been worth the death toll. We would have been victims yet again, and fighters to the end."

Brandon looked at Belinda's expression of abject fury. He couldn't imagine believing this if he was in her position. It would seem like a nightmare. Like the world had turned insane. He turned back to Treadwell. "What about my memory?"

"You were injured," Treadwell said casually. "You lost your memories. We gave you new ones. We even cleaned up your overly-stained military record."

Brandon lurched forward, his heart bursting with passionate rage. His right foot shot up with lightning speed, kicking the pistol out of Treadwell's hand. With both hands, he gripped the older man's throat. "I'm gonna fuckin' kill you, Treadwell!"

"Brandon, stop it. Stop it now!" Belinda pleaded.

Through the haze of rage, he saw the face of his nemesis assume a dark shade of purple, alerting him to what he could become if he continued. Immediately, he released him.

Treadwell sank to his knees gasping for air. After a few moments, he caught his breath and stood. "Oh my, there's still some of the old you in there, after all." He paused again, and then unleashed the ultimate torture upon Brandon. "You have no mother in New Mexico, no father who had a position in the army, and you never had an unscrupulous grandfather with a small fortune in a cabin in the snow."

You have no mother. The words resonated in Brandon's soul like shards of ice. But how could that be? He loved her so deeply and eagerly wanted Belinda to meet her. She was his only family. The hope of the three of them being together someday had been his anchor, his dream of a time when all the horrors of running and the conspiracy had come to end. He remembered his mother with such clarity—the color of her hair, her perfume, her smile, everything about her.

In numb devastation, he looked at Treadwell again. "Why?"

"Because I wanted the perfect soldier, Brandon. A covert operative who was a born killing machine, but who was brilliant, under my control, and unlikely to turn against me. I wanted *you,* and I was willing to do anything to make you mine."

"For what?"

"It doesn't matter anymore, other than to say, there is another out there who won't rest until he has what he wants from you. I've already set your final test in motion. A killer who's, arguably, even more merciless than you were."

Desperation came over Brandon. He found himself becoming almost drawn to Treadwell for comfort. "Please tell me this isn't true."

"It *is* true."

"I-it can't be. Who the hell am I?"

"Your name is Brandon Drake. That much is true. But nothing else is."

"So, what is?"

Treadwell laughed maniacally, as though he was on the verge of madness. "You thought you were the only one who knew about this cabin. You thought the money in the basement was a secret. Don't worry, it's still there. It'll be a moment before the two of you are the only people on earth who know about this place."

"You son of a bitch!" Brandon spat.

"I was alone when I narrated the details of this cabin to you during your memory-revision procedure. Not even the neuro-specialist I hired to perform your reconditioning has any knowledge of it. The only person who was sure to maintain its secrecy was the one who was programmed to do so." Treadwell picked up the pistol, sat back down in the recliner, and placed the gun to his temple. "You're a puppet, Drake. Sayonara, genius. You've got yourself one hell of a mystery to uncover."

"No!" Brandon shot forward in an attempt to seize the gun, but he was too late. Treadwell pulled the trigger and a spray of crimson painting the back wall.

Belinda screamed, her hands instinctively covering her eyes.

Brandon looked down at Treadwell's lifeless body. The shock took him completely. The senator's feet twitched and knocked against the recliner in his death throes.

The blood drained from Brandon's face as he tried to process the absurd. He didn't know who he was. He didn't know where he'd come from. He had memories of a mother he'd cherished, a father he had fought with, and a grandfather he barely remembered disliking as a boy.

None of them had ever existed.

He stood motionless with Belinda sobbing hysterically behind him. His greatest enemy, the man who could have answered all of his questions, lay dead before him. The answer to the mystery of his identity flickered in the candlelight, vanishing into the smoke, and into the shadows of the night.

Thirty-Four

Crushed

3:14 a.m.

Questions swirled around in Brandon's mind chaotically. The worst of all was his mother. She symbolized peace and family to him, and he loved her so deeply. He couldn't come to terms with feeling so strongly toward someone who didn't exist. *"Annabelle Drake isn't real"* echoed in his mind repeatedly. She'd been nothing more than a fictional suggestion that had been planted into his brain, but his memories of her were so real.

The rage he'd felt for his father was compelling. His grandfather had been so unpleasant that thoughts of the man continued to instill him with fear. But these men were complete fabrications also, leading to further questions— such as who was Brandon Drake? And where had he really come from?

It all affirmed his empathy with Belinda. They had both been victims of authority, and they had both been violated by it. They'd violated his mind as surely as the priest had violated her body. He could no longer see that authority existed for any reason other than to bully, control, and destroy.

The question why authority even existed pounded inside his head. Was it to maintain order? If so, how was he to define the nature of order now? Laws changed daily, and varied dramatically from nation to nation. There was no set, tried and tested method of assessing right and wrong. Yet, this clearly erroneous system continued to be imposed upon all. Regardless of its arguable necessity, who could possibly impose it? Men like Treadwell? Fallible, corrupt charlatans who had no superiority or immortality to validate their positions?

Such was how Brandon viewed the lifeless husk he'd pulled uphill for two miles in deep snow. He glanced down at the body bag containing the remains of Garrison Treadwell as he arrived at the north plateau. Clad in heavy, cold weather gear, exhaustion from his effort brought him to his knees. His interlude in L.A. had resulted in the loss of his acclimatization to the mountainous altitude. Given the low oxygen level, he realized he should've used the Turbo Swan, but he hadn't been thinking clearly. Shock had taken a powerful hold over him.

He saw the helicopter ahead of him and threw the straps from his shoulders.

It took a few minutes for him to deliver the heavy sack to the helicopter, pull the corpse from it, and strap it into the left pilot's seat. With his leather-gloved hands, he placed the pistol carefully into the fingers of his deceased foe.

A packed parachute on the pilot's seat caught his attention. His plan was to create the illusion that Treadwell had shot himself inside his own helicopter—anything to protect the cabin. He didn't know why a parachute would've been on the seat, although Treadwell and his intentions had proven to be far from usual.

He considered the possibility that Treadwell faking his own death in a helicopter crash and bailing out prior to impact might have been his original intention. Perhaps he'd realized in his final moments that there would have been no life to which he could escape. Only minutes before his death, he'd been protective of the location of his other cabin. What difference would it have made if he knew he was going to die all along?

Whatever Treadwell's twisted thoughts were, the parachute gave Brandon an idea. He reached over, grasped it, and gazed at it for several minutes. Still in shock, emotionally and physically exhausted, he shook his head in an attempt to clear his mind.

He carefully examined the parachute. It would've been in keeping with Treadwell's persona to have sabotaged it in order to set him up. After an initial peripheral examination of the gear, all looked to be in order and he put it on.

Having secured Treadwell's body in the left pilot's seat, he then strode through the snow to the other side of the helicopter. Finally, he climbed in.

Dazed, he started up the rotors, and waited until the blades came up to speed, creating a snow-storm in the darkness.

He looked upon the shattered, bloodied face of the corpse sitting next to him with vitriolic loathing. "You son of a bitch."

Once the rotors had achieved the required speed, he pulled the collective lever and the helicopter began to rise. The light at the nose of the aircraft illuminated the crystalline snow of the mountains as it ascended. Once he'd attained the required height, he set his plan into motion.

After ten minutes, he was approximately thirty nautical miles afrom the cabin. He glanced at Treadwell's body one last time, then looked ahead to see another mountain ahead of him.

He released the controls and threw the door open. The helicopter was already unsteady without his hand gripping the controls, and he was mindful of the tail rotor catching him when he bailed out. The powerful, chilling wind beat against his face reviving him from his weariness. It was almost impossible for him to open his eyes. He'd bailed out of helicopters before in the desert, but never in such extreme cold.

Gently allowing himself to slip from the edge of the cockpit, he fell out and arched his body into earth-fall position ready for deploying the parachute. Despite having checked it, the paranoia that Treadwell had set him up with a sabotaged 'chute gripped him again.

The wind chill beat against his face as he plummeted toward the ground. He deployed the main parachute and sensed the familiar feelings of deceleration and being stood up.

As soon as he was able to open his eyes, a sound similar to a thunder crack in the distance alerted him. He looked to his left and saw a faint orange glow grazing the bottom of the mountain. The helicopter had spiraled out of control and exploded on impact. Treadwell was incinerated.

He continued to glide down, not entirely sure where he would land, but hoped he was flying in the direction of Aspen. Of one thing he was certain—he faced a considerable trek through the snow after he landed.

He watched his ground track as he descended to the south. At least that was a step in the right direction, although he wished he would fly just a little farther. The snow below him took on an ethereal shade of blue in the moonlight.

Using all of his remaining wits, he braced himself for impact and flared the canopy for landing. His feet brushed the snow. He ran across it momentarily before his entire bodyweight sank down.

He waited for the parachute to float to the ground and collected it up in a tight bundle. Having removed the harness from his shoulders, he crudely stuffed the canopy back into the container. Ultimately, most of it hung out but it didn't drag on the snow once he'd fed his arms back into the pack.

He took out his compass and switched on the light, adjusted his position until he found north. He then plotted his course back to the cabin.

With minimal energy, he began his torturous hike, crunching his way through deep snow.

Relentlessly he continued, often uncertain as to whether he was dreaming. He was desperately tired and found himself slipping in and out of consciousness. As he came around each time, his heart palpitated with the realization he might have dropped the compass. Nevertheless, it was always grasped tightly in his glove.

Two hours passed. He began to worry he'd landed farther out than he'd originally thought. Finally, he noticed the smoke from the cabin's chimney in the distance and smiled weakly. The smoke meant he was nearly home and Belinda was still awake.

He looked to his left and noticed the impression in the snow where Treadwell had landed the helicopter. *Just another two miles.* Pushing himself forward, he prepared to descend the deep slope of the ridge. It was a harrowing ordeal with his body exhausted and his spirit crushed.

At just past seven in the morning, Belinda heard a knock on the cabin door. She hadn't been able to sleep all night.

She made her way to the door and opened it and saw Brandon standing before her. His eyes appeared sunken, his lips were blue, and his skin seemed a frozen shade of gray-white. "Brandon. What happened to you? I've been worried out of my mind."

He tried to reply but his lips were clearly frozen. "I-it's over. Treadwell's gone f-forever. N-need s-sleep. Walked eight miles in deep snow." He stepped into the cabin, the warmth from the log-fire embracing him. Shivering, he cast the parachute onto the floor.

"Oh, my God, you jumped out of the chopper," she said. "Let me help you."

Between the two of them, they managed to get him out of his boots and arctic vestments swiftly. He then staggered into the bedroom.

As soon as he was stripped down to his underwear, he collapsed onto the bed, and fell asleep.

Belinda knelt beside him and stroked his hair with deep concern.

After a few moments, she stood, pulled the duvet over him, and climbed in herself. Whatever had to be discussed would have to wait until the afternoon.

Thirty-Five

Road to a Collision

Gary Payne sat on the edge of the bed in a cheap motel room on the outskirts of Cedar City, Utah. Disheveled and on the run, he knew his only means of escape from America was in the hands of another fugitive.

He looked around the basic room. There was no television, a worn, lime-green carpet, and a bathroom in need of cleaning. However, it served his purpose for the moment. Before he could ascertain what his next move would be, he needed answers to vital questions. Who was Brandon Drake? Who were his contacts? Who were his friends? In order to find clues, he needed to delve into the man's history.

He reached into his suitcase, took out a laptop, and searched through the files. Finding nothing, he decided to initiate a secure internal search for Brandon Drake, using an SDT access code.

Quickly, a statistics file appeared on the screen. Strangely, however, key areas of Drake's life were blacked out, including the names of his birth parents and—his *foster* parents. All information pertaining to Brandon Drake prior to two years ago was deemed classified.

He screwed up his lips in annoyance and studied the only information the computer screen offered:

```
Sergeant   Brandon   Drake,   82nd   Airborne
Division.
Base: Fort Bragg, North Carolina, USA.
Commanding   Officer:   Colonel   Darren
Woodroffe.
Head   injury   incurred   during   rescue   of
colleague, Sergeant David Spicer.
Transferred   to   Mach   Industries,
Arlington, Virginia, 12/6/12.
Immediate   superior:   Senator   Garrison
Treadwell.
```

"You bastard, Treadwell," he growled. "He was your goddamn operative all along."

One particular line on the screen came to his attention. Drake had been injured during the rescue of one of his peers. His former commanding officer would be the last person on earth Drake would contact after going AWOL with a fortune in military tech. But someone whose life he'd saved was a strong possibility.

The more he contemplated the particulars, the more he became satisfied he'd found his man. "That's the one. Spicer."

***

Brandon awoke at seven o'clock in the evening. As his eyes opened he noticed through the drapes that it was dark outside. He hadn't seen daylight in twenty-six hours. For a moment, he hoped he'd simply dreamed the events of the previous night, but then quickly realized the magnitude of his reality.

He sat upright and saw Belinda sitting on the bed beside him.

"Hi," she said. "How are you feeling?"

"Groggy."

"You've been asleep for twelve hours. What happened last night?"

Brandon yawned and gathered his thoughts. "I took him to the helicopter. I wanted to make it look like he shot himself in it. I didn't want any trace of the son of a bitch near the cabin. I noticed a parachute and helmet in the chopper, so I took it up about thirty miles away from here, bailed out and let it crash in the mountains."

"Why'd you do that?"

"Because when, I mean *if*, anyone finds it, it's far enough away from here and the explosion will have hopefully obliterated any trace of him having been here. It'll look like he just crashed." He stood up out of bed and made his way toward the bedroom door.

"Where are you going?"

"Coffee."

"Brandon, let me get the coffee. You go watch some TV."

Almost zombie-like, he turned toward the living room and a desperate hope struck him. He was certain he had a photograph of his mother in his wallet.

Urgently, he returned to the bedroom, opened up the wardrobe, and took out his denim jacket. He reached into the inside pocket and seized the wallet. Frantically, he took the bills out, but there was nothing. He searched the credit card slots and the small, inside pockets but there was nothing else in them. He could've sworn he remembered putting a photograph of his mother in there.

Devastated, he made his way back into the living room. He sat on the couch and barely noticed the log fire was ablaze. Belinda had neatly folded up his clothing and parachute and placed them on the recliner.

He looked around the room. Wouldn't he have had family photographs mounted on the walls? He questioned why he'd never realized there were no such photographs in the cabin. How could he have missed something like that, especially since it was supposed to have belonged to his father and grandfather? Wouldn't there have been photos of his grandfather, or something relating to his life?

He looked at the back wall and his heart missed a beat. There was no blood on it. Could all that had transpired the night before have been a dream?

"I washed it off while you were asleep," Belinda said, as though knowing his thoughts. "I spent much of the afternoon on it. It was revolting and I couldn't stand the sight of it."

He turned and looked up at her. "I'm sorry. I was miles away."

"I can see that."

"Thank you for what you've done. It must have been horrible for you. I wish I'd have been conscious so I could've done it myself."

She smiled appreciatively. "The water has boiled. I'll get the coffee."

She returned to him minutes later holding two large mugs. Having spent his time in the cabin catering to just himself, he only had his own preferred, macho-sized mugs in the cupboard. Even that raised a question. Were they really *his* mugs? Or had Treadwell put them there, along with his memories of buying them?

236

Belinda handed him his coffee and sat beside him. She placed a comforting arm around his shoulders, unable to recall seeing such a tortured look in the eyes of another. He was such a contrast to the man she'd met only nineteen days earlier on the Carringby rooftop. *'Hold on!'* he'd said to her with such cool, cavalier confidence in the midst of such a hazardous situation. It had surely been his finest hour.

Her heart broke at the thought of what he must be suffering. Compassionately, she tried to imagine what she would have gone through if she'd been told that her mother wasn't real and her past never really happened. What if, perhaps, she'd never been to college, she hadn't really worked at Carringby Industries, and it had all been a series of fictional constructs? What if everything that made her who she was had been a fabrication, and she had no idea where she'd really come from? Could there be anything more terrifying?

And yet there she sat, holding the only man she had ever truly loved, who was suffering that horror. She had no words of comfort for him. She could tell him she loved him, but she knew he would only ask, "Love who?"

"I have to find out . . . ." he whispered.

"What, sweetheart?"

"I have to find out . . . who I am. There's only one man who can help me. Only one man who knows the truth, and I need to see him."

"Who's that, baby?"

He gazed at the sat-scrambler phone on the liquor cabinet.

"Who, Brandon?" she repeated. "Who's the only man who can help you?"

Finally, after an excruciating silence, he said, "David Spicer."

Thirty-Six

Bugged

Gary Payne gazed at the entrance door from the corner booth of Hooters restaurant, close to Fort Bragg army base in North Carolina. Several days' facial growth and a pair of window-glass spectacles enabled a makeshift disguise. Typically for five o'clock in the afternoon, the restaurant had only five customers.

Having kept a close watch on the news, Payne was confident his TV appearance had not been repeated after its one re-run. His name and the names of the two agents who'd been with him hadn't been released to the public either. From that, he knew there had been some interference from higher up the ladder. The question remained—what did they have planned for him?

For now, his most pressing concern was what he needed from Drake.

An attractive blonde approached his table and gestured to his empty beer glass. "Can I get you another, sir?"

He was about to reply when he noticed three men in civilian dress entering the restaurant. The last of them he recognized as David Spicer. "I'm fine, thanks." He made his way over to them, timing his arrival at the bar to coincide with the soldiers.

As the television played behind the bar, Payne noticed the casually-conversing troopers turning their heads to the screen. He followed the direction of their gazes and saw the face of Garrison Treadwell on the TV.

Spicer attracted the barmaid's attention. "Excuse me, Sally. Do you think you could turn the TV up, please?"

"Sure," she said, and took the remote control from underneath the bar.

The image switched from Treadwell to Tara Willoughby at the news desk: "It remains unknown why Senator Treadwell was in Colorado last night, or what caused his helicopter to crash. So far, authorities are saying it's an accidental death."

"Can't say that I'll mourn for the guy," Spicer said.

"What the hell is going on?" one of the other soldiers said. "We get called to either bring Drake in or take him out, and now we can't turn the TV on without seeing something Drake-related."

"It's a mystery all right," Spicer said. "I still don't get those broadcasts he made either. He seemed so different. Even his face looked different. Nicer."

"I'd have to see it to believe it," the other said.

"Captain Ward saw it too."

"And hundreds have seen Bigfoot, but I still don't buy it."

Payne decided to make his move. "Excuse me, gentlemen. Are you in the army?"

"Yes, sir," Spicer said. "Eighty-Second Airborne."

"Thought so. I heard this Drake guy was a queer, is that so?"

The soldiers were silent.

After a moment, Spicer retaliated. "What'd you say, man? I don't appreciate bigots, racists—or thugs." He moved toward Payne and lightly pushed him with an angry glare.

Payne continued to goad them with an intimidating stare. "Actually, I heard you all were. You all take it up the tailpipe, is that right?"

Spicer spat through his teeth, "Man, I think you'd best get the hell out of here while you still can."

The other two soldiers towered over Payne, making it clear they were ready to set upon him at any moment.

"Cock-sucking contests in the barracks?" Payne continued eyeing Spicer at all times. *Come on, go for it. Just go for it.*

Spicer's eyes glowed with rage, and Payne decided to force the issue. "Wouldn't you like to suck mine?"

Spicer lunged at Payne, his fist colliding with his intimidator's jaw. Payne's fake spectacles flew from his face as he fell against the bar.

The other two moved in, but David reached Payne first, grasped him by the lapels, and pinned him over the deck. "I don't know what you're playing at asshole, but you picked the wrong division to pull this shit on!"

Payne reached up as though he was attempting to persuade Spicer to release him, and placed his fingers on the soldier's right arm. Keeping his gaze fixed on Spicer's, he slid a small transmitter with a self-locking pin from between his fingers and attached it behind Spicer's lapel.

Within seconds, the manager of the bar hurried out of the back with the barmaid. "OK, boys, break it up. What seems to be the trouble?"

"No problem, Billy," Spicer said. "I think this clown just needs some air."

"Actually, I heard everything," the barmaid said. "That guy started provoking them for no reason."

The manager turned to Payne angrily. "These men have been regulars here for the past year. They fight for our country, and if you can't show them the respect they deserve, I want you to get the hell out of my restaurant. You're not welcome here, you understand?"

Spicer released his grip and stepped back.

Payne brushed himself off and walked away without saying a word. Looking back, he saw the four servicemen watching in bewilderment. He then stepped outside.

Spicer caught sight of Payne's spectacles on the floor and picked them up.

"Who the hell was that guy?" one of them said.

"I don't know," Spicer replied. "But something about him seemed familiar, especially when these glasses came off."

The other one laughed. "He's going to have trouble getting around in the dark without those."

Spicer put the spectacles on and immediately noticed there was no change in his vision. He took them off again, looking in the direction of the entrance. "I don't think so."

The evening continued in Hooters with the three troopers discussing the particulars of their lives. Spicer's two companions, Corporal Steven Wassell and Staff Sergeant Barry Stockton, had been with him in Wyoming on the day of the confrontation with Brandon Drake. Confusion remained as to why *they*, in particular, had been flown out that day, and why, under congressional orders, they'd been given a month's leave immediately following it. The validity of those thirty days leave came into question the moment Treadwell disappeared, coinciding with Drake's claims. With their lives in limbo, they found themselves frequenting Hooters.

"Let's face it. We stood up for Drake against that asshole earlier," Stockton said. "But none of us were sorry he got transferred after the explosion."

Defensively, Spicer said, "Drake saved my life. He fought for America, and he was lethal on the field, no matter how much of a pain in the ass he was. *That* is what we stood up for."

"Come on, Spicer. We all know why he saved your life. The guy hasn't got a noble bone in his body."

"Maybe, but he was one of us. Don't ever forget that. He was an incredible fighter, and would probably have made lieutenant by now if it wasn't for—"

"Being the worst human being any of us have ever known?" Stockton said.

David didn't answer, but finished his beer and stood to leave.

"Where are you going?"

"I think I've had enough. I'm taking an early one."

"Wimp," Stockton jibed.

"Sue me."

Spicer made his way out of the bar and stepped into the night air. He heard the faint jingle of his cell phone in his hip pocket, took it out, and frowned as the LCD displayed caller: unknown. "Yeah, hello?"

There was a momentary silence before he heard Brandon Drake's voice say, "Don't say my name."

Spicer's blood ran cold. "What do you want?"

"It's extremely important that I see you. I have nowhere else to turn."

"Forget it. I'd have to turn you in if I even had an inkling of where you were."

"Some things are more important than duty, David."

"Did you kill Treadwell?"

"No, but I was there when it happened. I can explain everything if you would just agree to meet with me. When are you on leave?"

"I'm on it now."

"If I was to come to you, say, Cherry Mountain Plain, in . . . three days from now. Friday?"

Spicer was stricken with an attack of conscience. The image of Drake sprinting across the sand, wrestling him to the ground, and grenade shrapnel catching Drake in the forehead, flashed before him. *But I know why you did it, you asshole.*

Regardless of his reasons, Drake had been seriously injured while saving his life. His motivation for saving him may have been questionable. But to David there were things in life that went beyond duty—and that was exactly what Drake had just suggested. In his heart, he knew he had to accept his former colleague's plea. "What time?"

"Ten hundred hours. You know the spot."

Spicer deduced the place Drake alluded to was the site of their first training exercise together—a barren stretch of wilderness situated near a canyon, a hundred-fifty miles from Fort Bragg. "Done."

In the cabin, Brandon sat back on the couch next to Belinda with a sense of relief. Although David's reaction came as a shock, he considered perhaps it was exactly what he should've expected. His memories of his friendship with David were now unlikely to be reliable. However, it was a weight off his mind that he'd been able to persuade him. He only hoped he'd correctly calculated the time required to purchase another inconspicuous vehicle and drive it fifteen hundred miles across America.

He looked at Belinda and smiled. "He went for it. We'd better get packing."

***

In a run-down motel, two miles from Hooters, Gary Payne listened through an earpiece, and wrote down every word Spicer had said: *Yeah, hello—What do you want?—Forget it. I'd have to turn you in if I even had an inkling of where you were—Did you kill Treadwell?—I'm on it now—What time?—-Done.*

From that, he was certain Spicer had been speaking to Drake. He silently rejoiced that contact had been made only a couple of hours after he'd pinned the transmitter to Spicer's jacket. The question remained, at what time of which day were they due to meet? And where?

Whenever it was going to be, it sounded imminent. As such, he knew he had to put David Spicer under twenty-four hour surveillance.

Thirty-Seven

Familiar Strangers

Under disguise again, Brandon purchased a gleaming, black, four-year-old Jeep Grand Cherokee SUV for $18,000 from a dealer in Aspen. His fake 'Kyle Summers' driver's license had convinced the salesman without question. It was his third such purchase in less than a month. With fuel and living expenses, he'd already spent almost fifty thousand of his $1.2 million. He knew this had to be the last time. He planned to meet with David Spicer, learn the truth about himself, and then return to the cabin to live out his life in peace with Belinda.

Switzerland, he now realized, was a hazard-ridden proposition. The cabin offered them an opportunity afforded to so few—a life of anonymity and freedom from oppression. He would never again consider letting it go.

His inability to invest his money, and the difficulty in either himself or Belinda finding a job while under constant disguise were pressing concerns. He knew he'd have to solve the problem of how they were going to survive, but now wasn't the time. His identity had to come first.

Belinda insisted she accompany him and he agreed. He was eager for her to meet David. At least he was someone from his past who *was* real, and this time, they weren't going out to stir up any trouble. His only concern was the possibility of David turning him in given that he had no reason to trust his memories of their friendship.

As a precaution against any potential dramas, he decided to equip himself with one of the attaché cases.

It was almost midnight when they arrived in Missouri. Needing sleep, they stopped at a motel, incurring another eighty dollar charge.

The following day they traveled across Missouri, through the southern regions of Kentucky and Virginia, and then finally into North Carolina.

It was almost midnight again when Brandon checked them into a motel thirty miles from Cherry Mountain Plain. On both nights, he'd awoken coated with perspiration, his fears, doubts, and tortured dreams, unrelenting.

***

9.56 a.m.

David Spicer stood beside his Buick Estate Wagon before a run-down shack in the middle of a deserted plot of land. He took in the barren, rocky location with nothing other than cliffs and hills all around. The winter wind cut through his shirt and jacket forcing him to wrap his arms around himself.

He watched the SUV come into view blowing dust across the terrain. As it came closer, he could make out Drake's face at the wheel, alongside his stunningly beautiful blonde companion.

The SUV finally came to a halt. Brandon looked into Spicer's eyes through the windshield. Slowly, he opened the door and cautiously stepped out. "David," he said warmly.

Spicer screwed up his lips. "Don't give me that shit, you son of a bitch. You really think I'm gonna buy this nice guy act? When did you ever call me *David*?"

As Belinda exited the SUV, Brandon gently reached out to Spicer with both hands in a beckoning manner. "You're my friend. I saved your life, remember?"

"The only reason you saved my life is because I owed you money, Drake."

Brandon's mouth fell open. "What are you talking about? What money?"

"The five hundred dollars I owed you from poker. I'm getting a little tired of this charade." Infuriated, David made a move to climb back into his Buick.

Brandon hurried after him. "Stop, please."

David outstretched his hand warily. "Stay back, Drake. I know what you're capable of. Now, just take it easy."

"This is crazy, David. All I wanna do is talk. I think I can explain everything." After a painfully difficult pause, Brandon said, "What do you know about me? I know that might sound strange, but please, humor me."

To David, the face of his former colleague seemed so wholesome and gentle. It wasn't the Brandon Drake who'd pulled him away from the incendiary. Surely, a con artist wouldn't have been able to perform an act that could actually soften the facial features—unless he truly believed what he was saying. "Who are you?" he muttered.

"It's me, Dave. It's Brandon."

"You never called me *Dave*."

"I do now. That's what a friend would call you."

Belinda came up behind Brandon, placed her fingers on his shoulders, and looked into David's eyes. "You see?

He's not the same anymore. Now, I don't know what he was. But I know who he is."

David raised his chin, looking downward with suspicion.

"Please," Brandon said. "I mean, come on, man. Treadwell can't have messed with my head that much. You know me."

"That's the problem. I do know you Drake, and you're a serious hazard to everyone around you."

"Tell me, please."

David studied Drake's look and began to feel it was far too genuine to be the work of an actor. "OK, gimme your version."

"I don't think you're gonna believe me, but I need you to tell me what I . . . used to be like."

"Why do you need me to tell you what you already know, Drake? You trying to get some kind of approval out of me? If so, forget it."

Brandon took a deep breath. "The point is I don't know anything. Before Treadwell died, he told me my memories had been changed. He said they messed with my personality after the explosion."

Spicer continued to stare at him with doubt. He didn't trust him, and clung to his distrust as a matter of self-preservation. "You killed him, didn't you?"

"No. He killed himself, right in front of us."

"It's true. I was there," Belinda said.

David looked from one to the other. Once he was satisfied he was dealing with something beyond his comprehension, he made a decision to open up a little. "What do you want to know?"

"What was I like? What kind of a person was I?"

"You were a total son of a bitch. You were The Scorpion."

Perspiration formed on Brandon's brow. "Treadwell referred to me with that term. W-would you please explain what it means?"

"You were cold, Drake. You were cruel, without compassion, and totally self-centered. You were a maniac. As a matter of fact, just before we were shipped out to Helmand, you were sent to the brig for beating the crap out of Colonel Woodroffe."

"So how the hell did I get shipped out with you then?"

It was clear to David that Drake was consumed with the need to find even a shred of doubt. "It was war, and I suppose we needed you on the team because of your technical expertise and skills on the field. You were due to go back to the brig when we returned, and then . . ." He decided he didn't need to rehash the chain of events surrounding the explosion. "You were sent up to Arlington later that year to work at Mach Industries, and that was the last we heard."

Brandon's lip quivered as he tried to maintain his composure. "D-do you know where I came from? Who were my parents?"

Spicer cringed. "You sure you wanna know?"

"Yes."

Belinda held Brandon even tighter and David noticed. What he was about to tell him was going to be traumatic information. "Your birth father was an alcoholic. Apparently, he got drunk and stabbed your mother to death before hanging himself. You were four years old at the time."

Brandon swallowed hard and Belinda looked away in horror.

"You were fostered by some family. I can't remember . . . *Cassidy*, I think you said they were called. When you got drunk one night, you told me you were beaten throughout your childhood by your foster father. You took karate when you were fourteen. You had a criminal record at sixteen for causing serious bodily harm and fencing stolen property. This continued until you were nineteen when you were given a choice."

"What choice?"

"The state pen, or the army. You'd only open up about anything when you were hammered. It was the only time any of us saw even a glimmer of humanity in you."

Tears streamed down Brandon's cheeks as he gazed into the ether. Everything David was telling him about his former self sounded familiar. He realized Treadwell had entombed his entire natural personality into another character—his phantom 'grandfather.' It explained why he sensed his grandfather when he saw the vision of his other self torturing the Afghan operative with the blow torch. It had been the essence of his true persona all along.

He'd needed to know the truth, but it was unbearable. Everything he was hearing confirmed his worst fears. At the same time, he empathized with David's position. How could he possibly convince him?

David moved slowly toward him, appearing almost sympathetic. "Look Drake, for whatever reason, I can see you're not the same guy anymore, so this is really difficult for me."

Brandon sobbed with relief. "I remember . . . being close to you, like a brother. I saved your life because I loved you."

David cringed. "Loved me? *Loved me?* You didn't have the capacity to love anyone, not even yourself." He reached into his pocket and took out his iPhone. "Come here if you want to see who you were, Drake. Come here and face your sins." He gestured to Belinda. "But this isn't something a lady should see."

David moved around to the back of the shack and Brandon followed. He watched as David searched through the files. After coming to the recording, he handed the palm-sized screen to him.

"I was with you in Helmand when Stockton filmed this, Drake. We were all afraid of you. We'd seen you wipe out gangs of thugs in bars, single-handedly."

Brandon brow crumpled. "Filmed what?"

"When I got your call, I thought I had to arm myself with something—a reminder of the truth after I'd seen this new you on the news. After all, when you see a monster acting like an angel on national TV, you've got to be careful."

Brandon looked at the screen on the iPhone. It took a moment for his eyes to adjust to the horror being displayed. It was him. But it wasn't *him*. He saw himself torturing the captured Afghan with a blow torch. There was no compassion in the Brandon Drake on screen. His face seemed distorted as he acted in a savage, animalistic frenzy. There was brutal heartlessness in the image. He heard his own voice roaring through the tinny sound of the iPhone speakers:

252

We can keep this up all night, you son of a bitch. Now where are they?

It was the vision that had flashed before his eyes during the fight with the gang in Los Angeles.

"That is what you were, Drake," David said firmly, "and I've got to say, I'm still not sure this good-guy-with-an-erased-memory gig isn't just another one of your dirty tricks."

Brandon sank to his knees barely hearing him, his soul filled with horror and shame.

The distress in Drake was undeniable. It was a look of pure anguish and David could see it. Despite flitting between belief and disbelief, he knew the old Drake wouldn't have been able to act out a performance of this caliber.

"W-what happened to this man?" Brandon whispered.

"He told us where the rest of his cell was holed up, and then you killed him. The next day we went in to take them out, and that's when you caught the shrapnel from the grenade." Spicer gestured to the phone in Brandon's hand. "I could never get over that animal look on your face."

Brandon's reaction seemed to indicate a concurrence. The terrible sight had reduced him to a sobbing wreck.

David's emotions had been batted around from anger and intolerance, fear of a psychopath who had once saved his life, confusion, pity, and sadness, all in the space of five minutes. It had finally taken its toll on him. *Command* was where he felt the most comfortable. "Come on, get up, Drake. I don't have time for this crap."

But Brandon didn't seem to hear him. "T-this can't be t-true."

The sound of a car pulling up on the other side of the shack interrupted the conversation. David became concerned the authorities had tracked Brandon. If it looked as though he was consorting with him, his liberty and position in the army could be at stake. "Drake, I'm duty-bound to turn you in. I could be court-marshaled for harboring you, you son of a bitch. Now get the hell up!"

But Brandon simply knelt, weeping.

"Drake, I can't deny you're like somebody else now. You look familiar, but you're a stranger to me, all right?"

And then Belinda screamed.

Brandon instantly revived from his despondency, stood, and ran around to the front of the shack.

David's concern shifted its focus also. For the briefest moment, he felt as though they were soldiers on the battlefield again.

As they came around the corner they saw Payne with Belinda in his grip, her hands cuffed behind her, and his pistol trained against her temple.

Payne grinned victoriously at Brandon. "It took me a while, but I've finally got you, asshole."

David recognized the assailant as the man he'd attacked in Hooters. The beard was gone but there was no doubt it was the same guy. He cautiously stepped forward and reached out, urgent to pacify him. "Just let her go. We can work this out."

"Stay out of this, soldier," Payne said. "This doesn't concern you. Drake's the one I want."

Thirty-Eight

White Knuckle Ride

Brandon looked into Belinda's terrified eyes, gripped by the most profound sense of protectiveness he'd ever known.

"You k-killed my colleagues," she said.

Payne turned the pistol on Brandon. "Where's the money?"

"What money?"

"My one million, two-hundred-thousand dollars in cash for services rendered that Treadwell left with you. Sound familiar?"

Brandon realized he was referring to the money in the cabin, which he'd believed had been placed there by his 'grandfather'. Most likely, it had been Payne's reward for the hoax terrorist attacks.

So many thoughts raced through his mind. It was yet another revelation amidst a combination of traumas. He'd just learned he'd been a brutal savage, a monster who'd only thought of himself—everything to which his current persona was opposed. And yet, that current persona had been given to him by a man who killed indiscriminately. Treadwell had no moral compass, and manipulated others, including the man who held his only loved one at gunpoint.

The irony struck him like a thunderbolt. His ultimate enemy had given him his soul, and that man's legacy now threatened to take the woman he loved.

He couldn't reveal the location of the money for fear of destroying their only safe haven. He could only start a war with Payne. "What are you talking about?"

Payne laughed and gestured at Belinda. "If you want the bitch, you'll stop playing games, asshole."

"I don't know what money you're talking about."

"Don't tell him anything, Brandon," Belinda shouted in a moment of titanic courage.

But Brandon's heart sank as she'd inadvertently revealed they both knew where the money was.

"On second thought, it seems I have my answer right here." Payne fired in the direction of the two men and pulled Belinda toward the Mustang.

Brandon and David instinctively jumped behind the shack and the bullet blew a gaping hole in the wooden door frame.

Payne continued to fire, keeping them at bay long enough to reach the Mustang while Belinda struggled.

"David, we have to stop him." Brandon ran from behind the shack toward Payne and Belinda.

Payne fired again, forcing Brandon to dive behind the SUV. Edging around the bumper, he saw Payne forcing Belinda into his car and was seized with a dilemma. He could make a run for it and try to reach the Mustang on foot. But if he failed to get to it before Payne drove away, he would have no way of finding her. He knew he couldn't take the chance.

Driven by panic, he opened up the SUV's back door, took the attaché case off the back seat, and threw it open. He took a semi-circular half-globe-like object from a sponge cut-out, and ran toward the Mustang as Payne fired it up. He hurled the device, watching intently to ensure it adhered magnetically to the Mustang, a few inches beneath the trunk.

The Mustang spun around with the door open. Brandon ran toward it again and came close enough to glimpse a cardboard box on the passenger's seat. For a fleeting second, he could see the box contained a few grenades. "Oh, my God." Frantically, he sprinted the last few yards to the car. However, the door closed and the Mustang sped away, momentarily blinding Brandon with dust.

Shielding his eyes, he turned and ran back to the SUV. "David, get in the car."

David climbed in as Brandon hurled himself into the driver's seat. Tires screeching, the SUV sped ahead onto the canyon road.

"Oh God, I've got to get her back," Brandon said. "When he turned that car in our direction, I saw a box of grenades by his side."

"Oh, shit."

"We've got to watch for whatever flies out of that goddamn window."

"You got it. But what's this money he was talking about?"

"I'm not sure anymore, but it's already about fifty grand short."

"There's something I have to tell you," David said.

"What's that?"

"On the night you called me, I had an altercation with that asshole in Hooters."

Brandon glanced at him for a moment, intrigued. "Are you serious?"

"Yeah. He must've been tracking me since then. I just can't figure out—"

257

"What?"

"Oh, my God. This jacket I'm wearing."

"Jacket?"

"I was wearing it in Hooters. I had him pinned over the bar." David ran his fingers along the insides of his lapels and immediately came to something stuck to one of them. Angrily, he tore it off. "Dammit!"

Brandon glanced at the small, electronic device in David's hand. "He bugged you?"

"Yeah. I led him to you without even knowing it." David tossed the device out of the window.

Brandon focused his attention and gunned the SUV along the narrow mountainside. To his right, there was barely enough space to accommodate another vehicle before the cliff edge and a one-hundred-fifty foot drop.

"Look out!" David shouted.

Brandon noticed a grenade flying out of the Mustang's window. It landed by the roadside and exploded a few feet ahead. Swerving to avoid the debris, he barely avoided slipping over the edge of the precipice. The road shuddered under the force of the explosion.

"I have to save her," Brandon said, his knuckles white as they gripped the steering wheel. There's no telling what that bastard's going to do to her." He couldn't contemplate grief as terrible as the thought of harm coming to Belinda.

He saw her looking at him with tears in her eyes through the back window of the Mustang. Keeping his gaze fixed on hers, he sensed his rage overcoming him.

The road became narrower. Any oncoming traffic would have to wait in the wider area and allow others to pass before going any farther. However, all was clear.

The SUV's wheels clipped the edge of the road again, startling Brandon out of his emotional distraction. He twisted the wheel desperately in order to avoid flying over the edge.

"Drake, take it easy, man," David said. "If we slip over that edge they're going to be cleanin' us up with a blotter."

Prompted to action, Brandon reached across, opened up the glove compartment, and felt around inside. He quickly found a small, palm-sized cell-phone-type gadget, and dropped it into his inside jacket pocket. He then grasped a metallic pistol-like device with a small targeting sight atop a bulbous end and handed it to David. "Take this. We may have no choice."

Spicer took the object with a look of recognition. "You've gotta be kidding me."

Another grenade flew out of the Mustang's window and rolled under the SUV. Seconds later, they heard the explosion behind them.

David exhaled with relief at how narrowly the grenade had missed them. "Shit. How many of those babies does that son of a bitch have?"

Belinda watched as Payne reached into the case for another grenade. "Don't do this," she pleaded.

"So long as I've got you, he's just another pain in the ass." He checked the rear view mirror and coldly pulled the pin out of the grenade with his teeth. He waited for three seconds until he was about to turn a corner. "This time," he said, and hurled it out.

Belinda looked back again, feeling as though her soul had been torn away. Horrified, she watched as the grenade detonated under the SUV, the explosion annihilating it.

Metal and upholstery sprayed across the road and over the edge of the cliff. "No!" she cried.

Thirty-Nine

Manhunt

Brian Malone had been driving his new Mercedes-Benz for three hours. He pulled over in the wilderness just north of Asheville, North Carolina. His wife, Angela, sat beside him. Their eighteen-year-old son, Joe, sat in the back seat.

"I need to take a leak," Brian said, and stepped out of the car.

Angela rolled her eyes impatiently. "Couldn't you have gone before we left?"

"That was three hours ago."

Joe climbed out and joined his father.

"Do you think we'll get there this year?" Angela said. She received no reply.

Brian and Joe wandered into the wooded lot until they found a couple of trees to relieve themselves against.

"I don't know how you put up with all that earache, Dad," Joe said as he unzipped his fly.

"The joys of marriage, son."

They heard the faint sound of a female screaming in the distance.

Joe's head snapped up. "You hear that?"

Brian nodded and pointed to his left. "I think it came from over there." He shook himself off and walked in the direction of the cry.

Joe followed as another scream came wailing through the trees.

"You killed him, you bastard!"

Brian and Joe ran through the woods until they saw an abandoned gas station on the other side of the trees. Outside, some guy was manhandling a woman. Her hands looked as though they were cuffed behind her back, but she kicked frantically as he pulled her out of a Mustang.

"You're going to be joining him, if you don't shut the fuck up, bitch."

Brian studied the victim, the assailant, and memorized as much as he could before they disappeared into the gas station. Finally, he turned back to Joe. "Whatever you just saw, remember as many details as you can. We just witnessed a kidnapping."

They turned and ran back through the woods.

As they reached the Mercedes, Angela's scornful face was clearly visible through the open window. "What on earth took you so long?" she said.

After what he'd just seen, Brian's intolerance surfaced. With his index finger in her face, he said, "Shut up, and pass me my cell phone."

She appeared to be stunned by his aggression.

"Now!" Brian said, and held his hand out.

Angela reached into the glove compartment and handed the phone to him.

Hurriedly, he punched in 9-1-1.

***

Director Elias Wolfe studied the files on his desk with obsessive focus. His life had become consumed with getting to the bottom of the Treadwell mystery. The moment he first realized the Delta Unit's contact number on

McKay's cell phone contained a high-level security SDT prefix code, his blood had turned to ice.

Almost immediately afterwards, Drake turned the camera on Payne and his two accomplices, Ogilsby and Woodford, for the entire nation to see.

Now, Treadwell was dead, Payne was missing, and the more Wolfe delved into Treadwell's affairs, the more he realized how far the man's operation extended. He'd uncovered mentions of Everidge, Carringby, and Colton Ranch, but he couldn't ascertain if there were cells of the Central Intelligence Agency involved, or if was restricted to SDT. Treadwell's personnel would have bypassed their annual polygraph tests. With nothing known of Treadwell's operation, the test questions wouldn't have been relevant. There was also the likelihood they would have learned polygraph bypassing techniques from outside the intelligence community.

Wolfe had discovered connections between Treadwell, a corrupt arms dealer, and several independent mercenary groups. The senator had negotiated billions of dollars' worth of arms deals over a ten year period. Hundreds of millions had been siphoned away to a bank account in Switzerland, enabling him to finance his entire murderous operation. It had all occurred right under the radar of the US government and two presidents, without even a hint of exposure.

Particularly intriguing to Wolfe was the discovery of several payments made by Treadwell to a neurobiologist based in New Hampshire, and the repetition of Brandon Drake's name on all associated files.

He was startled out of his deep thoughts by a knock on the door. "Come in."

Deborah Beaumont, Wolfe's assistant, stepped into the office. An officious-looking brunette in her late thirties, Wolfe had always appreciated her deep commitment to professionalism. "Agents McKay and Wilmot to see you, sir."

"Send them in." Wolfe turned to the two operatives with a humorless expression. Deborah closed the door behind her. "Are Ogilsby and Woodford *singing*?"

"Not yet, but we think Woodford is getting closer to loosening up," McKay said. "Ogilsby has a will of iron."

Wolfe rubbed his chin in contemplation. "I'm going to propose a deal to them. The death penalty, or parole after thirty if they surrender information leading to the capture of Gary Payne."

"Yes, sir."

"And make sure this is kept away from the TV and radio stations. I don't trust that Hobson, in particular. That little weasel would start a goddamn civil war just to pay for his next vacation."

"No details have been leaked. We've made sure of that, sir," Wilmot said. "They're not even certain Payne, Ogilsby, and Woodford were with the agency."

"Good. Now you two get back out to the jail and find out what you can about Payne. You absolutely have got to track that animal down."

"Yes, sir."

Wolfe waited for them to leave and rubbed his eyes with his thumb and forefinger. "Heaven help us all."

***

McKay and Wilmot followed two stern-eyed corrections officers along a bleak, dimly lit corridor in a remote section of DC Central Detention Facility.

Wilmot and McKay knew they were fortunate not to have spent time in the jail themselves for their part in assisting Treadwell. Ultimately, their claim of being ignorant of any knowledge of what the senator had been doing had been accepted.

They finally reached a door at the end of the corridor. The guard to Wilmot's right took a key card from his belt, inserted it into the reader, and opened the door. The two agents stepped inside the gray, sterile-looking interview room. McKay closed the door behind them.

Ogilsby and Woodford sat handcuffed, wearing customary orange prison uniforms at a long desk in the middle of the room. After being transported from the Los Angeles Police Department, they'd been confined to solitary. This was their first hour out of the hole.

McKay had studied the information that had, so far, been prized out of the two killers. They'd been cautiously recruited by Treadwell six years previously. Both were ambitious, and it hadn't taken Treadwell many months to determine that power and money were their primary interests in life. Ogilsby and Woodford were highly-trained, experienced killers, completing the perfect criteria for the senator's agenda.

McKay sat at the table opposite the prisoners and wasted no time getting down to business. He eyeballed Timothy Ogilsby on the left. "We have a proposition for you."

"And what would that be?" Ogilsby's cruel eyes and towering frame seemed threatening even through the cuffs and the jumpsuit. His short-cropped, army-style haircut further enhanced his rugged square jaw.

"Look Ogilsby, don't be a wise guy. We're here to offer you a break. Or do you enjoy the décor in here?"

"What break?"

"Right now, you're both looking at the lethal injection," McKay said. "If you cooperate, Wolfe will pull a few strings to reduce it to life with the possibility of parole in thirty."

"Thirty years?" Ogilsby barked. "I'll be sixty-fucking-nine, you son of a bitch."

"And the innocent people you gunned down will still be *fucking* dead."

"You can't prove who killed who, ass-wipe, so don't give me any of that. I wanna see a lawyer."

"You know that's not going to happen," Wilmot said. "You were involved in attacks against government installations, treason, mass murder, and conspiracy. You're a national security risk with access to inside secrets. That's why you're being detained here, away from the rest of the prison population."

"I've still got my goddamn rights, *Andy.*"

McKay shook his head smiling. "The Patriot Act *and* the National Defense Authorization Act. They can keep you here on suspicion of picking your nose if they want to, and for however long. You know that."

Woodford looked at Wilmot and finally spoke. "What do they want from us?"

Ogilsby rolled his eyes as though he perceived his co-conspirator's compliance as weakness. He turned back to Wilmot and McKay, cutting off their response. "Don't give us any of your self-righteous crap. You were involved too."

"I was in the dark, and I certainly wasn't a party to the killings," McKay said.

Wilmot interjected. "They don't want the two of you anywhere near as much as they want Payne. Now, we need to know. Where is he likely to be?"

There was an uneasy pause as Ogilsby and Woodford looked at one another in a short moment of silent conference.

"Information leading to capture will save your lives," Wilmot prompted them.

"I have no idea where Payne is, believe me," Woodford said, almost pleadingly.

"Well, can either of you give us any indication of his characteristics? You worked much closer with the guy than we ever did. Anything to help us build up a profile. You know the drill. The smallest details can lead to a capture."

After a moment of silence, Ogilsby said, "Drake."

McKay looked at him, puzzled. "Drake? What did Payne have to do with Drake?"

"No, no, you're not getting me. He hasn't got anything to do with him. He just needed to catch him."

"Why?"

"For some reason, Treadwell left money he owed to Payne with Drake. He needed to get to Drake in order to find out where it was, and then he was going to get out of the country. He was going to pay Woodford and me a hundred grand each for helping him."

McKay glanced at Wilmot. If Payne wanted Drake, they knew they were talking to the wrong men.

"So, did Belinda Reese have anything to do with the attacks, or not?" McKay said.

"No, of course not."

"OK, let's look into Drake," Wilmot said. "If we can locate him, we might, just *might*, nail Payne."

Woodford began to perspire. "What about us?"

"What about you?"

"C-can you get us a deal?"

Wilmot shrugged and stood to leave. "It isn't up to us."

Ogilsby stood sharply. "Hey, hey, now wait a minute. I just gave you two bastards a lead. Now you do your part."

Wilmot reached into his inside pocket, took out a pen and a folded piece of paper, and placed them on the desk. "The names of each and every operative involved in Treadwell's plot, and we'll see if we can get you the thirty-'til-parole."

McKay knocked on the door for the guards to release them.

Moments later they were gone, leaving Ogilsby and Woodford to their fears.

An hour later, McKay and Wilmot stood in Wolfe's office, conveyed what Woodford and Ogilsby had told them, and awaited directions.

Wolfe stood facing the back wall with his hands clasped behind his back. "I'll have the all-points bulletin on Belinda Reese lifted immediately. As a matter of fact, I should have done that some time ago. Any fool would've seen she had nothing to do with it."

Wilmot stepped forward. "Sir, the Dodge Sprinter Drake abandoned on the highway in Wyoming was traced to a dealer in Aspen, Colorado. Maybe that's a lead on where he could be located."

"Thoroughly investigated," Wolfe said. "The description of the man who bought it was twice Drake's age. Of course, that could have been Drake in disguise, but the kid's an itinerant. The location of anything he bought wouldn't tell us a damn thing about where he's really holed up."

There was a knock on the door. "Come in," Wolfe said.

Deborah Beaumont entered.

"Yes, Deborah."

"Sir, we've just had word that the police in Asheville, North Carolina, received a report of a man answering Agent Payne's description assaulting a woman matching Belinda Reese's. It's believed he's kidnapped her."

Wolfe's demeanor assumed a note of urgency. "All right. I'm going to call for back up on this one."

"Sir, we could get an investigation team out to Ashville right away," Wilmot said.

"No. Until we get to the bottom of this, I want SDT kept out of it. We don't have any way of knowing who's with Payne and who isn't. This is going to require outside intervention and personnel with powers of arrest."

"Who?"

"Who do you think?" Wolfe circled around his desk and picked up his phone. "The federal task force."

Forty

Excruciating Payne

Belinda's eyes darted around the interior of the disused gas station. Her breathing came in rapid gasps, almost causing her to black out. Payne was most likely preparing something unthinkable in the back room.

Having only one pair of handcuffs, he'd bound her to the dusty wooden work bench with ropes. She pulled with all her might against them, which caused a constricting pain in her wrists. She thought if she could loosen even one of her hands she might have been able to pull it free and then untie the other. Once her hands were released, she could then untie the ropes binding her ankles to the dusty wooden work bench.

But it was no use. She quickly realized she had no chance of escaping.

She heard his every move coming from the room behind her. Every shuffle echoed like a prophecy of doom.

Her tears continued to fall with persistence. Thoughts of Brandon filled her mind, and how much she'd grown to love him in such a short space of time. Now he was gone. He'd been so extraordinary; a soldier of the most moral kind, and one who had saved her life repeatedly. She felt certain there was no other man for her after him. All that remained of him were her memories, and even they were now threatened.

Payne was going to kill her. Of that she had no doubt. But she also knew he was going to torture her first.

Through her unbearable sadness, she was going to be subjected to intolerable pain. Even if she relented, she was going to die anyway. Payne wanted the money, and nothing was going to stop him from doing whatever he could to force her to reveal its location.

She heard footsteps coming closer from the back room and shivered.

"This is going to be extremely unpleasant," Payne said in a calm and professional manner. "However, you must appreciate that you leave me with little choice."

Weeping, Belinda tried to speak, but her words were barely more than a whimper. "W-what are you going to do to me?"

"Excuse me?"

She didn't repeat it.

He came round to the front of her and knelt down, his demeanor assuming an almost-sympathetic front. "Now, please. Let me help you. If you tell me where the money is, I swear I won't hurt you. I'll let you go, and that'll be the end of it."

Consumed with terror, she was sorely tempted to tell him what he wanted to know. What would it have mattered if she told him the location of the money? Brandon had no need of the cabin any longer.

But it was about so much more than that. The cabin was where she had been the happiest she'd ever been. It was a paradise. She remembered the night she'd made love to Brandon for the first time. They both believed he was losing his virginity in front of the log fire, with the snow falling outside the window. There had been nothing but frozen wilderness all around them. She now knew he probably hadn't been a virgin, but neither of them knew that at the time. The absence of that knowledge enhanced the moment for them in a way that could never be duplicated. They were not only in ecstasy together, but they were safe. Nobody could have found them. They were untouchable.

On the night they returned from Los Angeles to find Treadwell sitting in the living room, the dream was shattered. But within minutes, hope was restored as they watched the monster destroy himself. The cabin was still there, safe from predators.

She resigned herself to the belief she was going to die, regardless of what she revealed or didn't reveal. But perhaps, *just perhaps*, she would be reunited with her one and only love on the other side. Maybe they could return to their utopia and live there together for eternity. Just on the chance it might happen, she was not going to permit Payne to take it away from them.

She closed her eyes and tried to forget her fear. She focused on thoughts of being with Brandon in the cabin. It wasn't a case of whether or not she believed it. She *had* to believe it. It was all she had to cling to.

It was all or nothing as far as Payne was concerned, and the more she refused to talk, the more desperate he became. He was a wanted man facing either life in a federal prison, or the death penalty. His only means of escaping was to find the money and disappear, perhaps to Panama. "Talk to me, and this will all come to an end," he said.

Belinda didn't respond. Her eyes remained closed with the subtle hint of a euphoric smile edging from the corners of her mouth.

Payne raised his right hand to her face and waved three slender, sharpened wooden sticks, a little larger than toothpicks. "Do you know what these are?"

She didn't answer, react, or even open her eyes.

"These are crude, but effective in inflicting extreme pain, Belinda," he said with continual, chilling calmness. It wasn't the first time he'd interrogated another human being in this way.

He grasped her right hand. "I am going to ask you once more. Where is the money?"

Belinda remained static. Payne considered the possibility that she'd slipped into catatonia, but he wasn't about to allow that to impede his task.

He dipped his hand into the side pocket on his denim jacket and took out an electric stun baton. As he squeezed the two sides together, an arc appeared. "OK." He touched the arc to her chest where the skin was exposed between the buttons of her blouse. The shock tore through her and her eyes opened involuntarily. He knew the pain was horrific, but no sound emerged from her. Her entire body froze and her arms and legs were useless. He grasped her shoulders in order to keep her body steady on the bench. "Now, I hope that got your attention."

She lost consciousness. Five minutes passed before Payne noticed she was beginning to stir. "Ah, I see you're with me again. Now, let's try it again. Where's the money?"

Once again, she refused to answer.

"My, my, you are tenacious, aren't you?" He showed one of the sharpened sticks to her again. "The correct method of using these is somewhat of an art. It's always been a specialty of mine. I must say, I find the procedure most enjoyable."

He took Belinda's right hand and grasped her index finger. Carefully, he placed a wooden spike underneath her fingernail. "One last time. Where's the money?"

She didn't answer.

He gently pressed against the spike, easing it under the nail knowing knew that almost immediately, the pain would send signals screaming through her nerve endings.

She cried out a bellow of harrowing agony. Gradually, he forced it farther into her until her cries became a squeal of unbearable anguish. Perspiration fell from her brow, and blood dripped from her fingertip onto the dust-laden ground.

"Where's the money?" Repeatedly, he forced the spike into her.

She'd never known such excruciating pain, but she continued to keep the vision of being with Brandon in the cabin at the forefront of her mind. *The pain will lead to the cabin. This bastard will not take our afterlife from us.* She was now more certain than ever that her life was over.

The image of Brandon holding her in his powerful, gentle arms as they soared away from the Carringby building on that first night, flashed before her eyes. In her mind, she was no longer afraid as she glided five hundred feet above ground with him. It appeared as a fairy tale to her. He was Peter Pan and he was flying her away to Neverland. He was Superman and she was Lois Lane, flying through the clouds to the snow-covered mountains.

And then there was Snooky the bear, the beautiful little furry creature that was so entrancingly linked to Brandon and the cabin. He was waiting for them, standing on hind legs, beckoning her, welcoming her home.

She tried to latch onto what Brandon had said to her as they stepped off the edge of the roof, but the pain of the spike impeded her train of thought.

Hold on! It came back to her. *Yes. That's what I must do. Hold on! Hold on!*

Payne grasped her forefinger and inserted the second spike under the nail. She screamed for only a moment before her endurance gave out. As her consciousness slipped away again, her lips mouthed the words, "Hold on."

Payne stood in frustration and released her hand. He searched his mind for other extraction techniques, realizing she had a will of titanium. He'd interrogated soldiers—*warriors*—who weren't as resilient as she was.

Without care or grace, he tore the spikes from underneath her nails. The shock of the terrible, stinging pain revived her momentarily, but she was notably senseless.

He walked out the back and found the bathroom. There was a faucet and sink still attached the back wall, but he knew the water would be turned off. Soiled rags and rotted towels were strewn across the filthy floor.

Scanning the area, he noticed a large bucket of liquid in the corner. He strode over to it, knelt down, and smelled what was in it. It wasn't gasoline, but from the stench, he deduced it was merely stagnant water. He glanced at the ceiling and noticed where the water had come from. There was a hole in the roof directly above the bucket, where rain had fallen through. "Perfect."

With the bucket in his hand, he collected a handful of the aged rags from the floor, and made his way back to Belinda.

Forty-One

The Window

Belinda watched in terror as Payne returned to her. He placed the bucket and rags on the floor, and looked around the gas station.

His gaze seemed to latch onto a heavy wooden table at the far side of the room. It appeared covered with dust, and severely scratched and battered. She thought it had probably found its way into the gas station when the place was being cleared out, probably in the 70s.

She followed his movements as he pulled the table into the center of the room. She had no idea what he was doing, or what it meant for her.

Closing her eyes again, she tried to lose herself in the dream of the cabin. The unbearable, tender pain in her fingertips continued to gnaw at her ability to concentrate.

She heard Payne walking toward her, but tried not to allow him to distract her from her beautiful vision: Brandon. The cabin. Snooky the bear . . .

The footsteps stopped. She listened to him picking up the bucket and rags and walking away again. But she soon heard him coming back.

Then his hands were upon her. She winced as he unbound her wrists with the cuff of his jacket sleeve brushing against her bleeding fingertips.

He untied her ankles and then grasped her under her armpits. Her body was severely weakened by the stun baton and the incredible agony in her fingers. He shook her by the shoulders. Her eyes opened for a moment, but closed just as quickly.

With the loose ropes in his hand, he picked her up, cradling her in his arms. Brandon had held her in the same way, and the thought of this beast carrying her as he had sickened her. Consequently, she was unable to hold back another burst of despondent tears.

Payne laid her on the table. Her back and head rested on the surface, and her legs fell over the bottom end at her waist. He pulled her arms down to the sides and bound her wrists to the table legs. As the blood rushed into her hands the sting in her fingertips sent shock waves coursing through her.

Finally, he bound her ankles to the table legs. He then took one of the dirty rags from the floor and folded it repeatedly.

Keeping her eyes closed, she knew Payne was leaning over her. She forced herself to believe she wasn't there. She was still in the cabin with Brandon.

"Once more," he said. "Where's the money?"

She didn't answer.

"All right, have it your way." He bound the folded rag-towel around her head, across her mouth, nose, and eyes.

She was seized with the distinct sensation of being smothered. The stench of stale motor oil soared into her nostrils, and her heart pounded with exhausting persistence. *Is he trying to suffocate me?*

A flood of liquid cascaded onto the rag, soaking her face and filling her mouth with the most rancid taste. She couldn't understand it. The solid table was beneath her. But she was underneath an ocean of . . . what was it? Sewage? She couldn't decide. Whatever it was, she was drowning in it. As much as she wanted to see Brandon on the other side, her lungs begged for air. She wanted to take a breath so badly, but couldn't. The involuntary panic began, causing her body to convulse. Then the liquid stopped falling.

Payne grasped the rag, tore it away from her, and she lurched upward, choking.

"Waterboarding is the current torture of choice in intelligence circles. Personally, I find it quite tedious," he said matter-of-factly. "Where's the money?"

Belinda's gaze wandered across to the window on the right. It seemed so remarkable that it wasn't broken or cracked, considering the condition of the rest of the building. Light beamed through it, giving her a sense of the time of day. Mid-afternoon perhaps? She'd lost her sense of time.

"OK, let's try it again." Payne bound her face again and picked up the bucket. In a carefully-controlled movement, he poured another steady stream onto her.

She was drowning in the sewage ocean again. She threshed in her bonds after only ten seconds. Mercilessly, he let her suffer it for another ten before stopping. He tore the rag away again and her head reached forward, vomiting forth the dregs of the terrible liquid.

"Where's the money?"

Sputtering, she tried to take a deep breath before the next time, but he didn't give her the opportunity. He tied the towel back around her head and resumed the insidious procedure.

Repeatedly, he tormented her with the stagnant water. Each time, she was sorely tempted to reveal the location of the money. Anything for the torture to stop. Every time he put her under, she focused on being in the cabin with

Brandon, and that only by dying was she going to reach it. Such was the extent to which her terror had taken her. There was no other way but for her to welcome her death, and her own delusion.

The horror of being unable to breathe became so terrible she was losing sight of her fantasy. As Payne drew the towel from her face for the last time, the word automatically leaked from her lips, almost inaudibly. "C-cabin."

He brought his ear to just above her mouth. "What did you say?"

As the air flowed into Belinda's lungs, her resolve was restored. She wanted to be in the cabin with Brandon and that was all there was to it. "Go to hell."

"Bitch!" he roared, and slapped her harshly across the face.

Her head twisted to the right under the force of the blow, and she saw the bucket was empty. His options were now exhausted.

He drew his pistol from its holster and pointed it directly at her forehead, his eyes wide with desperate rage. "Where's the money?"

She looked into the barrel of the gun, but all she could see was Brandon and the cabin. A serene smile formed across her lips.

Payne slowly lowered the gun, slipped it into his holster, and stepped back slowly—as though a sinister thought had occurred to him. "As annoying as you are," he said, "you're a stunning-looking woman, and I don't relish the thought of having gone to all this trouble for nothing."

She hoped he'd just said that to scare her. But what if he hadn't? *Oh, God, no.*

He moved to the end of the table, unbound her ankles, unbuttoned her jeans, and tore them down, followed by her panties.

Filled with dread, Belinda craned her neck to see what he was doing. He wasn't bluffing. He intended to go through with it. "Please. I'm begging you. Don't do this. Not *this*."

Payne smiled and drew himself out.

Of everything he had done to her, this was, by far, the worst. In her heart, she knew that, under no circumstances, must any man touch her after Brandon. He was her one and only. The thought of this evil, raping piece of scum taking what was Brandon's was beyond her ability to endure.

She watched as he spat on his palm and made a move to lubricate her. With his fingers inches away from her, she cried, "Stop! I'll tell you where it is!"

He stopped abruptly and hurried around the table to her face again.

"You can kill me," she said, weeping. "But please don't do *that* to me. I'm begging you."

"Where's the money?"

"It's in a cabin." Her soul died in that moment, for she knew, in just a few seconds, she and Brandon would have no paradise to go to. Her only consolation was that she would still be his, and only his.

"What cabin? Where is it?"

She was about to answer when they were startled by a rustling noise coming from the roof. Payne looked up and drew the gun from his holster. "Who's there?"

There was no reply.

"I said who the fuck is there?" He fired at the ceiling, causing a shower of dust to fall upon him.

Belinda screamed with all her might, "Somebody help me, please!"

Payne slapped his hand across her mouth. The silence continued, and fear showed in his eyes.

The seconds ticked by and nothing happened. Nobody was outside and her brief moment of hope was shattered. They were inside an old gas station that was practically falling apart. It was inevitable there were going to be a few creaking sounds.

Payne seemed to have come to the same conclusion, and resumed the interrogation. "Now, where were we? Oh, yes. You were about to tell me where the money was."

Suddenly, the remarkably-unbroken window on the right exploded into a million splinters. Two heavily-booted feet followed through to collide with Payne's head, hurling him cleanly over the table. The assailant let go of the cable he'd swung through the window with and landed next to where Payne had fallen.

Belinda turned her head and gazed with wonder into the face of her rescuer. His clothing was torn and his face was cut, bruised, and blood-caked, but there was no mistaking who it was. She knew she wasn't dreaming because she would never have dreamed *him* up in this condition. But how could it possibly be?

"Brandon?" she said with a combination of shock, bewilderment, exhilaration, and above all, indescribable joy.

"Hi, honey. I'm sorry I'm late," Brandon said breathlessly. "I got held up."

Forty-Two

Ultimate Vengeance

"Brandon, look out!" Belinda yelled.

Payne was stunned by the impact of Brandon's boots, but only momentarily. He stood and attempted to lunge toward his assailant. Brandon sidestepped him with ease, causing Payne to fall again.

That was when he saw Payne's open zipper. He glanced at Belinda. In the heat of the moment when he'd swung through the window, he hadn't immediately noticed his lover's nakedness from the waist down. Instantly, he knew what Payne had been preparing to do to her.

And he knew what *he* had to do.

Possessed by a murderous rage, Brandon hurled himself upon his adversary. He saw Payne reaching for his gun, apparently unaware he'd dropped it on the other side of the table.

Shaken and struggling to stand, Payne attempted to punch Brandon in the groin. Brandon's right foot shot up with dazzling speed and curled inward, breaking Payne's arm in one move.

Payne's scream and the terror in his eyes seemed to feed Brandon's inner beast. Hatred for the man before him possessed every iota of his being.

Or perhaps it wasn't *only* Payne that was causing such hatred within him. This monster could have been likened to the incarnation of himself he'd seen in David's video. Was it truly *just* Payne he wanted to destroy? Or was Payne simply a convenient scapegoat? *No! I know what you were going to do to her.*

Infused with an overwhelming sense of justification, he grasped Payne by his broken arm and an ear-piercing cry filled the building. "You bastard!" Brandon roared.

"P-please stop."

Brandon dug his steel-like fingers deep into Payne's fractured bone and pulled him to his feet. "You hurt the only woman I ever loved, the only family I have, and you were going to rape her, you son of a bitch." With that, he bludgeoned his fists into either side of Payne's face with ferocious speed.

The scar on Brandon's forehead deepened and Belinda finally realized what it meant. It was the injury that had led to the end of his former persona and the birth of the new. She couldn't be sure if it was an effect caused by increased blood pressure, or something in his subconscious. But it always became more pronounced during times of extreme stress, appearing almost as a harbinger for a visitation from his true self.

She watched as he rendered Payne senseless. Blood spewed from Payne's nose and mouth. Crimson strings flew from Brandon's knuckles.

She'd seen it before on the day in the woods in Wyoming. It had disturbed her at the time, but not now. Payne had shown her no mercy. He'd been vicious in his treatment of her, and the unforgivable fact was that he'd enjoyed every minute of it. He was going to rape her as a final gift to himself before killing her. Payne was someone who existed only to be cruel: an irredeemable parasite and an opportunist who could only find pleasure in the suffering of others.

She would never forget what he'd done to her colleagues and her employer. She again recalled her absolute terror as she watched him through the restroom's air vent grill. At any other time, she wouldn't have condoned what Brandon was doing. But there was one thing of which she was absolutely sure—the world needed to be rid of the savage he was beating.

Brandon grasped Payne by the hair and looked into his blood-caked face. The fugitive agent was unconscious, perhaps even comatose, but Brandon wasn't satisfied. Tears of rage rolled down his cheeks as he thought of Belinda's terror and how Payne had violated her in almost every conceivable way. The sudden uncontrollable impulse consumed him again, and he drove Payne's head into the wall repeatedly. "Die!" he cried with every thrust of his arm. "Die! Die! Die!"

The bludgeoning continued in a frenzy of ultimate vengeance. Payne's bloodied face caved in and became a mangled, unrecognizable crater by the time Brandon had exhausted himself. He finally pulled away leaving his foe's blood spattered across the wall. The lifeless body slipped from his fingers into a heap on the floor.

Physically and emotionally drained, he fell to his knees beside his victim.

"B-Brandon," Belinda said quietly behind him. "It's all right, Brandon. I'm OK."

He came to his senses, stood, and turned to his half-naked lover tied to the table. "Oh, my God, baby, I'm so sorry." Urgently, he ran across to her, untied her wrists, and noticed her bleeding fingers. "Oh, God. What did he do to you?"

He helped her to her feet and she hugged him tightly. "It doesn't matter," she said stoically.

"Yes, it does, goddammit. Yes, it does."

Belinda broke the embrace, picked up her panties and jeans from the floor, and pulled them back on. Brandon couldn't help noticing her wincing as her tender fingertips gripped the fabric. He was seized by an overpowering need to take the pain away from her, but was powerless to do so. He felt so helpless.

"I can't believe it," she said, shaking her head.

"Can't believe what?"

"You're here. You're alive. Just the thought of seeing you again . . . on the other side. It got me through."

"Alive? Of course I'm alive. Why would you think—?" And then he realized. "The grenade."

Belinda shuddered. "Yes. I saw the SUV explode. I saw you die."

"No, you didn't. You must have missed what we did. Come to think of it, it was just before a bend in the road when we jumped out."

"Jumped out?"

Sniffing his tears back, Brandon moved across to the dangling cable he'd swung through the window with. "You remember how I got you off the roof of the Carringby building that first night?"

She smiled fondly. "How could I ever forget? *Hold on!*"

Brandon cringed. Being quoted in endearing terms wasn't something he was comfortable with. "It's called a spider cable. When we saw the grenades coming at us, I gave one to David. We knew we had only seconds to act.

286

David threw open the door, fired the cable, and the claw dug into the edge of the cliff. With the car moving, it just pulled him out and over the edge. At the same time, I threw myself out the other side and banged myself up pretty badly on the roadside."

"You did what?" she exclaimed.

"Just in time too. It was a micro-second before the bend in the road. The cliff shielded me from the explosion. The grenade blew a couple of seconds after we bailed out."

"So, that's why you look the way you do . . . The torn clothes and the cuts and bruises." She threw her arms around him again. "Oh, thank God."

"I can't believe it," he said. "You thought I was dead?"

Belinda was startled as the garage door creaked. Brandon looked across to see David Spicer entering sheepishly with his arm in a makeshift sling.

"Is it safe to come in yet?" David said.

Brandon smiled. "Sure, man. Come on in."

David held up a small semi-spherical object. "I thought you might want this back. I took it off of that asshole's car."

"What's that?" Belinda said.

"That's how we found you," Brandon replied. "When he took you, I threw it onto his car. It's a magnetic homing device. When we bailed out of the car, the last thing I took out of the glove compartment was the tracking device. It led us straight here."

"Yeah," David said. "Dra—*Brandon*—had to pull me up a cliff, and then we had a four mile hike back to my car."

Brandon turned to Belinda and shrugged coyly. "Told you I got held up."

287

Belinda gestured to David's arm. "What happened to you, David?"

"He did."

"It happened when he hit the side of the cliff, but it's not that serious," Brandon said, initiating a little banter with his old/new friend. "Just a broken wrist. That's two you owe me, bud."

David walked past Brandon and Belinda and noticed Payne's body and the condition of his face. "Another Drake special," he muttered. The sight of Payne's corpse was so ghastly he questioned the degree to which Brandon had actually changed.

Then he moved over to the table and discovered the bucket, the ropes, and the filthy wet towel lying on the floor. *She's been waterboarded.*

As he looked across to see the two lovers in a loving embrace, it was clear they didn't want to let go of one another. David finally made up his mind. The old Brandon Drake would never have been caught holding a woman in such a way.

David questioned if he would have beaten to death a man who had waterboarded the woman he loved. In a heartbeat, he knew that he would have.

Breaking the embrace again, Brandon turned back to him. "Are you going to be able to drive with that busted wrist?"

"I really don't have much choice but to try."

Brandon approached David and extended his hand. There was an uncomfortable moment of unresponsiveness, but David finally took it with his good hand.

"Thank you for everything, David," Brandon said sincerely.

"Don't mention it. My biggest problem is going to be explaining this busted arm."

"This never happened, all right? You never met with me. You never saw me, no matter what. We make a pact. Agreed?"

"Whatever you say, soldier. I just pray we never have to call it in. But I really appreciate you thinking of my wellbeing. I never thought I'd see the day."

"It's been great seeing you again, Dave."

"And it's been a pleasure *meeting* you finally, Brandon."

After a moment, David let go of Brandon's hand and made his way out of the gas station.

Brandon and Belinda watched as David walked across the dusty yard, disappearing through the trees, and back to his car parked on the other side of the lot.

Brandon bowed his head as an attack of sadness came over him. He didn't know if he would ever see David again. His life was now that of a fugitive. Belinda was all he had, and it was essential he get them both back to their only home. The question remained, with all of his petty cash blown to smithereens, how was he going to get them back to Aspen?

He spotted Payne's car keys on the floor next to the table and picked them up. That, at least, gave them the ability to travel. However, even in the unlikely event the car had a full tank of gasoline, there was no chance of it taking them fifteen hundred miles. "Come on," he said. "Let's get out of here."

And then he noticed Belinda's gaze fixed on the table she'd been tortured upon—the table she'd come within a hairsbreadth of being raped upon. He desperately wanted to get her as far away from there as possible.

Without a word, she turned and hurried out of the building. Brandon followed her toward the Mustang.

She suddenly stopped in her tracks.

"What's wrong?" he said.

"What happened when you went behind the shack with David? You remember? Just before that guy grabbed me?"

He knew there was no way he could possibly tell her, especially after what she'd just been through. On the iPhone screen, he'd seen himself in a way that could have been likened to Payne himself. "It doesn't matter."

"It does matter."

He lowered his head again and a sense of shame came over him. What he'd seen on the phone wasn't a person he could relate to in the here and now. It was a doppelganger—a look-alike. It was a distorted reflection of how he perceived himself. But it was the truth. He could only mouth a barely-audible, non-specific response. "I was a monster."

The guilt in his tone was unmistakable and his face became contorted. He struggled not to lose control of himself, but it conquered him. He hadn't been given the opportunity to grieve. When David had been showing him the video of his former self, the love of his life was being taken from him. It had been immediately followed by a car chase, a leap out of a moving car, a four mile hike, a race to the rescue, and the murder of his lover's torturer.

He fell to his knees as the shock finally took its toll. His body trembled, his chest convulsed, and a fit of sobbing overcame him. The trauma caused him to vomit. "P-please . . . help me." He looked up for her response and saw her tear-filled eyes.

"It's all right," she said. "I'm here. Forget what I said. It doesn't matter what you *were*. It only matters who you *are,* and who that is, is the most wonderful, most incredible human being I have ever known."

For long moments, they held one another until his spasms of grief began to abate. He couldn't help but love her more for helping him through this anguish.

"Do you feel better now?" she said.

He looked into her eyes. "God, I love you."

"And I love you too, baby. Now, let's go home."

Brushing himself off, he stood.

As they walked to the car, Belinda seemed to be distracted by something in the distance. "Did you see that?" she said.

"See what?"

She pointed into the distance. There appeared to be a flash of light. And then it happened again, illuminating the dull gray of the overcast sky. "There. What is that?"

Brandon stepped forward to afford himself a clearer view. It wasn't an occasional flash, it was continuous and it was blue. And then another appeared behind it, and another, until there was a long line of them coming closer.

"Is that the police?" Belinda said almost rhetorically.

Brandon didn't answer until the lights came closer. Panic seized him. "Oh, my God."

"What?"

"That's not the police. That's a federal task force." He placed his hand on her shoulder and moved her toward the car with frantic urgency. "Let's get out of here, right now."

Forty-Three

To The End

Brandon and Belinda climbed into the Mustang. Dust filled the air as Brandon spun the car around, tires screeching across the earth.

He noticed the fuel needle showing the tank was a quarter full. "Oh, Jesus."

The reflection in the rear view mirror showed the task force convoy was alarmingly close. There was no way for him to speed away without them spotting him, but he had no choice. As far as he knew, Belinda was still wanted, and if they discovered him he'd be arrested and returned to Fort Bragg for his court-martial. That could mean life imprisonment, especially given the number of offenses he'd committed while absent without leave. With Payne dead, there was also the possibility of murder being added to his list of 'transgressions.' It all depended on what would be believed.

He bolted forward and raced onto the dusty, badly-maintained road. With his eyes on the rear view mirror he could see a number of task force vehicles racing onto the driveway of the gas station. However, four of them continued along the road and they were speeding up. It was obvious they'd seen them racing away from the scene.

"Oh God," Belinda said. "They're getting closer."

Brandon slapped his forehead as he realized his stupidity. It would have been safer for him to have run with

Belinda into the forest where David had parked his car. The feds wouldn't have even known they were there, but in his distress, he hadn't been thinking rationally.

Heart pounding, he pressed his foot to the floor. The car shuddered as it touched ninety miles an hour along a desperately ragged stretch of road. He and Belinda were thrown around mercilessly by the repeated bumps in the road, but he persisted.

They'd been racing away from the task force for ten miles when they finally came upon even road. Brandon accelerated to one-hundred-ten miles an hour, but the flashing lights were still in pursuit. The fuel needle was dropping rapidly and he knew he had to come up with a contingency plan.

The task force was approximately two miles behind them. On this straight, deserted back road, wherever they stopped would be noticed.

Up ahead, Brandon saw another wooded lot and knew it would likely be the last forest they would see before they ran out of gas. "All right, sweetheart," he said. "I'm gonna stop at those trees and we're gonna make a run for it. We stand a chance of losing them under cover of the woods."

"Are you out of your mind?"

"We're almost out of gas. We have no choice."

He brought the car to an abrupt halt by the trees and threw his side door open. "OK. Now, run!"

Belinda leaped out and sprinted into the forest. Brandon caught up to her in seconds. The federal agents were coming closer with each fleeting moment.

He grasped Belinda's hand and led her through the trees. The uphill climb quickly exhausted her.

"Brandon, I can't," she said, gasping for air.

"You have to. We can't stop."

Belinda felt faint and couldn't continue. Her legs felt leaden and stopped moving. Her lungs burned from the exertion and her breathing came in deep, desperate gasps. It had been over a month since she'd last seen a gym, but even if it had been a day, she wouldn't have been prepared for such exertion. What she was doing required Olympic-level fitness. She knew Brandon was already used to it from scaling the ridge behind the cabin every morning.

"I am so sorry I got you into this," he said.

"Don't be. I'm with you . . . to the end." She pulled her fingers up from her lap as her breathing gradually became easier. "Do you hear me, Brandon? To the end."

She saw his sad smile. His eyes misted over as though he was filled with guilt and the belief he wasn't worthy of her.

He turned his head toward the bottom of the hill. "This *is* the end."

She followed the direction of his gaze and saw at least eight men decked out in Parka and Liner field attire with their pistols drawn. "Oh, God," she cried, and instantly resumed running.

Brandon followed and they continued sprinting together for almost a mile. Belinda's survival instinct infused her with adrenaline.

From the beginning of her adventure with Brandon, it had been as though she was the Princess in the Tower. He had been the dashing, handsome prince who'd rescued her from certain doom and taken her to his castle, far away. Now, she ran with him from the forces of oppression, never leaving his side.

It seemed hopeless, when suddenly they heard the unmistakable sound of a freight train just beyond the trees. They raced toward it and could see it was approaching at a relatively slow speed, perhaps twenty miles an hour.

Brandon turned to run parallel with the train. An open car approached behind them. "This is it, babe. Take my hand." He slowed his pace as her fingers interlocked with his.

She glanced behind her. Three agents were almost on top of them.

With perfect timing, Brandon leaped into an open car, but he lost Belinda's hand. "Oh, shit." He reached out to her. "Run, baby. Take my hand."

With one last burst of energy, she sprinted toward him, their fingertips barely touching. Quickly, they were joined again. She cried out as the pressure of his grip pulled on her skewered fingertips.

The hand of a task force operative brushed her shoulder, but Brandon had her in his grasp. With one powerful curl of his arm, her feet left the ground. Steadily, she found her footing on the edge of the car as the train traveled farther away from their pursuers.

"Easy baby. I've got you. You can do it," he said. "Hold on!"

She braced the soles of her feet against the edge of the car, but the pain in her fingers prevented her from gripping tightly enough. As the stabbing sting ripped through her hand, her left foot slipped off the edge, and in an instant, she was gone.

Brandon watched as she fell to the ground, the train taking him farther away with each passing second. No matter what, he couldn't leave her. *To the end*, she'd said.

He leaped from the train and rolled on the ground, picking himself up again in one graceful, fluid movement.

He reached her within moments, only to find her weeping with despondency. "Baby, don't cry. We've both done enough of that to last a lifetime." He glanced up to see the agents were less than a minute away.

"I'm so sorry I couldn't hold on this time," she said. "They're going to separate us, Brandon. They're gonna lock us away."

"No. They haven't got anything on you. Any fool could see that. But I'm going to have to go away for a while."

"Why, Brandon? Why did you jump after me? You were free."

"Are you kidding? I could never abandon you."

"I love you with all my heart."

"I'm going to worry about you, but I don't want you to be alone."

"W-when that guy was torturing me in that gas station . . . When he was about to rape me . . . I just knew," she said tearfully.

"Knew what?"

"I knew I couldn't bear the thought of anyone other than you touching me. If I can't be with you, I honestly don't want to be with anybody, baby."

The agents were seconds away and Brandon didn't waste a moment. Embracing her, he shut out the sound of the cruel, corrupt world. This was *their* moment—their last precious bonding opportunity, and he treasured every fleeting instant of it. They emotionally bonded with one another in a way that couldn't be broken: a marriage of the purest kind, requiring no institution.

The operatives finally came upon them and harshly tore them apart. "You are under arrest," was all he heard as they pulled him up by his armpits. They cuffed his hands behind him, with three loaded pistols trained on his chest.

Five more agents emerged from the trees to join the cadre. One of them gently grasped Belinda by the shoulders. "Are you all right, ma'am?"

Brandon watched as she glared at the man and shook his hands off her. After a moment, she turned back to Brandon.

As they led him away, he turned his head, his eyes fixed on her at all times. It felt as though as long as he could see her, he hadn't got a care in the world.

Then, she disappeared from his sight.

***

In a DC Central Detention Facility interview room, Timothy Ogilsby turned a sheet of paper around on the desk. He aggressively pushed it toward Wilmot and McKay. Wilmot studied the list of names written in ballpoint pen that filled the page.

"Is that everybody?" McKay said.

Ogilsby glanced at Woodford on his left in a final moment of conference, and then said, "That's everybody."

"Now, we have something to tell you," Wilmot said.

"What's that?"

"Payne is dead."

The two prisoners looked at one another again, their expressions indicating panic.

"D-dead? Dead how?" Woodford said, stammering.

"He stopped breathing, that's how, you prick," Wilmot said sarcastically.

"They think Drake killed him," McKay said. "Made quite a mess apparently. He's in custody at the moment. They're arranging for him to be sent back to Bragg for his court-martial."

Ogilsby's lower lip quivered as the impact of McKay's words reverberated in his mind. "B-but that means—"

"That's right," Wilmot said. "The deal you were offered—information leading to capture—is no longer valid." He coldly stood to leave.

Woodford stood up sharply. "Now, wait a minute. We gave you that list."

"That wasn't a condition of the agreement."

With fear in his eyes, Ogilsby stood up beside Woodford.

"Please, Wilmot," Woodford said. "You've got to help us. What can we do? Please!"

McKay opened the interview room door without saying a word.

Wilmot turned back to Ogilsby and Woodford for a final moment of gloating. "Wait for your execution date. That's what you can do now."

Incomprehensible bellows of horror were immediately silenced as the door slammed shut behind the two agents.

"Well, that's the end of that," McKay said. "I've got to admit, for a minute there I felt a mild sense of sympathy for those two. But I keep reminding myself of what murderous sadists they actually are. They deserve everything that's coming to them."

"You got that right."

"I'm still a little concerned, though, about how much that goddamn task force knows."

"Nothing," Wilmot said. "Wolfe arranged it. They were sent in to investigate 'a serious terrorist threat and a female hostage.' No names. As luck would have it, all they found was Drake and Reese."

McKay exhaled with relief. "Wanna come back to my place for a few drinks?"

"Under the circumstances, why not?" Wilmot tapped his partner lightly on the shoulder. "By the way are you still seeing that hot model? What's her name?"

"Becky?"

"Yeah."

"Sure am. I think she's pretty keen."

"Have you screwed her yet?"

"None of your business."

Wilmot grinned devilishly. "You have, haven't you?"

"Well, you know, I never kiss and tell."

Wilmot laughed with juvenile glee. "You hound."

Together, they jovially continued along the airless corridor.

McKay loosened his tie and stepped into his apartment. He made his way over to the liquor cabinet and poured out two shots of bourbon. "I can't believe it's finally over."

They raised their glasses and clinked them together. "To a job well done," Wilmot said.

As they took their seats, Wilmot looked around the room admiringly. "I must say, you've fixed this place up nicely."

"To think how close I came to losing it all. And all because of Treadwell."

"Well, I shouldn't worry about it."

McKay frowned. "How can you be so easy about this?"

"I guess I've just had it up to my neck with it all." Wilmot dipped his hand into his pocket, took out the sheet of paper Ogilsby had given to him, and began to study it.

"I wonder what's going to happen to Drake."

Wilmot's eyes didn't move from the page. "Who knows?"

"How many names are there, approximately?"

"Thirty-nine."

"That's precise. When did you count them?"

No answer came and McKay became uncomfortable. "Do you think they're all there?"

"What?"

"Do you think they gave us the names of every operative in Treadwell's conspiracy?"

"Not even close."

McKay rested his bourbon on the table next to him, and turned to his partner uneasily. "What do you mean, 'not even close'?"

It took McKay a few moments for the sight of Wilmot's pistol to register. He heard the faint blip of the shot as the bullet was fired through the silencer—the last sound he would ever hear.

Wilmot swallowed the last of his bourbon and put the glass in his pocket. He calmly moved over to McKay's corpse holding up his right hand to the overhead light. His virtually-invisible fingerprint guard was still firmly attached to his hand. As he tilted it to the left and right, he could make out the slight sheen of transparent micro film.

He carefully placed the pistol into McKay's hand and wrapped his dead colleague's fingers around the cartridge holder and trigger.

After looking around the room, he spotted an ornate china plate ceremoniously adorning the wall. He took it and placed it on the desk next to McKay's bourbon glass.

After setting the list of agents' names alight, he watched the flame creep upward, spilling ash onto the plate. Within seconds, he was grasping a small shard of paper and released it before burning his fingers. He smiled as the last shred of evidence was incinerated on the china.

Finally, he turned away, exited the apartment, closed the door behind him, and didn't look back.

Forty-Four

Court-martial

"And that's everything? The whole story?"

Brandon nodded as Lieutenant Terrence Brock stared at him from across the table in a sterile Fort Bragg interview room. Brandon gazed into the ether, struggling to process his predicament. It had been two years since he'd worn his dress uniform, never imagining the next time would be for his court-martial.

Lieutenant Brock, a lawyer stationed at Fort Bragg, slipped his on reading glasses and perused his files. Although Brandon had the means to employ the finest counsel, accessing those funds would have involved revealing the location of the cabin. Consequently, he found himself in an extremely vulnerable position.

Five weeks had passed since his arrest in the North Carolina forest. After being taken into custody, he'd been transported back to Bragg to be detained, awaiting trial. Not wishing to delay the inevitable, he'd refused a pre-trial. As such, it was decided the most appropriate course of action was to take the matter directly to general court-martial.

His heart ached for Belinda. The most traumatic consequence of his capture was that he couldn't be with her. Everywhere he looked, he was convinced he could see her face, his heart drawing him ever closer to the edge of sanity.

He looked up at Brock and finally spoke. "How much do they have on me?"

"This isn't going to be easy. They've pulled in witnesses from across the country. They're eager to take you down, you do know that?"

"I know."

"I had a meeting in chambers with General Grant an hour ago and they're going to begin with an article thirty-nine, subsection A." Brock studied the list of witnesses the prosecution had for the day. "Colonel Darren Woodroffe, Professor Abraham Jacobson from Mach Industries, Captain Lewis Jordan of the Denver Police Department, Sheriff Earl Gillespie from Morgan, Wyoming, and Agent William Tremayne from the FBI."

"Should be a fun day then."

The lieutenant gathered up his papers. "Sergeant Drake, there's something you're not aware of, and I think now would be the time."

"What's that, sir?"

"The media is having a field day with this, as is a large section of the general populace."

Brandon stood, bemused. "A field day, sir? I'm not sure I follow you."

"You've become quite a celebrity. There's a parade of them outside the gates. Do not engage them. Is that clear?"

"Yes, sir," Brandon said, eyes front. He relaxed momentarily as his curiosity got the better of him. "May I ask why, sir?"

"They are antagonizing to General Grant as well as the prosecution."

"Yes, sir." Brandon saluted as Brock opened the door.

"We are coming to you live from Fort Bragg, the base of the Eighty-Second Airborne Division, where today, Sergeant Brandon Drake is due to face a general court-martial for desertion, and a series of further crimes, including the murder of a Homeland Security agent," Tara Willoughby said into a microphone before the cameras outside the front gates. "However, there are those who believe Drake is not the villain the army and the police want to make of him. Rather, he is a man of courage, who sacrificed himself for the sake of others in his fight against a corrupt and tyrannical conspiracy."

As she said those words, screaming cheers filled the air behind her.

Brandon walked out onto the front of the base accompanied by Lieutenant Brock and ten members of the military police, and headed toward the courthouse. Despite Brock's orders, he was unable to restrain himself from glancing across at the commotion. There were approximately two hundred people outside the gates. He saw at least four TV camera crews and scores of placards bearing slogans: 'We Love You Brandon,' 'Down with Tyranny,' 'Set Brandon Free,' and 'Superheroes are 4 Real!'

Brock flicked his knuckles onto Brandon's forearm. "Eyes front, Drake."

"Yes, sir."

An attack of apprehension took hold of Brandon as he was led up the steps to the new courthouse. Walking between the pillars into the building, a sense of doom came over him, but he held his head up high. He marched along the corridor and up a stairwell with Brock, barely noticing the array of paintings on the walls or the ornate décor of the new building.

When they came to the end, one of the MPs opened the courtroom door and led Brandon inside.

Lieutenant Brock gestured to a long table just ahead of the judge's bench. "Over here, Drake."

Without a word, Brandon moved along the line of seated, off-duty servicemen and curiously, a couple of civilians who didn't look like reporters. He wondered who they were and what they were doing in the courtroom. However, his curiosity couldn't overcome his anxiety.

Brandon sat to Brock's left noticing Wassell, Stockton, and the newly-promoted Master Sergeant David Spicer sitting behind him.

Brock acknowledged the opposing counsel sitting at an adjacent bench.

Brandon recognized his opponent as Captain Hugo Arrowsmith, a man with whom he'd only had fleeting acknowledgements in the past. The irony struck him. His adversary was a man who didn't even know him.

Or was that only as Brandon remembered it? He could no longer be certain of anything relating to his past.

He noticed the jury of five. They were, appropriately, strangers to him, except for Captain Andrea Ward, whom he'd only known in passing. His unease was compounded by the fact that none of them made an effort to look at him.

The door behind the judge's bench opened to the chilling sound of an officer's call: "All rise."

General Thaddeus Grant entered the court. A tall man of fifty-five, with graying hair and a thick moustache, his very presence conveyed authority, compounding Brandon's sense of foreboding.

Brandon felt unsure of the general's opinion of him now that he knew about his past 'Scorpion' persona. The situation didn't inspire his confidence.

Nevertheless, Grant was duty-bound to remain impartial. He sat and gave his notes a final glance-over. "You may be seated." When he finally looked up again, he met Brandon's gaze. "Sergeant Drake, for the purpose of this general court-martial, you are charged with desertion, theft of army property, the murder of an SDT agent, conduct unbecoming an officer, including evading arrest by the police, assaults against three police officers, an escape from police custody, and the reckless endangerment of civilians. How do you plead?"

"Not guilty, sir," Brock said.

Grant nodded and turned to the prosecution. "Captain Arrowsmith, call your first witness."

With no apparent emotion, Arrowsmith stood. "Yes, sir. The prosecution calls Colonel Darren Woodroffe."

From the back of the court, a tall, uniformed man in his late thirties approached the witness stand.

Once Woodroffe was in position, Arrowsmith asked him to state his name, and then began his line of questioning.

With tight knuckles gripping his seat, Brandon listened intently as Arrowsmith questioned his former commanding officer. He recalled David telling him he'd assaulted Woodroffe prior to being shipped out to the fateful mission in Helmand Province.

But to Brandon's shock, Woodroffe sang his praises, conveying his viewpoint that Drake was a true born warrior, and an example of what kept America safe. However, the colonel admitted Brandon had difficulty leaving his killer instinct out on the battleground. He couldn't deny that Drake did, in fact, present a public health hazard, even though Brandon may not have been entirely to blame. He argued that the army thrived on training combatants, but didn't relish the consequences of doing so.

The fact that no record of Brandon assaulting Woodroffe could be found was raised, but Woodroffe couldn't explain it.

As Brandon listened, he remembered something Treadwell had said to him on the night of his death. It came back to him as the voice of a ghoulish specter: *We even cleaned up your overly-stained military record for you.*

Brock could see no purpose in questioning Colonel Woodroffe. The man had answered honestly and was clearly a hostile witness who was reluctant to sell out one of his own. There was nothing he'd said that could possibly be discredited.

The next witness to take the stand was Professor Abraham Jacobson, a balding man in his sixties, and director of weapons development at Mach Industries. Brandon had been assigned to him following his head injury and memory revision.

As Arrowsmith interviewed him, it became apparent that Treadwell had arranged for Brandon to be posted at Mach Industries, accompanied by a team of agents who oversaw the entire operation. Brandon already knew Treadwell had a close involvement with the facility. Without that involvement, he wouldn't have come into contact with the senator's plans to attack army-contracted corporations. But he didn't realize it had all begun when he'd arrived. From what the professor was saying, Treadwell had marched in and taken over Mach Industries.

Brandon screwed up his lips at the injustice. The professor was a kind and gracious man with whom he'd developed a fine friendship. The thought of Jacobson being oppressed by scum the likes of Treadwell caused a flutter of anger to fester in him.

Jacobson went on to stun those in attendance by expressing his astonishment at Brandon's skills and intellect, which had enabled him to create the miniature engines for the Turbo Swan. He confused the jury profoundly by showing deep emotion when describing Brandon as a gentle soul, whom he'd grown to love like his own son.

While it caused Brandon a degree of bashfulness, it was clear nobody else could associate the professor's words with the psychopathic warmonger they knew Drake to have been.

However, as supportive of Brandon as Jacobson was, he couldn't deny the equipment Brandon had stolen was the property of the United States Army.

The hearing extended into the afternoon, with the testimonies of Captain Lewis Jordan from the Denver police, Sheriff Earl Gillespie from Morgan, Wyoming, and Agent Eric Tremayne from the FBI, who had been present at Brandon's arrest in North Carolina. Each of the men gave descriptive and captivating accounts of their experiences with Drake, which was detrimental to Brandon's case. Two escapes from the police, a jail break, an assault against a police officer, beating a man to death, and a car chase with the FBI, were damning incidents.

After an intense day, General Grant decided recess was in order. "We will reconvene tomorrow at oh-nine-hundred."

The following morning, the trial resumed. It had been an angst-ridden night for all concerned. Brandon hadn't slept. He was vacant and unresponsive, as though he wasn't in his right mind. Brock had serious reservations about how he intended to proceed. He was beginning to doubt Drake's suitability to stand trial.

Nevertheless, the judge and jury had heard from everyone except the one who could have put the entire situation into perspective for them.

Grant entered the courtroom and everyone stood. "Be seated," he said. "Does the prosecution have any further witnesses?"

"Just one, General. The prosecution calls Belinda Carolyn Reese."

Brandon's gaze shot up from the floor. He watched, wondering if he was dreaming as an MP escorted Belinda into the courtroom. She looked stunning to his eyes. Her hair had grown a little, and she'd reverted back to her natural brunette color. Her eyes were visibly moistened. She seemed to take a sharp breath when she saw him, but he assumed she was just surprised to see him in his military uniform.

It occurred to him that his adversary had brought her into this. Then he noticed the MPs hand grasping her arm as he led her in. She was in no danger and wasn't being manhandled, but his mind was not sound at that moment. His adrenaline surged and his aggression ignited, destroying his rationality. "Get your hands off her, you son of a bitch!" He sprang up from his chair and leaped over the witness stand in a single bound.

Forty-Five

Sting of the Scorpion

Arrowsmith recoiled instinctively, and the jury members stood in alarm.

"Leave her alone!" Brandon roared.

Grant gestured to the four officers who were standing at the courtroom door. "MPs. Stop that man!"

Belinda watched as Brandon charged toward her, but she knew he wouldn't hurt her. The whites of his eyes became bloodshot and the forehead scar deepened, this time assuming a dark shade of purple. His face contorted into the grimace of a beast. However, as comforting as it was to see him acting so protectively toward her, she was devastated by what he was doing to his case.

Brandon's foot flew into the MPs jaw, knocking him over the bench. Brock darted out of the way as the man crashed into the oak surface beside him.

Four MPs were on Brandon within a heartbeat, but their efforts were futile. He was down on the floor in an instant. His left leg swept around in an arc, taking two of the MPs' feet from under them.

He leaped onto the desk, using it as a springboard before leaping off toward the two who remained standing. The heel of his right shoe collided with the chin of the man in front of him. Simultaneously, his left foot kicked back into the solar plexus of the MP behind him. It all occurred in one fluid movement before he landed.

The first two fallen MPs got to their feet and one grabbed Brandon around the neck. Brandon reached backward, gripped the back of his assailant's head, and hurled him over his shoulders.

The last remaining MP stepped in front of him and threw his fist toward Brandon's face. Brandon's left arm rose up with dazzling speed and blocked the strike. Wrapping his arm around the MPs, he drove his palm up under the man's chin, rendering him unconscious. The man fell to the floor onto his three senseless colleagues.

Brandon lunged toward Arrowsmith, but he was suddenly halted by an attack of complete bodily paralysis. A second squad of MPs had entered the courtroom and hit him with a shot from a taser. He fell to the ground with wires protruding from his back.

Belinda trembled, sobbing as she watched him twitching on the floor.

David Spicer ran from among the spectators and gently held her shoulders. She noticed his sad expression, and suspected he was taking a serious risk given that he wasn't supposed to know her. She hoped that perhaps he could pass it off as common compassion for a woman in distress.

Grant stood from his judgment seat with one cold word: "Recess."

The trial resumed in the afternoon, and Belinda took the stand. Brandon sat in a chair with his wrists shackled to his ankles via long chains.

"Agent Payne inserted wooden sticks under two of my fingernails," Belinda said.

The members of the jury winced as she related her horrifying tale.

Belinda noticed Brandon shaking with rage. She paused to collect herself and then resumed her testimony. "He kept asking me about the money, but I told him I didn't know what he was talking about. Then he tied me to a table and wrapped filthy rags around my head. He poured dirty water onto my face." She became tearful as she remembered her terror.

"I understand this is difficult for you, Ms. Reese," Arrowsmith said gently, "but please, try to tell us what happened."

"When that didn't work, he was about to shoot me, and then thought better of it."

"What do you mean, Ms. Reese?"

"He made a move to . . . rape me." She struggled to retain her compose as the words spilled out of her.

Brandon looked up from the corner of the room. "You bastard, Arrowsmith."

Grant alerted a new group of MPs at the door. "Recess. Escort Sergeant Drake from the court."

After a brief recess, Brandon was brought back into the courtroom, still restrained by shackles. He looked across the crowd of personnel and off-duty soldiers. He glanced at the two civilians he'd noticed earlier, a young man, and an older guy with a snow-white beard. For a moment, his eyes locked with the younger man, whose expression seemed to show sincere concern. Brandon didn't recognize him from anywhere specifically, but there was something about him that seemed strangely familiar.

"To resume, Ms. Reese," Arrowsmith said. "You say Agent Gary Payne was going to rape you. Is that correct?"

"Yes, that's correct."

"And what happened?"

"Brandon came in through the window and . . . stopped him." Belinda's tone lifted as she recalled the wondrous moment.

"By stopping him, do you mean beating him to death?"

Brock stood. "Objection. Badgering."

"Sustained," Grant said.

"He did what he had to do to stop an armed man from raping and killing me—"

"Thank you, Ms. Reese," Arrowsmith cut her off abruptly, but he was too late. The jury had heard her. "Where did he take you after each of these *fantastic* rescues you mentioned?"

"Motels."

"Motels?" Arrowsmith gestured to the off-duty personnel. "We have soldiers in this room today, who were present in Morgan, Wyoming on February seventeenth, when Drake took off in the Turbo Swan with you. Where did he take you?"

She was silent for a moment as though she was trying to think of a story that couldn't be discredited. "I don't remember. I was in shock. I think we ended up at another motel."

"And where did he leave the Turbo Swan?"

"I don't know."

Arrowsmith held her gaze for a moment before concluding. "No further questions. The prosecution rests."

After a break for lunch, Grant sat in his judgment seat and wasted no time resuming the proceedings. "Lieutenant Brock, you may call your first witness.

Brock stood. "Thank you, sir. Defense calls . . . Sergeant Brandon Drake."

Brandon's feet shuffled as he was escorted to the stand.

"State your name for the record, please."

"Sergeant Brandon Drake, Eighty-Second Airborne Division, sir."

"Sergeant Drake, would you please tell the court the circumstances that led to your arrest."

Brandon felt emotionally exhausted, and it took several moments for him to gather his thoughts. "When I was working at Mach Industries, I was researching ways of increasing the load that could be taken by the engines on the Turbo Swan."

"And what happened then?"

Brandon shook his head, trying to clear his mind. "I was in the facility's mainframe when I came across a deleted file that clearly shouldn't have been there."

"What was the nature of this file?"

"It was a folder from an untraceable location, which mentioned attacks against army-contracted facilities by an undisclosed cell operating from Langley. An attachment within the folder contained a series of crypto-numeric codes for the dates, times, and locations for the attacks."

Brock's slight smile indicated he was now in a more comfortable place. Brandon knew his attorney was trying to defend his true intentions as being those of an honorable soldier, and not a deserter.

"Please continue, Sergeant."

"The first two I decoded a few weeks later were Everidge in Dallas, and Carringby in Denver. It seemed the government I was serving was involved in attacks against itself."

"So why didn't you report it?"

"Report it to whom? Who could I possibly trust? I was already working within a high security operation. Do you honestly think I would have lived to see the next sunrise if I'd said anything about this?"

"So what was your solution?"

"The base was heavily guarded, and my whereabouts had to be accounted for. I couldn't have just walked out, so I escaped in the Turbo Swan."

"Thank you, Sergeant. Why did you take so many items from the lab with you?"

"I knew that in order to have any chance of stopping what was going to happen, I'd need the right equipment. I tried to employ a non-confrontational tactic, but it failed."

"And what was that?"

"I phoned in a warning to Everidge using a sat-scrambler phone, but it was disregarded as a hoax." He paused for a moment before adding, "I don't think I need to say how many died as a result."

As David Spicer listened, he figured it hadn't been possible for the jury to avoid hearing stories of what kind of a character Drake used to be. This new incarnation was the same 'Drake' Captain Ward, had seen on television. Descriptions of his new persona had spread throughout his division to all who'd missed the broadcasts. Most were convinced it was an act he'd designed to ingratiate himself, and level an attack against the authority of the US government.

Only David knew the truth, but he was sworn to secrecy about what he knew and how he came to know it. The situation made his position agonizing, and he suspected what questions were coming. He could clear up the question of Brandon's altruism once and for all, but at what cost? For now, Brandon was doing well, if he could only keep his cool. For the sake of a promise he'd made to Brandon, and for his own career in the army, he had no choice but to remain silent.

Brandon continued. "I worked out the date and a time for the attack against Carringby, and decided to intervene personally. The rest is history."

"As the police pursued the van that night, why didn't you stop and explain yourself to them? Why all of the pyrotechnics and the escape in the Turbo Swan?"

"By that time, I trusted no one. If they took me in, I knew I would've been the victim of assassination within hours. When we reached Wyoming, we discovered they'd targeted Ms. Reese."

"And that's the reason you incapacitated two police officers with a . . . just a moment." Brock put on his reading glasses and sifted through a slew of papers. "A UX-E5 sonic force emitter?"

"Yes, sir."

"And afterward?"

"The van was stolen from the motel while we were sleeping. I learned the thieves had been taken into police custody along with the van, so I set about reacquiring it."

"Thank you, Sergeant Drake. No further questions for now."

Grant looked across to Arrowsmith. "Do you have any questions, Captain?"

"Yes General, I certainly do." Arrowsmith approached the witness stand.

Brandon's eyes burned into those of his adversary, and he sensed his rage beginning to resurface. *Keep it together. Don't lose it now.*

Forty-Six

Cross Examination

"Sergeant Drake," Arrowsmith said, "at the time you speak of, you were without a vehicle. You were far away from anyone who might have been trying to kill you. So why did you break into the police impound yard?"

"You're right. I wasn't in any danger at that time," Brandon replied. "Treadwell knew I was responsible for interfering with the Carringby operation, and yet he still made sure my name stayed out of the media."

"So why did you break into the impound yard? You'd taken equipment that belonged to the authorities and it had found its way into official hands. What right did you have to take it again?"

"Belinda . . . Ms. Reese, had been targeted and we were out in the cold with no means of transportation or defense, no weaponry, and all our money was in the van." Brandon's voice increased in volume. "Now, what the hell do you think I should have done, asshole?"

General Grant slapped his hand upon the desk. "Sergeant Drake, outbursts like that will not be tolerated. Is that clear?"

Brandon sat back in an attempt to compose himself. *Dammit. Why can't I hold it in?*

Arrowsmith resumed. "Sergeant Drake, the FBI reports show that on March thirteenth, you were driving away from a deserted gas station approximately thirty miles north of

Asheville, North Carolina, in a Mustang identified as having been purchased by one Carl Perry."

Brandon shook his head, confused. "Who?"

"The car was traced to its previous owner in Washington DC, who said he'd sold the vehicle, one month before, to a man named Carl Perry. When shown a photograph of Agent Gary Payne, he confirmed that Perry and Payne were one and the same."

"What does that have to do with me?"

Arrowsmith stepped closer to the witness stand. "The man was found beaten to death with such ferocity that the only way he could be identified was through his fingerprints. Even his teeth had been shattered, and you were seen driving away in his car. What happened?"

Brandon clenched his fist with the eyes of all in the court upon him. "Belinda and I were driving to Florida," he lied. "I stopped outside an old storage shack to take a leak."

"Where was this?"

"Cherry Mountain Plain, around seventy miles northeast of Asheville."

"What happened?"

"Apparently Payne had been following us. When I came from behind the shack, he was holding Belinda at gunpoint, and he demanded money from me."

"Why would he do that?"

"He seemed to think I had money that Treadwell owed him."

"And what happened?"

Brandon pinched the bridge of his nose as he tried to find the right words. "I threw a homing device onto Payne's Mustang and gave chase. Payne hurled grenades out of his car toward me. I jumped out of the SUV moments before a grenade took it out."

"What happened then?"

"I had the tracking device, but some of the equipment I'd taken from Mach Industries was destroyed in the explosion."

"What time of day, and whereabouts did this happen?"

Brandon shrugged. "I don't know. Ten, maybe ten-thirty hours. It was on a narrow road by a cliff edge around four miles ahead of where Payne found us."

"And at what time did you arrive at the gas station?"

"Around fourteen-thirty hours."

Brandon saw Brock covering his eyes with his hand as though despairingly. *Have I just said something wrong?*

"How did you get there, Sergeant Drake?" Arrowsmith said.

In his fatigued state, Brandon couldn't grasp the nature of the question. "I followed the homing signal on the tracker."

"No, I mean what did you get to the gas station . . . *in?*"

Brandon instantly realized he was defeated. Struggling to keep his gaze away from David, he tried frantically to think of a way he could have gotten from the mountain road to Belinda without involving his friend. *I ran? No, that's ridiculous.* "Somebody gave me a ride," he said, but feared his delay had been too suspicious.

"Who?"

"I don't know. Some old guy with a truck."

"So," Arrowsmith said in summing-up fashion, "you can't tell us how you arrived at the gas station, and yet you ran from the FBI in the victim's own car after savagely beating him to death."

Brandon felt his rage beginning to resurface. "No. I saw what that bastard did to her. He'd skewered her fingers, waterboarded her, and he was about to rape her at gunpoint when I got there. I had no choice."

"You said *some* of the devices you took from Mach Industries were destroyed when a grenade hit the SUV?"

"Yes."

"That's convenient. Where's the Turbo Swan?"

Brandon was silent. It was one question he couldn't answer, no matter what. He could almost feel everyone's eyes upon him while he sat gazing at the floor.

"I will ask you again, Sergeant Drake. Where is the Turbo Swan?"

Caught in a vacuum, Brandon didn't utter a word.

General Grant said, "Drake, I am giving you a direct order. Now, answer the damn question!"

Finally, he raised his head to the general. "I've told you everything that happened. If you don't believe me, there's nothing I can do about it."

Grant turned to Brock. "Lieutenant, would you like to redirect?"

Brock stood with a look of hopelessness. "No, sir."

***

The particulars were discussed among the jury members over the following two days. Belinda was granted permission to remain at Fort Bragg until the verdict. It was a harrowing ordeal for all concerned.

The jury questioned how they would decide Brandon's fate. Aside from the matter of how he'd managed to reach the location where Belinda had been tortured, everything he'd said had the ring of truth, and Belinda had corroborated all of it. There was no reason for any of them to believe she'd been complicit in a conspiracy with him. His earlier outburst had been a reaction to her being brought into the court. This was highly persuasive that he had no knowledge she would even be attending the trial. He hadn't had any contact with anybody since his arrest.

Treadwell was dead and so couldn't be tried, but everybody knew at least three SDT agents had been involved in the Carringby attack. The Channel 7 incident had been blatantly obvious as to where the guilt lay.

However, during the course of events, Brandon had committed acts contrary to the law, and his violent behavior and attitude in court had been damning. Conversely, although his behavior had been typical in its hateful aggression, there was a persuasive difference. This time, it was on behalf of another. His words during his earlier attack resonated in their minds: 'Leave *her* alone,' as opposed to 'Leave *me* alone.' It seemed to lend credence to his entire defense. His so-called crimes and acts of violence were all in the defense of others. Of Belinda Reese, in particular. Bewilderment overwhelmed the jury's ability to come to a swift decision.

Anxiously, Brandon awaited his fate.

Forty-Seven

Hollow Judgment

Closing arguments had been delivered. Brandon sat on the bench in shackles with Lieutenant Brock, while Belinda sat among the off-duty soldiers three yards behind him.

General Grant sat in the judgment seat and addressed the jury. "Have the members reached a verdict?"

Captain Ward stood with their decision in her hands. "We have, sir." She handed the paper to the general.

Grant opened up the folded sheet and perused it for a moment. "All right. Sergeant Drake, please stand."

Brandon and Brock stood. Brandon looked back at Belinda who was pinching her knuckles. "I love you," he mouthed to her.

"And I love you," she whispered.

"On the count of desertion, the members find the accused—" There was a pause as Grant looked into Captain Ward's eyes, as though uncertain about what they'd written. Or perhaps, merely disappointed. "Not guilty, on the grounds of necessity."

Belinda's eyes glowed joyously at those words, but Brandon tried to remain composed.

"On the charges of conduct unbecoming an officer, including assaults against three police officers, attempting to liberate government property from police detention, and an escape from police custody, the members find the accused . . . not guilty, on the grounds of necessity."

Brandon exhaled with relief. Life in the cabin with Belinda was in sight.

"On the charge of the murder of an agent of the US government, the members find the accused not guilty, on the grounds of necessity.

"On the charge of theft of government property, the members find the accused not guilty on the grounds of necessity, contingent upon Sergeant Drake's disclosure of the location of the test aircraft known as the Turbo Swan."

Brandon looked back at Belinda in horror. They were asking him to reveal the location of the cabin. *Their* cabin.

"Sergeant Drake, I am going to give you one last chance to tell this court where the Turbo Swan can be found."

Brandon made an impulsive decision. The cabin was the one, unrepeatable chance for him and Belinda to be free of authority, corruption, and the horrors of so-called civilized society. If all else failed, he could disclose the location at a later date, but for now, he had other plans. He looked at General Grant with contempt-filled eyes. "Go to hell!"

Belinda stood and called across to him desperately, "Please tell them, Brandon. It's not worth it."

His anger and resentment for Grant superseded his fears, feeding him with a rebellious burst of overconfidence. He turned to her again and whispered, "Wait for me."

"All right," Grant said. "Given your violent temperament and your blatant contempt for this court—"

"You're a joke, General," Brandon interrupted him, thus beginning an exchange of the general ignoring him and Brandon ignoring the general.

"—and your assaults against officers of this court—"

"—a puppet whose only power is a delusion."

"—I sentence you to an indefinite period in the United States Disciplinary Barracks—"

"You can never contain me."

"—your release contingent upon your disclosure of the location of the Turbo Swan."

"You can never take my freedom from me, Grant. Nobody can!"

The jury looked away.

"Upon your release, you will be dishonorably discharged from the United States Army. We are adjourned." Grant struck the gavel and retired to his chambers.

David Spicer looked at Brandon with profound sorrow and confusion. Against all odds, he'd had his freedom in his grasp, but he'd refused it simply to avoid giving the Turbo Swan back to the army. There was no possible reason for it. He certainly wouldn't be flying it around at Leavenworth.

Ultimately, David concluded that the man who had saved his life in Afghanistan had lost his mind—a violent, dangerous individual who had always been destined for tragedy.

All except Belinda turned to leave. Four MPs grasped Brandon by the arms and led him past her.

Brock moved with him and Belinda heard him say, "I believe we may have grounds for appeal."

She presumed Brock's thoughts were that, due to his head injury, Brandon might have incurred cranial damage, which may have been causing his irrational behavior.

Brandon turned his face to her as they led him toward the courtroom door. She fought back her tears and gazed at him longingly for what was likely going to be the last time.

She knew he was a good man. Thinking along similar lines to Brock, whatever was inside him was well-intended, no matter how volatile. His mind had been violated by Treadwell, and no one could say how it might have impaired his judgment in times of stress. The circumstances were so terribly cruel. She wanted only to put her arms around him, return to the cabin, and spend the rest of her days there with him. It made so much sense. He wanted to be away from the world, free, where nobody could hurt him, and where nobody could be hurt *by* him.

But then she remembered his words to her a few minutes earlier—"*Wait for me.*" Did he have something planned? *Oh, God. What are you going to do, Brandon?*

In that moment, she realized. He was going to try to take it all: his freedom, the cabin, his happiness with her, and they would never find them.

But what if he was wrong? What if he failed? How could she talk him out of whatever he was planning when he was so sure of himself?

The courtroom door closed and Brandon was gone. Belinda sat alone, knowing her period of waiting was just beginning.

Brandon's eyes were totally vacant as he was led along the corridor outside the courtroom. He didn't appear to notice the young man and his elder companion with the snow-white beard standing several feet away from the courtroom door.

Belinda exited the court, but she didn't notice them either. Her eyes conveyed the same numb, empty, vacuous shade of devastation.

The bearded man turned to the young man at his side. "I think you should go talk to her."

"I want to, but I don't think now is the right time. I couldn't tell her anything that would take away her pain."

"All right. I understand."

"So, this is where it has led," the young man said sadly.

"I don't know what to say."

"Isn't there something you can do, Dad? I mean, for Christ's sake he's—"

"Gone, Son. He made his choice. If you ask me, you're better off without him after that little scene in there."

The young man turned to his father, outraged. "Don't say that to me. I've been searching for him for most of my life, and now you're telling me to abandon him?"

"I just don't want to see you get hurt, that's all."

"I can take care of myself. And if you can't do anything, maybe I can."

"What difference does it make? You've got everything you'll ever need. Don't do anything to jeopardize that."

The young man exhaled as he watched Brandon disappear around the end of the corridor. "He's my brother."

***

Lightning filled the sky and rain fell onto the military police unit as it transported Brandon to the gates of Fort Leavenworth. It was six in the evening, two days following his sentence, when he was led out of the storm into the facility.

The image of Belinda's face was with him constantly as they guided him into the ante-chamber. He was ordered to strip, but was oblivious to the humiliation.

From the moment of his arrival, he began studying the outside architecture of Leavenworth—the security system at the gate, the code-key entrance systems, the corners of the ceiling, the walls, the lighting system, and the carpentry. It was all relevant. His silent plan was already set in motion.

As he was searched, he watched the walls with rigid calculations. He heard every word, even conversations outside the door. Nothing would escape his notice.

They pulled him up again, but he refused to be a victim. Every moment provided him with information. His mind absorbed every sound, every routine, and every move.

"He's clean," he heard a hard-sounding voice say. "Dress him and take him to his cell."

As he was led away, he scanned the most trivial of details—the fact that the ceilings were designed in straight lines. The corners led to further corners. It might have all seemed insignificant to a regular prisoner. But to Brandon, it was the beginning of an incredibly intricate web—a maze he was determined to conquer. *There has to be a way out of here.*

However, as more of the architecture and security system became apparent, a sinking feeling consumed him. There was no way he was going to succeed in the few weeks he'd thought in his irrational, rebellious rage. Leavenworth might as well have been a fortress, The realization he'd made a grave mistake was devastating. But he couldn't give up, no matter what. Belinda was counting on him.

He stepped into his cell and his gaze darted around the small, sterile room. There was a sink, a toilet, a bunk, no windows, and everything was fixed with bolts. Possibilities quickly came to his mind, but he knew he had so much to learn.

He faced the back wall of his cell and heard the metallic clang of the door behind him. With his head turned away from his jailers, nobody saw the slight smile edging from the corners of his mouth.

Epilogue

Two years later

February 13th, 2016

Belinda found a new job working as a secretary at an insurance company in Denver. She'd continued her life to the best of her ability. It was all so terribly boring. It seemed as though every time she stepped out of her apartment, or met somebody new at work, she was bombarded with questions about Brandon and the Carringby escape. In the beginning, she'd been hounded by the press relentlessly.

Brandon was always in her thoughts. He was the most incredible human being she'd ever known, but now he was gone; caged by his own people. She hadn't been able to come to terms with his incarceration, and had long since realized that whatever he'd planned at his trial hadn't succeeded. She'd become a bitter woman, whose life was a living memorial to him.

She'd rejected all advances from other men. No man could ever compete with her memory of Brandon. He was perfect. Who could possibly follow him?

She returned to her apartment after work and switched on her fourteen-inch, flat-screen television set with abandon. Tara Willoughby's voice was so familiar it had become a piece of monotonous background noise.

That is, until that fateful evening. Her head snapped toward the screen urgently. The kettle of boiling water slipped from her hands onto the kitchen floor.

"Unruly celebrations are taking place tonight," Tara said with unusually-unprofessional joviality, "following the escape from Fort Leavenworth of the man many have called a national hero—Brandon Drake.'

Belinda's hand came across her mouth.

"To repeat," Tara continued, "the man Time Magazine rebelliously voted the ultimate hero, Brandon Drake, has escaped from Leavenworth. Drake was sentenced to an indefinite period, his release conditional upon his surrendering stolen military hardware two years ago. It is still not known why Mr. Drake refused to comply with the order."

In that moment, Belinda knew her life was renewed. She knew Brandon, and she knew exactly where he was heading. Her life and love with him was about to be resumed. They were finally going to be reunited.

Her face shone with excited, tearful elation as she made a hurried move to pack her belongings. She hadn't a moment to waste lest the authorities be on her trail. She would be vigilant, watchful, never averting her eyes from what might be behind her. One way or another, she was determined to reach him.

In her mind, she was already in the cabin, holding him, kissing him, loving him.

"I'm coming, Brandon," she murmured. "*Hold on!*"

To be continued in

Go!

Hold On!—Season 2

Go!

Hold On!—Season 2

Excerpt

Belinda entered the ticket court, relieved she'd made it. It was crowded and easy for her to lose herself among the commuters. Excitedly, she joined a line to one of the ticket vendors. Immediately, another commuter stepped in behind her. She glanced around trying to spot anything alarming, but there was nothing. Everything was perfectly normal.

As she reached the halfway point in the line, she noticed a man in a suit talking on his cell phone close to the station's entrance. There was nothing unusual about that. But it was the way in which he just glanced at her as he spoke into the phone. She looked away.

And then she slowly looked back. Their eyes locked. In an instant, she knew, and could see he did too.

Her breathing became shallow, her palms were damp, and there was a heaviness in the pit of her stomach.

She gently eased her way out of the line and looked back again for a fleeting instant. The man was talking into his cell phone with a sudden urgency in his eyes, and he was persistently looking back at her.

She darted forward only to be halted by a hand on her shoulder. She looked around to see it was the man who'd been standing behind her.

"Belinda Reese?" he said.

That was enough. Without hesitation, she drove her fist into the man's nose and he recoiled with blood trickling onto his lip. He was stunned by her unhesitant assault, which gave her the moment necessary to run.

A number of men in suits emerged from the crowd like a swarm. Belinda barely missed being grasped by one of them as she dashed through the exit.

Out in the street, she ran as fast as her legs would carry her. The suitcase was slowing her down, her breathing was labored, and she didn't know how long she could keep up the pace.

Out of the corner of her eye she saw men she thought must be CIA or federal agents appearing on street corners all around her. "Oh God, no!"

The memory of what Payne had done to her filled her mind again. It would most likely result in a repeat of the ordeal if they caught her. That was unthinkable.

She saw a crowded street ahead and sprinted into it, trying to steal herself among the pedestrians in order to slip back into one of the alleyways.

She quickly saw her chance and darted back into the alley where she'd almost been mugged. Her emotions flitted between fear and rage. It was all so terribly unjust. She only wanted to be with her man and live her life in peace. Neither she, nor Brandon, had any desire to harm anyone, and yet both of them were suffering such overwhelming persecution. She questioned what right they had to do this to them? Why couldn't they just leave them alone?

Hopefully, Brandon would have the Turbo Swan sent back to the army, and that would be the end of it.

She continued running, but agents came up behind her within moments.

Seconds later, she lost her footing and found herself on the ground. A brawny agent twisted her arm behind her back, and she swore loudly with the pain. She didn't know what was going to be worse. The sticks under the fingernails? Or the suffocation of waterboarding? She hadn't been able to decide on that before. They were both completely different types of horror. Consumed with panic, her tears flowed with unbearable dread.

"Take it easy lady and this'll all go smooth," the agent said. "We only want to talk to you."

She could hear the footsteps of several more agents hurrying toward them.

"Good job, Rogers," she heard one of them say.

And then, Rogers collapsed. The others followed, falling like dominoes beside her.

She rubbed her eyes and looked around her. It was such a familiar scene—being captured by the authorities and the authority figures just falling unconscious in front of her. It brought back a harrowing memory. Moore, Wyoming. She smiled with relief and excited exhilaration at the only thing it could mean. "Brandon."

Beaming, even through her exhaustion, she turned around to a sight she hadn't seen for two years. He stood before her in his black, bullet-resistant suit and the smooth black helmet with the visor. It was what he'd been wearing when he'd rescued her on that fateful first night. In his right hand was the sonic force emitter pistol. She realized the agents had been rendered unconscious by an intense concentration of ultrasound wave jolts.

Looking up she saw more agents turn down the alleyway behind him. The leader, a tall man in his mid-thirties, took out his cell phone, close enough for her to hear. "Sir, four men are down, but we have Reese in sight, and an unidentified individual. I think it's Drake."

There was a pause on the line.

And then the reply came through. "Take him out."

Belinda heard and saw the official drawing his pistol. "Brandon, look out!"

The agent fired and the bullet struck him in the back, knocking him to the ground.

"No!" she screamed, and ran to him.

However, he rolled onto his back and fired at the agents with desperate speed, taking down four of them. But more were coming.

She knelt down beside him and held him tightly. "Are you all right, sweetheart?"

"I'm fine. It's Kevlar. Bullet proof."

"Of course."

Something wasn't right. His voice was different. He seemed to have some kind of a Southern hint to his accent. *Surely, he wouldn't have picked that up in Leavenworth.*

"Run to the end of the alley," he said. "Help's coming."

"Help? What help?"

"You'll see when you get there."

She frowned, confused. In addition to the new voice, his manner wasn't as it used to be.

He lifted his visor.

She looked up and saw it was Brandon's face—his eyes, his mouth, even his nose. But something was wrong. "B-Brandon?"

He didn't answer.

"Who are you?"

"Later. There's no time now. You've got to go." He pointed to the end of the alley.

Perplexed, she stood and picked up her suitcase.

Immediately, another three agents appeared at the opening of the alleyway, and they were closing in.

The man who looked like Brandon got to his feet and a bullet struck the armor of his left arm. Dropping the visor back into place, he fired at the agent who had shot him, but the sonic jolt missed its mark.

Belinda heard a familiar sound behind her. She turned to see a white van with blacked-out windows pull up at the far end of the alley. Her heart leaped. Was the real Brandon inside? It couldn't drive any nearer because the alley was too narrow. Seeing the problem, she ran toward the van.

The man in the Kevlar suit fired and took down another agent, but two were still coming. He got to his feet and started to run backward while firing at the remaining two pursuers. But nothing happened. His sonic force gun had depleted its charge. "Piece o' shit!" he spat.

Belinda glanced behind her. "Come on. Hurry."

He turned and ran toward her, but the agents were gaining on him. "Go!"

"Come on!"

"GO!"

About the Author

Peter Darley (P.D. to his friends) is a British novelist, whose professional history is in showbusiness. He is a graduate of the Birmingham School of Speech and Dramatic Art, and he studied television drama at the Royal Academy of Dramatic Art (RADA). His television credits include guest-starring roles is UK productions such as BBC's *Crime Limited, Stanley's Dragon* for ITV, *The Bill*, Sky One's *Dream Team*, and numerous TV commercials. He also worked as a model, presenter, and voice-over artiste for ten years, and has been an agent for several variety acts.

His lifelong admiration of heroes, and love of roller-coaster-style thrills have been a huge influence on his writings.

He is a keen athlete and body builder, and lives with his wife in rural England.